STORM
RISING

ALSO BY DOUGLAS SCHOFIELD

Time of Departure

STORM RISING

DOUGLAS SCHOFIELD

MINOTAUR BOOKS ☙ NEW YORK

STORM RISING. Copyright © 2016 by Douglas Schofield. All rights reserved. Printed in the United States of America. For information, address St. Martin's Press, 175 Fifth Avenue, New York, N.Y. 10010.

www.minotaurbooks.com

Designed by Omar Chapa

Library of Congress Cataloging-in-Publication Data

Names: Schofield, Douglas, author.
Title: Storm rising / Douglas Schofield.
Description: First edition. | New York : Minotaur Books, 2016.
Identifiers: LCCN 2016016263 | ISBN 9781250072764 (hardcover) |
    ISBN 9781466884625 (e-book)
Subjects: | BISAC: FICTION / Mystery & Detective / Police Procedural. |
    GSAFD: Mystery fiction. | Suspense fiction.
Classification: LCC PR9275.C393 S76 2016 | DDC 813'.6—dc23
LC record available at https://lccn.loc.gov/2016016263

Our books may be purchased in bulk for promotional, educational, or business use. Please contact your local bookseller or the Macmillan Corporate and Premium Sales Department at 1-800-221-7945, extension 5442, or by e-mail at MacmillanSpecial Markets@macmillan.com.

First Edition: November 2016

10 9 8 7 6 5 4 3 2 1

Every sweet hath its sour;
Every evil its good.

—Ralph Waldo Emerson,
  Essays

STORM RISING

SOCCORSO MORTO

It sickened him.

It sickened him that after so many years, so little had changed.

Peppino was gone.

Barely ten years old, and dead.

The laws had changed a century ago. No more child labor, they said. No more six- and seven- and eight-year-old boys, the exploited *carusi* of past centuries, forced to work in the mines. No more naked children working fourteen-hour days in the narrow tunnels and the stifling heat, carrying impossible burdens of sulfur ore from the working face to the gill ovens—the toxic, lung-destroying furnaces on the surface.

Yes, the laws were all there, all written in black and white, filling those fat books he'd once seen lining the shelves in the office of a *notaio*, but laws are meaningless unless they are enforced. This was Sicily, where stubborn tradition never died, and never yielded.

Yes, changing times had forced the owners to raise some workers' wages, but it was mainly the *picuneri*, the pick-men, who had benefited. In the remote defiles of *la zona di Gallizzi*, behind the forested slopes overlooking the main shafts and far beyond the apathetic gaze of torpid mine inspectors, the child labor laws were still ignored. Young boys were still being transformed into old men before they reached their late teens, deformed from long years spent in crushing physical work while their bodies struggled vainly just to grow to normal size.

He had been lucky. His *carusi* years had not begun until he was full grown. Unlike many of the boys, he hadn't been sold to a heartless mine owner by desperate, starving parents. He hadn't been surrendered in return for a payment of money—money to be repaid over long years from the meager earnings of the child.

Soccorso morto, they called it.

The Death Loan.

Aid for the family; death sentence for the child.

They had visited when he was barely five, sizing him up, preying on his mother's poverty. Her solitude. Her desperation.

When he was six, they returned, with their cold-eyed smiles and their lulling words.

But his mother had steadfastly resisted their offers and their promises. She had worked and begged and scraped, and, yes, she had even stolen, to protect him. She had sometimes, for small payments, hidden rival *Mafiosi* in the two-room hovel they called home. But when he was fully grown, eighteen and strapping, he had gone himself to see the mine manager. With his cap in his hand, he had volunteered for the work.

In the mine, he had quickly proven himself. He was promoted to join the ranks of the *picuneri*. Every week he collected his pay and gave most of the money to the indomitable woman who had saved him from a childhood of torment.

He was so productive that the *capo* of his shift had assigned three *carusi* to work for him. He was different from the other *picuneri*, many of whom abused their *carusi*, often physically, and sometimes sexually. He tried his best to protect them, these boy-men. Although he was paid by the weight of ore he sent to the surface, he often sacrificed income in order to ease their burdens. It was always a balancing act. If it became too obvious, his *capo* would take one of them away from him. Maybe even two.

So he worked the face, swinging his pick, and tried his best to do right by his charges.

Yesterday, he had sent Peppino on an unimportant errand into a neighboring shaft, more to give the boy a rest than for any necessity of work. Unwittingly, he had sent the child to his death. A pocket of leaking gas, a spark from a pick, a flashover explosion, and it was over.

They'd recovered the bodies this morning. He'd held Peppino's mother in his arms when she collapsed, smearing her clothes and her skin with the dirt and the soot and the stink of the mine that had murdered her son.

They both knew that her torment had just begun. She had lost her son to the death loan, but the loan remained unpaid.

Peppino had two younger brothers.

Her family would never be free.

Numb with exhaustion, he trudged up the cliff trail from the train station. Crickets crackled at his approaching step. Behind him, the vast valley was white and silent under the heat haze of the late summer sky. A profusion of wild poppies bordered the path he now climbed. It led to the ancient *comune* of Valguarnera Caropepe. This had once been a well-traveled road, but fifteen years ago, the rotting supports of a long-abandoned mine under the town had collapsed without warning, destroying both the roadway and a dozen homes along the top of the escarpment.

In ten days' time, the train service that had carried him to and from the Floristella mine for every working day of his life would be abandoned as well.

Those thieving Christian Democrats, and those lying PCI swine, the loud-mouthed *comunistas* who never wasted a stray thought on Sicily's miners or peasants—all those self-serving politicos who constantly talked of progress—all had promised that things would change, that things must change, that nothing would stay the same.

Nothing . . . except illiteracy and poverty and disease and death.

Nothing . . . except the raw abuse of power, and the fearful silence of the defenseless.

Everything was fluid, and yet . . . petrified.

It was no wonder that the *Mafiosi* had always come out on top.

He sank his pick into the broken earth of the hillside and used it to pull himself up the last few feet to the top of the escarpment. Pneumatic drills had long ago replaced the pick, but he always kept his by his side. There were some things that could only be done by hand—like digging yourself out of a cave-in when all sources of power had been cut off.

He threaded his way through the rubble that marked the northernmost terminus of Via Roma. The prospect before his weary eyes contrasted starkly with the avenue's grandiose name. Cobbled in basalt from Etna's quarries, laid down decades ago, the narrow roadway plunged steeply toward the center of town, a trash-strewn ravine of decaying tenements, cluttered catwalks, and sagging clotheslines.

He trudged south toward home.

One hundred and sixty meters later, his life changed forever.

As he was passing the cathedral, Valguarnera's *Chiesa Madre*, he heard a child scream.

He turned to see a black Lancia Flavia sedan parked on the exit ramp from the church's small parking area. He recognized the model instantly because he knew a lot about cars—mainly because he couldn't afford one. But his attention was immediately drawn to the disturbing scene that was unfolding behind it. As he watched, a burly priest seized a fashionably dressed young woman by the front of her dress and drove a fist into her face. The woman flew backward onto the hard pavement.

Simultaneously, another priest was dragging a shrieking little girl toward the open rear door of the Lancia.

The miner recognized both men. He knew they were not priests.

The Lancia's powerful engine revved up.

He ran.

He rushed along the driver's side of the car and smashed the butt end of his pick handle through the open window, knocking the wheelman out of the fight before he could join it.

The thug holding the child went for a gun. The miner took him out with a powerful swing that drove the blade of his pick deep into the man's skull. Bone fragments and blood and brains splattered the child as he yanked the steel out with one violent pull.

The man was dead before he hit the ground.

Released, the weeping child fled toward the cathedral.

The miner spun to face the woman's assailant, and found himself staring into the barrel of a pistol.

He tensed.

BOOM!

The gunman's body jerked and twisted. He struggled to raise his weapon.

BOOM!

He collapsed to the pavement and lay still.

The miner slowly turned.

A handsome young man stood at the base of the shallow steps that led from the church's main door. He was holding a heavy revolver. He was impeccably dressed in a pin-striped three-piece suit, his shoes shone like mirrors, and he wore a boutonniere on his lapel.

The weeping little girl clung to his pant leg.

The man tucked the weapon into his jacket and hoisted the little girl into his arms.

The miner rushed to attend to the fallen woman.

PART
I

1

It started on Christmas morning.

At least that was when Kevin threw his first tantrum.

Later, looking back, Lucy realized that she hadn't been paying close enough attention.

There had been the nightmares. Too many to count. Thank God they had recently stopped.

And, there had been the boy's silences. She would find him staring into space, his face frozen in concentration. Or was it deep longing? She couldn't tell. But the very adultness—was that even the word for it?—of her little boy's expression had at times unnerved her.

She knew her son was different. There had always been an almost preternatural stillness about him. Even during the so-called "terrible twos," she had known him to sit for hours in the presence of his mother, his aunt, and his uncle without fidgeting.

But these long, solitary silences were something different.

They were something more profound.

Today's trouble began when Kevin tore the wrapping from a present, revealing a plastic construction set. It was a gift from his cousin

Pauline. A few moments earlier, Lucy had patiently read the label to him while he'd been busily collecting his trove of presents into a serviceable pile.

He stared at the gift. His mood seemed to change. He jumped to his feet, raised the box high over his head, and threw it at the wall.

He threw it with surprising force for a four-year-old.

Pauline's blissful humming abruptly ended. Jovial coffee talk among the adults died. Lucy moved quickly. She kneeled at the agitated boy's side. "Kevin! That's your present from Pauline! What is it? What's wrong?"

"I want to go home!"

"What? You are home, sweetheart!"

"No! I want to go home!"

"But this *is* home! Here with Auntie Ricki and Uncle Jeff and Pauline." Lucy hated the note of pleading in her own voice, but she was confounded and embarrassed.

"*No!*"

Ricki interceded. "Where do you want to go, Kevin?" she asked gently. "Where's home?"

"*Home!*" He burst into tears. His voice rose to a shriek. "*HOME!*"

He ran crying from the room.

Lucy and Ricki stared at each other.

"What the hell was that?" Jeff muttered.

Pauline abandoned the present she had just opened and ran to her father. "What's wrong with Kevin, Daddy?" she asked querulously as Jeff folded her in his arms. "Doesn't he like the gear set we got him?"

Lucy started after Kevin.

"Did you notice?" Ricki asked.

Lucy broke stride. "Notice what? That my son just threw a tantrum, and he's never done that before?"

"No. That he's limping. It looks bad."

Lucy hurried out of the room.

She found Kevin on his bed.

Fast asleep.

An hour later, the boy was wide awake and back to his old self. He was playing cheerfully beside the Christmas tree with the same Gears! Gears! Gears! Super Set he had tried to smash. It was as if nothing had happened.

Except for one thing: He was limping, favoring his right leg. And he didn't seem to want to use his right arm.

When Lucy asked him if he'd hurt himself, he answered with a blank look.

"Your leg, honey. Did you hurt it?"

"No."

"Then why are you limping?"

"What's 'limping,' Mommy?"

"You're walking like this . . ." She demonstrated.

"No, I'm not."

But the limp didn't go away. On the twenty-seventh, Lucy took him to Coral Gables Hospital. Twelve hours later, after a battery of tests and a hefty medical bill, she was told there was nothing physically wrong with her son.

"Perfectly healthy boy," the doctor said. "Nothing abnormal."

"But he limps! And his right arm—he doesn't want to use it! How is that normal?"

"It can only be psychosomatic. Something may be deeply affecting your son, and this is just its manifestation. I'll refer you to a child psychologist. In the meantime, you need to think carefully about the stressors in your household."

So, Lucy Hendricks thought about stressors in her household.

Since before Kevin was born, she'd been living with her sister Erica—the gorgeous and inimitable "Ricki" to friends and family—and Ricki's husband, Jeffery Barnett. Her brother-in-law's busy legal practice had easily supported the purchase, a dozen years ago, of the couple's spacious Coral Gables home. Sprawling over two acres, Casa Barnett boasted an imposing main residence, a separate guesthouse where Lucy and Kevin nestled in significant comfort, a swimming pool, and a tennis court.

Over the past four years, Lucy had devoted most of her time to raising Kevin and caring for her niece, Pauline, now a precocious eight-year-old with thick black curls and her mother's startling hazel eyes. With the benign indulgence of Jeff and Ricki, she'd been able to live rent free in return for helping out as Pauline's part-time nanny. The arrangement had worked well for both sides. It enabled Ricki to take over management of *Il Bronte*—"the Bronte" to locals—their ailing father's bar and restaurant in Coconut Grove. And it permitted Lucy to bank her modest police widow's allowance, and to use the rent she collected from her house in Bayonne to pay down the remaining balance on the mortgage.

But the pain was unending.

In the weeks and months after her husband's death, horrified disbelief had slowly faded into utter desolation; desolation into numb exhaustion. Her life had seemed meaningless; her nights blistered by feverish dreams, her days a barren wilderness, empty of hope. *Dolore immenso* her father had described it, after the death of Lucy's mother, his beloved Giulia, when Lucy was only twelve.

Immense grief.

It was a despair so deep and deadly that at times it had threatened her sanity. There had been moments when only her sister's devotion, and her pregnancy with Jack's child, had prevented her from taking her own life.

She had survived, but five years on, the keenness of her loss remained an ever-present anguish, informing her moods and haunting her relationships. Her days were consumed with a futile effort to stop herself from thinking. Time after time, the past rose to the surface. There were still days when she felt so sluggish with depression she could barely move. She had never come anywhere near the so-called "closure" that pop psychologists always prattled about. The term itself, she knew, had been lifted from the legitimate literature of psychotherapy and devalued by constant misuse. Nowadays, it was used to embrace every conceivable emotional circumstance.

And then there was the police counselor's talk about grief being a "journey" to be worked through, with its own pre-prepared checklist of emotional states. If Lucy hadn't been so lost in her wasteland of sorrow, she would have laughed in her face.

The fact was that none of the theories and the chit-chat and the checklists mattered. The only thing that mattered was that Jack Gabriel Hendricks, her soul mate, her protector, her lifeline—the man she had loved almost from the moment they met—had been brutally murdered, and the crime had never been solved.

In other words . . . forget closure.

Recently, Lucy had made a sincere effort to emerge from her shell. She'd signed on to work as a substitute teacher in the local school district, and she'd even spent a few evenings each week helping out behind the bar at the Bronte.

Not that the activity had sweetened her dreams, or lessened the ever-present throb of loss on the margins of her waking thoughts.

So, yes, there was at least one significant stressor in her household.

It was her.

2

"Sorry about Parrish. Met the guy once . . ."

"Oh yeah?"

"Back at the Academy. He filled in for an instructor who was off sick. Seemed like a good man."

"He *was* a good man." Detective Ernie Tait thumbed the remote, opened the rear door of their unmarked Dodge Charger and dropped his briefcase on the backseat. Then he squeezed his heavy frame behind the wheel.

Jack Hendricks took a deep breath of the cold night air. The ice storm of two days ago had changed back to sleet before finally easing off early this morning. The guy on the Weather Channel said the system had been a headache to forecast because its track was so erratic. One thing was sure: The roads were going to be treacherous. Jack wondered if he should have insisted on doing the driving tonight. The four months he'd spent at the Army's Northern Warfare Training Center in Alaska had included a driving component; he wasn't so sure about this aging detective's skills.

He bent to release the lock on the passenger seat and shoved it all the way back to make room for his long legs.

"I would've driven, you know," he said as he yanked the passenger door closed.

"My car, my rules. You'll get your chance."

Tait twisted the key. Jack felt the powerful engine respond. They pulled out of the lot.

"How long were you and Cal partners?"

"Seven years, eight months, ten days."

"Good friends, then."

"Yeah."

Tait swung north on Avenue C. He stayed in the outside lane, tires alternately crunching and splashing, moving with the subdued traffic flow. Ahead of them, a sedan fishtailed as it swung into traffic. Even here in the center of town, the roads were still slick.

"How did he end up behind that warehouse alone?"

Tait turned to his new partner. "Look, kid," he said in his low rumbling voice, "if you want us to get along, you won't bring up Cal Parrish again."

"Sorry."

"Hen-dricks . . ." Tait rolled Jack's surname off his tongue. "Sounds a lot like an old Bayonne name."

"One of the oldest."

Tait gave him a sideways look. "How's that?"

"Dutch settlers . . . from way back."

"How far back is 'way back'?"

"If you believe the stories, my family took up their land grant in the 1650s. Didn't last. Indians drove 'em out. They finally made it back a few years later."

Tait grunted. "What'd they do? Call in the troops?"

"No. They did it the Dutch way. They negotiated an agreement, and then they kept their word."

"So . . . old family . . . old connections. Explains how you got into plainclothes so fast."

"Meaning?"

"You were only in uniform for, what, a couple of years?"

Jack exhaled. "I applied. I got the transfer. Last cop in my family was back in the thirties, so I don't think my name helped much."

"Sorry, kid. Took me a lot longer to get down the hall. Always figured it was because I'm a FOOT."

Jack knew what that meant in local slang: *fucking-out-of-towner.* He replied carefully. "I've heard that before. People saying locals look out for each other. One guy said it was like the Freemasons."

"Yep."

"I can't say . . . I grew up here, went to school here, spent time in the Army, and came back. My name never opened any doors."

"Maybe. But you're sitting in this car."

First Cal Parrish. Now this . . .

Jack decided to change the subject. "Where are we heading anyway?"

"Captain wants us to talk to a witness. Guy was sitting in his car outside Irv's Liquors when that robbery went down. Said he was afraid to come forward last night, but his wife talked him into calling us."

"Whose case is it?"

"The guys who caught the file are off tonight. Blackburn asked us to take the hand-off."

"I haven't even seen the file."

"In my briefcase."

Jack twisted in his seat and reached back. Just as he snared the briefcase, their radio came to life.

Seven-Five-One . . . Respond Code One . . . We have a report of a carjacking Hook Road and Four-Forty. Female victim unconscious.

Witness describes two male actors, heading north on Four-Forty in the victim's dark blue BMW SUV. We've got a partial—begins Mike Two Eight, repeat Mike Two Eight.

Jack keyed the mike.

"Five-Eight-One, myself, and Five-Eight-Two are uptown, we'll head to Four-Forty and the Av C ramp."

Dispatch came back instantly.

Received Five-Eight-One.

At Tait's nod, Jack lit them up and hit the siren. Tait punched the accelerator. Too hard. The rear tires spun. Jack grimaced. Tait backed off, waited for the tires to grip, and then started edging up their speed. The traffic cleared obediently, and they made it to the Route 440 ramp in less than five minutes.

At the top of the ramp, Jack killed the lights and siren as Tait swung the Charger up over the left-side curb onto the verge. They waited behind a brake of juniper bushes, conveniently evergreen even in the depths of winter.

A few minutes later, a dark blue BMW blasted by.

Jack got back on the radio.

"Five-Eight-One . . . we have that vehicle north on Four-Forty from Av C. We're in pursuit."

Jack hit the lights and siren as Tait rolled the Charger back onto the ramp. They merged onto Route 440 and took up pursuit.

Bayonne received. All units clear channel one.

After three-tenths of a mile, the roadway bent left into the notorious 440 loop. It was an apparently pointless curve that inexplicably forced northbound traffic south, then abruptly north, toward Jersey City. The Bayonne police had long cursed the road design for its sharp curves. Local towing companies, not so much . . . overturned tractor-trailer units were the norm along the section's half-mile length.

"Five-Eight-One . . . entering the loop, speed forty-five, surface slush, target vehicle speed estimated sixty."

The north zone supervisor took over.

North Super received. I have it, Dispatch—notify Jersey City. Five-Eight-One, use care!

"Five-Eight-One, received."

A warning sign ahead displayed a switchback arrow and a twenty-five-mile-per-hour warning. Tait was already backing off their speed. "Idiot's going to roll that thing," he muttered as the BMW disappeared in a spray of slush around the bend at the bottom of the loop.

True to prediction, they rounded the corner in time to see the target vehicle in a broadside slide. It capsized, rolled, and came to rest upright on the far side of the median. Oncoming cars swerved.

"Five-Eight-One . . . north bend on the loop. He lost it. We're out of the car."

As the Charger slid to a stop, Jack bailed, weapon ready. He rounded the nose of their car and started moving toward the BMW. He heard Tait behind him, then heard him yell, *"Kid!"* and suddenly found himself facedown in the slush and the dirt. Tait landed heavily right next to him. In the same instant, a spray of automatic gunfire whipped just above their heads and chewed up their car. Almost simultaneously, they heard the wet slide of braking traffic and the boom of a collision on the road behind them.

"Fuck this," Tait said. He took careful aim with his Glock and fired three quick rounds. A black barrel protruding from the SUV's driver's-side window jerked upward and disappeared. An instant later, from their ground-level vantage point, they both saw a pair of boots hit the ground on the far side of the BMW and start running away from the scene.

Jack and Tait jumped wordlessly to their feet, separated, and made a weapons-ready run at the vehicle. Tait jerked the driver's door open and swung into position, flashlight on, gun ready.

A scruffy male, mid-twenties, lay sprawled across the seats. There was a neat hole in his cheek just below his right eye and the back of his head was missing. Blood and gray matter dripped from the seat back and the ceiling above him.

Jack lifted an automatic weapon off the floor of the vehicle, where it lay among a litter of shell casings. "It's an AR-15."

He straightened and stood for a second, noting the stopped traffic to his right . . . the vehicles trying to reverse . . . the few men who had emerged from their cars jogging back up the line of traffic, waving arms and shouting. He shifted his attention to the figure of the other car-jacker, running and slipping, silhouetted against the lights of the Rut-kowski Park entrance and the Port Newark container terminal a half-mile across the bay beyond.

"He's heading for the park," he said thoughtfully.

Tait guessed what he was thinking.

"Don't do it, kid! We'll get him!"

Sirens were closing in from two directions.

Jack started moving. "The name's Jack. And yes, we will." He strode into the middle of the highway. He held up a flat palm to make it plain to the goggling drivers at the front of the line that they'd better not move.

As if anyone was going to argue with a mud-covered man packing an assault rifle.

Tait yelled after him. "Jack! Not in the back!"

Jack raised the rifle and took aim.

"Jack!"

The young detective squeezed off a single shot. The distant figure dropped.

The sound of the gunshot hung on the heavy night air.

Jack strolled back to the BMW. Tait was staring at him in dis-belief.

"Thanks for getting my name right," Jack said evenly. "Scratch one tibia. It's going to be a while before he runs from the cops again."

The downed man's squeals and moans reached their ears.

"I thought you Dutch guys would rather negotiate."

"He didn't have anything to trade."

Tait allowed himself a faint smile. "I think maybe you and I are gonna get along."

Jack nodded. He gestured toward the writhing carjacker. "I better go get him."

"I'll do it." Tait jerked a thumb at traffic chaos behind their Charger. "Check for injuries back there. And make sure someone called the medics." His dark eyes cut to the BMW. "And the M.E."

"Right. And, Ernie . . ."

"What?"

"Thanks for the save."

"My pleasure. I thought you'd rather eat slush than take a bullet."

3

Kevin's first visit with Megan Avedon, the child psychologist—a kindly woman in her forties with a welcoming smile—hadn't been very productive. He was still limping, although not all day, every day. He wouldn't engage with Dr. Avedon at all, either in or out of Lucy's presence, even to discuss his apparently painful gait. At the end of the session, she reported to Lucy that Kevin had just stared at her with "those old-soul eyes" and asked her if she had a gear set he could play with.

The psychologist had wanted to interview Lucy ahead of time, alone. Lucy told her that she'd need time to arrange a sitter for Kevin because her sister Erica was busy at their father's bar. So they'd made two appointments for later in January—one for Lucy, and a later one for Kevin.

The babysitter excuse wasn't precisely accurate, but it had given Lucy some breathing room.

Some time to prepare herself.

The fact was, the whole process left her cold. She'd already been down the grief counseling road, and she realized this would be more of the same, just under another name. She'd never been someone to share her deepest feelings—except with Jack, who was now lost forever in unreplying death—and she dreaded having to explore them with an-other pretend-friend analyst.

On the other hand, she knew she owed it to her son. Especially since, at least once a day for the past two weeks, Kevin had burst into tears for no apparent reason. At least, for no reason that he could be persuaded to explain.

Then, today, just after four o'clock in the afternoon, something hap-pened that rocked Lucy's perception of reality. Kevin crawled into her lap, hugged her, looked up into her eyes and said, "Mommy, it's time to go home."

Lucy's heart sank.

"I don't understand, honey. What do you mean by 'home'?"

"Home to b-bay . . . to Bay-onne."

Bayonne.

Lucy was shaken.

She had left New Jersey before Kevin was born.

He had never been to Bayonne.

Lucy had been four months pregnant when her sister Ricki arrived to move her back to Florida. She'd been dealing with the indifference of pension board bureaucrats, trying to sort out a payout and allowance. The constant rumor-mongering that Jack had been corrupt, the attitude of the police toward her, the attitude of fellow teachers at the school—it was all too much. The last straw was when she returned home from an appointment with a specialist ob-gyn physician in Manhattan to dis-cover that her home had been burglarized and ransacked. The uniformed patrol officers who answered the call had seemed almost indifferent, and the actions of the BCI crime scene technician cursory and slipshod. Ricki had been trying to persuade her to move back to Florida; now Lucy was ready to agree. Wallowing in her loss, and feeling increasingly isolated, she began to believe that if she didn't get away from the whispers and the stony looks, she would lose her sanity.

Ricki had driven thirteen hundred miles to help her pack up her life.

To save her from the *dolore immenso* that was sapping her will to live.

They'd moved most of her effects to a self-storage unit at the north end of town. Then they'd driven south—Ricki deliberately taking it slow, making the journey last, so they could talk. Well . . . so Ricki could *try* to talk to her silent, paralyzed sister. When they arrived in Coral Gables, Ricki and Jeff had installed her in a spare bedroom in the main residence so they could keep an eye on her until she made it past her period of darkest thoughts. She was remote and impenetrable, and they feared for her life. It wasn't until Kevin was three weeks old, when Lucy finally seemed to have found something to live for—some*one* to live for—that they'd agreed to let her move into the guesthouse behind the pool.

In the meantime, unable to help herself, Lucy had kept a watch on the New Jersey media websites. Stories kept appearing in the Bayonne and Jersey City press under headlines that seemed expressly designed to lacerate:

DEAD COP MAY HAVE BEEN INVOLVED WITH ORGANIZED CRIME
BAYONNE POLICE REMAIN QUIET ABOUT CORRUPT COP INVESTIGATION

Allegations that amounted to nothing more than rumor-mongering were regularly recycled. The main allegation was that Jack had been somehow connected to an unnamed New Jersey crime family. Lucy knew the reporters were talking about the infamous Lanza family. After spending several weeks tormenting herself with these articles, she finally terminated her online searches.

But the unwelcome reminders didn't end. Not long after her move south, she received a call from the owner of the compound where she and Ricki had rented the storage unit. Someone had cut the lock off her unit and rummaged through her effects. Exasperated, she asked the man to secure it with a new lock, mail her a key, and let her know what she owed for the extra expense. She promised she would include it in her next payment.

"But, ma'am, don't you want me to call the cops?" Whatever the man may have thought about all the rumors, his tone showed that he was sympathetic to Lucy.

"Thanks, but no. They won't do anything about it."

"But, why wouldn't they?"

"Because they're probably the ones who broke in."

Although she had never returned to Bayonne, Lucy hadn't been able to bring herself to sell the house that she and Jack had bought together. So she'd used the lump-sum payout from his police pension to make a balloon payment on the mortgage, and then left the property in the hands of a rental agency.

She cradled her little boy's head against her breast, searching her memory, trying to recall if she had ever talked to him about Bayonne, or to someone else in his listening presence.

But what came to her mind was something else.

She remembered his mystifying obsession with her old Rand McNally atlas. It had started early last fall. Poring over maps of the fifty states had seemed a strange interest for a four-year-old boy. The aging atlas's spine had deteriorated and some of the maps were coming loose. Concerned that he might damage it further, she'd taken it away when he wasn't looking. But he cried so piteously that she finally relented. After that, he'd spent days flipping back and forth through the book.

Stranger still, thinking about it, had been her later discovery of a clue card from his I SPY Preschool Game protruding from page 108. It was as if her son had deliberately bookmarked the map of New Jersey.

New Jersey.

The state she had left behind five months before Kevin was born.

His fixation on Bayonne made no sense.

For the last four years, she'd put her life on hold, waiting for something to happen—something to help her decide what to do next.

Maybe the universe was trying to tell her something.

What happened ten seconds after that very thought crossed her mind shook her to the core.

Her phone rang. The call display showed a number she didn't recognize, but an area code that she did: **201**.

It was one of the area codes for Bayonne.

Lucy's hand trembled as she answered.

"Hello?"

"Hi! Is that Lucy? Lucy Hendricks?"

"Who's speaking?"

"It's Garrett, Lucy. Garrett Lindsay."

She blanked for a second.

"Garrett?"

"Yeah, it's me. How are you, Lucy? It's been a long time."

"I'm . . . I'm fine. Can I ask how you got this number?"

"Teachers' Fed. Your last renewal."

"I thought I'd let that go."

"You did, but this contact number was on your form from '09. I took a chance."

"Okay."

"I've been thinking about you."

"Why?"

"I know you went through hell back then. I mean, pretty obvious why you felt you had to leave. Leave the job. Leave Bayonne. Everyone understood."

"Yeah. Thanks, but—"

"It's been a few years now. I mean—"

"Garrett. Why are you calling me?"

"Okay. I'll just come out and say it." He spoke quickly. "I'm calling because I'm hoping you're ready to come back . . . to, you know, move back. Come back to your old job. Okay, not *exactly* your old job, but come back, join my team, and—" He stopped abruptly, as if he was embarrassed by his rapid-fire sales pitch.

Lucy was completely unnerved. She looked down at Kevin. He was lying with his knees drawn up, his head on her lap, his face pressed to her stomach.

"Your team?"

"I'm the principal at Oresko. We had a resignation over Christmas, and I thought—"

"Oresko?"

"Sorry. The Nicholas Oresko School. It's the new one on the site of old P.S. Fourteen. They named it after the medal of honor winner. I guess you missed that."

"Yes, Garrett, I missed that."

"Well, listen, I've got a space for you and I want you to come."

"I thought principals weren't allowed to do any recruiting."

"We're not. But the mayor owed me. He had a word with Central Office."

"The old politics thing again."

"It's Bayonne, Lucy. If you can't change it, use it. Come back and work with me at a great new school!"

"Garrett, I have a son. I'm a single mom. I can't just—!"

"Yeah, I remember you were pregnant. Listen, we can help you work around that. We have pre-K in the school, and daycare facilities nearby."

"I still own the house down at the Point. If I remember correctly, kids have to go to the school in the district where they live."

"Lucy . . ."

"You fixed that as well?"

"Yeah, I did."

"You presumed a lot, Garrett."

"Yeah, I did."

Lucy took a long breath. "I don't know . . ."

"Lucy, do you know how many waiters there are in America?"

"What?"

"Just under two million! And do you know how many teachers?" He didn't wait for her answer. "Nearly four million!"

What is this man talking about?

"What's your point?"

"My point is that only five percent of those four million are top performers—natural born teachers who consistently lift their students' test scores. You're one of them, Lucy, and I want you back. I'll get you top of the scale. I promise."

Lucy didn't reply. She was watching her son, who seemed to be in a half-doze, and wondering what the hell just happened.

"Lucy?"

A few weeks ago, the tenants in her house in Bayonne had given notice that they wouldn't be renewing their lease. They'd be moving out at the end of the month. For the first time in over two years, the house would be vacant.

Was it time?

Was it time to stop leaning on her sister?

Was it time to grit her teeth and face reality?

Was the universe *really* trying to tell her something?

"Lucy? Are you there?"

"Yes, Garrett, I'm here."

"I know this is a bit sudden, but what do you say?"

"Are you talking . . . *now*? This term?"

"Yeah. If you agree, I'll use subs till you get here. As long as it's not, like, months."

Lucy took a deep breath. "Can you give me a day to think about it?"

"Of course!" He sounded elated. "Let me give you my number."

"I've got it. It's on my phone."

"Right. Okay, call me! I'd love to have you back on staff, Lucy!"

There were other things they could have discussed: Who else had he arranged to get transferred from their old school? Who got married?

Who had an affair? Who got divorced? But Lucy wasn't interested and Garrett Lindsay was too smart to introduce distractions. They said their good-byes.

Lucy already knew she wouldn't need a day to make up her mind. She resisted the temptation to walk over to the main house to talk to Ricki. And, although Jeff had always been a sensible adviser, she discarded the idea of calling him at the office. One word to either of them and she'd be drawn into a family conference. Her ailing father, who doted on his grandson Kevin, would be dragged into it. The discussion would become a swirl of logic mixed with emotion.

No, the decision needed to be hers and hers alone, unaffected by concerned advice from the people who loved her, and whose first instinct would be to protect her.

She eased out from under Kevin, who was now fast asleep, and went to the kitchen. She brewed a cup of peppermint tea. She settled into her favorite chair to think.

Forty minutes later, she picked up the phone and called her property agent in Bayonne. She instructed him to take her house off the rental market. Then she called Dr. Avedon's office and canceled their appointments.

When Kevin woke up, she told him they were going home.

"Where's that, Mommy?"

"Bayonne."

His reaction baffled her. He just blinked and then asked what they were having for dinner.

But, the next morning, she noticed his limp was gone.

4

The carjackers' victim had survived. The doctors said it had been touch-and-go. When the woman's head hit the pavement, she'd sustained a cracked skull and a subdural hematoma. But she was a tough lady. She'd pulled through without any mental deficits. When they showed her a photo lineup, she'd immediately pointed out the man who had yanked her out of her car and batted her to the ground.

It was the guy Ernie had shot.

Jack's own dead-eye performance before a half-dozen gaping motorists had earned hard questions from journalists and a stern letter of reprimand from his chief. But somehow that letter never made it to his service file. Official disapproval transformed to admiration when the full extent of Jack's subsequent actions was revealed. Although, miraculously, the carjacker's spray of gunfire had not struck human flesh, it had stitched the rear quarter panel of a passing car and shot out the tire. The crash Jack and Ernie heard behind them as they lay in the mud had involved that car and a plumbing company's service truck that was traveling behind it. The car went into a spin, took a broadside hit from the overtaking truck and slammed into a lamppost.

As Jack rushed toward the scene, he used his portable to tell the supervisor they needed an ambulance. "Make that two! And call the M.E."

The nose of the truck was jammed hard up against the side of a Hyundai sedan. The truck driver was vainly trying to start his engine, presumably to back it away, but the sickly whine of the starter underlined the futility of that effort. Jack could hear crying coming from inside the sedan. Several motorists were out of their cars, milling about, but keeping their distance. The strong smell of leaking gasoline explained their caution. Jack sprinted to the back of the truck, found a heavy pipe wrench, and then sprang onto the hood of the wrecked car. He smashed out the windshield and single-handedly extracted all three occupants—a father, mother, and their infant daughter. He had acted just in time. Seconds after they were freed, the car burst into flames. He yelled at everyone to move away and, with the help of the truck driver and a couple of male bystanders, carried each member of the injured family to a safer location. An ambulance crew arrived a few minutes later, followed shortly after by the fire crew Ernie Tait had called in when he spotted the fire from across the highway.

In the end, at a Memorial Day ceremony held a week ago at St. Henry's Church, both Ernie and Jack had received valor awards for their actions.

On top of that, based on leads Ernie and Jack developed, a carjacking ring had been rolled up. Its leader, a man with the unlikely name of Edward Tudor, ran an auto wrecking yard in East Rutherford. He was currently in federal custody because the Bergen County prosecutor's case against him was standing in line behind federal charges—those the result of a cache of military-grade weapons found on the wrecking yard premises. Apparently one of Tudor's employee-carjackers had decided to help himself to one of the assault rifles.

A week after the incident, Ernie admitted to Jack how he'd obtained their first lead. The procedure, he said, had involved a folding knife and a quiet threat. Well . . . quiet from Tait's side at least. As he'd hiked across to the Rutkowski Park entrance, he'd slipped his trusty Schrade knife out of his pocket. He kneeled next to the man that Jack's bullet had felled. He told him that he'd just have to wait his turn for an ambulance, because their first priorities would be the innocent road users his scumbag partner had shot up.

"Assuming," Tait added, "that it was *him* who did the shooting."

The thief was moaning with pain. "It was him, man! They call him Slider! He's fuckin' crazy!"

"*Was* fuckin' crazy. He's dead."

"It wasn't me, I swear!"

Tait ended this part of the discussion by shoving his knife blade up to the hilt into the wound in the man's shattered lower leg. He let the guy shriek for a few seconds, and then he withdrew the steel. Blood flooded out after it.

"What'd you do that for?" the thief gasped.

"Wound looks really bad. In fact, it looks like you're bleeding out. Bullet must've got an artery. I'm not medically trained, so I can't say how long you'll last."

"Pleeease! I need a doctor! I need an ambulance!"

"Yes, you do. I'll get one over here as soon as you tell me where you got that rifle. And who hired you."

"No one hired us!" he whined, but the lie was obvious.

"No? You just decided to pull some lady out of her fancy car, knock her unconscious, and leave her on the side of the road? You just decided, what the hell, let's take our trusty AR-15 along and hose down any cops that follow us? You did all that for a *joyride*?" Tait wiped down his knife on the guy's cuff, folded the blade, and put it away. He stood up. "Well, I guess I'll just wait here while you think about that."

Tait got exactly what he needed in less than a minute.

Now, three months later, the BPD investigation was complete and the charges against two other carjacking crews—four young males with long lists of priors—were working their way through the courts in Hudson and Bergen Counties. Tait's impromptu "interrogation" of the surviving carjacker, and the leads it provided, had helped break up a ring that had been operating for at least two years, if not longer. They'd been stealing luxury cars and high-end SUVs, presumably to break them up for much sought-after parts—although, strangely, not many auto parts directly traceable to stolen vehicles had been found on the wrecking yard's premises.

The Feds, meanwhile, had been trying to identify the actual owner of the operation in East Rutherford. Edward Tudor had only been the on-site manager. The U.S. attorney and the Bergen County prosecutor had both offered deals on sentence in return for his cooperation, but he was ignoring his own lawyer's advice and refusing to talk. He'd made it clear that if he rolled, he was a dead man. A frustrated FBI agent had told Jack that the wrecking yard belonged to a company incorporated in New York—one that was owned, in turn, by a company incorporated in Delaware. The Feds had relied on the U.S. attorney's subpoena powers to track their way through what turned out to be a network of shell companies. The trail had led from Delaware to Texas, Nevada, the Channel Islands, and back to Delaware before vanishing into an impenetrable maze of anonymous ownership. After weeks of relentless financial analysis, they still had no idea who was actually controlling any of the entities they had identified. "It's fucking easier to find out the beneficial ownership of a company in the Cayman Islands than it is in some of our U.S. states!" the agent complained. All he could tell Jack was that they suspected the Mob was involved, but that was pure conjecture.

Although he'd kept it to himself, Jack wasn't comfortable with Tait's revelation about his interview technique. Surprisingly, Michael

Ortega, the young thief Tait had tortured—and there was no other word to describe it—hadn't said a word about the knife incident to his attorney. Instead, in some unspoken trade-off, he'd taken a generous plea deal that Tait had helped arrange, and even agreed to testify if any of his fellow thieves forced a trial. The fact that the ATF had become deeply interested in Edward Tudor's activities led Jack to believe there were other incentives being offered behind the scenes. He wondered if Ortega would end up serving any time at all.

On the other hand, courtesy of Jack's marksmanship, Ortega would be walking with a limp for the rest of his life.

As summer neared, Jack wasn't thinking about carjacking rings, or roadside rescues, or sadistic interrogation techniques. He was thinking about the woman he loved. He was thinking about the approaching school vacation. He was thinking about taking some time off, flying down to Florida, visiting Lucy's family, scuba diving in the Keys . . . and maybe, finally, starting a family of their own.

He was thinking about that, and he was thinking about something else.

He was thinking Ernie Tait knew more about Cal Parrish's murder than he'd ever disclosed.

5

Moving north from Florida in the dead of winter hadn't been an attractive prospect, but Garrett Lindsay had begged Lucy to be ready to start by the first of February, so here she was.

Yes, here she was having an acute anxiety attack.

She'd agreed to take over a sixth grade class, at a school she'd never seen, five years after she'd ceased teaching full time. Now, after three days on the road, she was rolling down Broadway, Bayonne's anemic version of that iconic Manhattan thoroughfare, with Kevin asleep in his car seat behind her, returning to live in the state where the boy's father had been murdered in cold blood.

Returning, in part, because for some inexplicable reason her son had demanded the move.

And because, for some equally inexplicable reason, she knew she must rebuild her life in the place that had given her the greatest joy and the greatest sorrow.

Lucy Hendricks was wondering if she'd lost her mind.

• • •

Before they departed Florida, Lucy and Kevin spent an afternoon with her father at his assisted living residence near Tamiami Park. Lucy made lunch and, later, while Kevin kicked a soccer ball against the fence behind Joseph Cappelli's small apartment, father and daughter sat together on the patio.

Lucy had long ceased to notice the nasal cannula that was permanently attached to her father's face, or the low hiss of his oxygen concentrator. But what did distract her was a conversation they had toward the end of the day.

"He's a good boy, Lucinda," her father said.

The boy in question was at that moment shrieking with delight as he and Joseph's mutt terrier chased each other back and forth across the yard.

"Yes, he is."

"Here in Florida he has you, and he has this family. Up there, he will only have you."

"I know, Dad. But it's time for me to stand back on my feet. For me, and for Kevin."

"You will be alone, a single woman, raising a boy to be a man."

Lucy knew the signs. Although her father's eyes were tracking Kevin's joyful antics, his mind was focused elsewhere. She had a pretty good idea what was coming next.

"I'll be strong. I have Nonna's blood in my veins. Your grandson will be safe."

"Nonna saved my life."

"I wish I had known her."

"Some days she would walk miles—seven, eight, even ten miles—searching for wild greens. Filling sacks with wild cabbage, asparagus, chicory, fennel. Greens she could only sell for pennies, Lucinda! Pennies!"

"I remember the stories."

"And, snails! The vermicularas . . . they were the fat ones. She didn't need so many to make a stew. But they disappear at first light, so she'd get up at three or four in the morning. Sometimes she took me with her, but not often. She wanted me to get my sleep, for school. She wanted me to finish school."

"You told us."

"She was a great woman, your grandmother." His eyes were damp as he reached across the space between their chairs. She felt his bony fingers clasp her forearm. "It was just her and me. She would have killed to protect me." There was a deep coldness in his voice. Lucy wasn't sure how to reply, but he wasn't waiting for a response. "Instead, she sacrificed her own life to keep us safe. Me. Your mother. Erica, who had just been born. And, because of that . . . you, my dear daughter."

The words set Lucy's mind tumbling.

"What do you mean? You always said she died before you could bring her over! You always said everything was set, and she was planning to come!"

"It was, and she was. But the immigration papers didn't get to her in time."

"In time for what?"

Seconds ticked. The oxygen concentrator hissed and clicked, cycling faster.

"Never mind. Just protect that boy." His voice was gravel.

The temperature was hovering in the twenties and there was snow on the ground, but at least her Chevy's heater was working and the street ahead had been cleared. She rolled south toward Bergen Point.

Kevin's voice startled her. "We missed the turn!"

"What?"

"The street, Mommy! It was back there!"

Lucy checked the rearview mirror. Kevin was twisted in his seat, looking back.

She slowed and pulled to the curb.

"Honey, what do you mean?"

"That one! I want to go there!"

He was pointing at the corner of East Twenty-first.

"Why? Our house is this way."

Kevin's face contorted. *"I want to go there!"*

At once curious and uneasy, Lucy pulled back onto Broadway, cut left onto East Nineteenth and backtracked on Avenue E.

"That way!"

She checked the mirror. Kevin was pointing to their right.

Lucy suddenly knew where her son wanted to go, but she simply could not accept that he knew it himself. She tried to stifle the idea, to reject it out of hand, but her little boy's expectant expression, as he strained against the straps of his car seat, made it impossible to ignore.

She was assaulted by a nightmarish sensation.

She made the turn. East Twenty-first was a one-way street, and the plows hadn't scraped it as clean as Broadway, but it was passable. The road dove under the Hudson-Bergen Light Rail overpass. She stopped at the Prospect Avenue intersection, and then drove straight on.

In the backseat, her four-year-old was silent.

They neared the destination. As a final test, Lucy maintained her speed. She intended to drive on by if Kevin said nothing.

"Mommy!"

There was space at the curb on the right, next to an old yellow house with clapboard siding. She pulled over. She released her seatbelt and twisted around to look at her little boy. He was staring intently at a shabby three-story row house on the opposite side of the street. The building's siding was painted a sickly green. A bent old woman wearing a heavy coat, with an empty net bag slung across her shoulder, had just emerged from the residence. She completed her unsteady descent down a short flight of stained concrete steps, noticed Lucy watching, glared suspiciously, and moved away.

"Kevin?"

His face wore an otherworldly look. He pointed at the house and said, "Jossie."

A chill ran down Lucy's spine. Her mind raced, unable to credit what had just happened.

Kevin was pointing at the house where Jack grew up.

And he'd just used Jack's nickname for his kid sister, a Hollywood wannabe who had finally made it and was currently co-starring in a popular drama on cable TV.

She damned well knew she'd never used that nickname in front of Kevin.

She felt like she'd just plunged into an alternate reality.

Twenty minutes later they arrived at Lucy's house on West First Street.

Lucy was still stunned by the paranormal event she'd just witnessed. Based on Kevin's behavior, she'd expected a screaming fit when they drove away from Jack's old family home on East Twenty-first. Before she started the car, she tried to explain, as calmly as she could, that "we" didn't live in that house anymore. She told him that they'd bought a new house down near Bergen Point and that's where they were going.

To her surprise, Kevin hadn't protested. He just said, "Okay, Mommy," and reached for the battered toy car he'd been playing with off-and-on for the entire drive from Coral Gables. As she navigated the streets that brought them finally to the little white house across from Collins Park, Kevin matched every turn with the little car in his hand.

The driveway was a foot deep in snow, so Lucy parked on the street. Clearing the driveway would be Job One. She would be working alone when she emptied her packed storage unit and moved the contents back into the house. Rather than dozens of trips across the front yard, up the steps to the front door, and then around the tight corner leading from the foyer, it would be much easier to move everything straight through

the sliding doors at the rear. The two-story Radford bungalow was over
ninety years old and, although the interior had been updated—most recently by Lucy and Jack themselves—it didn't have the most accommo-
dating floor plan.

But it was *her* house and, despite the threat of painful memories, she
intended to live in it.

She unstrapped Kevin and helped him out of the car. He stood on
the sidewalk, looking up at the house, and then took his mother's hand.
They crunched along the walkway past the sprawling red oak. The path
had been shoveled, but a thin remaining layer showed the impressions of
footwear coming and going from the front steps—artifacts, Lucy deduced,
of the last tenants' vacating move.

She led Kevin up the steps and unlocked the door. She allowed him
to enter first, then followed.

Kevin hesitated for a second, and then ran through the foyer and
cut to the right toward the living room. No longer sure of what to expect
from her remarkable child, Lucy quickly followed. She heard his thump-
ing footsteps come to a stop.

She found him standing in the middle of the living room, looking
around in wonder. As she reached him, he took her hand again. This
time, he seemed to want to lead, so she let him. He escorted her from
room to room, saying nothing, stopping to take in each room, his face
wearing a serious expression. He reminded her of a grown man working
his way through an art gallery. Lucy followed, watching and confused.
They climbed the narrow stairway to the second floor. There were only
two rooms on that floor, the master bedroom and a guest bedroom, each
with its own en suite bathroom.

In the short hallway at the top of the stairs, Lucy noticed that Kevin
was limping again. He ignored the guest bedroom and led her to the master bedroom.

After lingering for long seconds just inside the doorway, he sighed,
looked up at her, and said, "Mommy, I'm tired."

When Lucy had moved out, five years ago, she left the house furnished.

Except for one room: the master bedroom.

She hated the idea of anyone sleeping in the bed she had shared with Jack for their entire married life, so she donated the bedframe, night tables, and dressers to Goodwill and sent the mattress to the landfill. Each set of tenants—there had only been two over the entire five years—had leased the house on the basis that they would furnish the master bedroom themselves. But when she'd called her rental agency a few weeks ago, she asked him to tell the departing tenants to take anything they wanted when they moved out because she was planning to refurnish completely.

The only thing they'd left was the old sofa in the living room. That didn't bother Lucy, because she'd packed air beds and sleeping bags for her and Kevin, and she'd budgeted for a major shopping expedition before she went back to work.

She and Kevin headed back down to the living room. He sat on the sofa and patted the faded cushion beside him. She sat. He laid his head on her lap and immediately fell asleep.

6

Over the months since the events on the 440 loop, despite the fact that they'd been jointly awarded medals for their exploits that day, and despite their subsequent "bonding," Tait had remained steadfastly close-mouthed about Cal Parrish's death.

Nevertheless, over those months, he'd let a few nuggets drop.

During one investigation, after they'd turned over a guy for unlawful possession of a firearm, Tait had picked the weapon off Jack's desk and muttered, "Cal was killed with one of these." The gun was a Baikal-Makarov .380, a Russian make.

Another time, on a quiet day, Tait mentioned his retirement date, which was eighteen months away.

"Any plans for a post-retirement job?" Jack asked.

"Looking at a few things. At least I'll still be fairly young"—he caught Jack's quizzical look and responded with a rare smile—"okay, *relatively* young. What they pay us . . . a man could starve to death if he stayed in this job too long. Point is: I'll have time for a second career. At least I'm not facing what Parrish was facing."

"What do you mean?"

"Must've been eight, ten years ago . . . before he and I partnered up. He had this son living out West—California, or maybe it was Nevada. Told me the kid got involved in some get-rich-quick scheme, a land speculation deal that went sour. Cal had to bail him out. Said it meant he'd have to delay his retirement, have to wait 'til he maxed out, maybe even go a few years past that. Dying when he did, he left his wife with a fuckin' mess."

Jack was thinking: *Money trouble . . . Russian-made murder weapon . . . the whole thing just doesn't sit right.*

Not long after that conversation, Jack took the leave time he'd promised himself. He and Lucy flew to Miami and spent several days at the Gables with Lucy's sister and brother-in-law.

Jack had always enjoyed visiting Lucy's family. After several years in the police, he harbored a certain ingrained cynicism when it came to attorneys, but he genuinely liked Jeff Barnett. The man's slightly rotund appearance and spaniel eyes belied the steel that lay within, and Jack imagined he would be deadly in a courtroom, consistently surprising strutting opponents who had underestimated him. He respected Jeff's quiet wisdom, and was highly amused by his obsessive devotion to Wellington, their enormous cat. (Jeff referred to the feline as "my son and hair.") And he got a real kick out of his sister-in-law, Erica, who somehow combined dazzling elegance with a quick and earthy wit.

He loved Jeff's story of how they had met.

"I was wandering through a shopping mall. There was this smoking-hot chick wearing shorts and a skimpy top walking along in front of me. There were three words stitched across the ass of her shorts: TAKE A NUMBER. She went into a store. I waited outside while she browsed. She came out and I followed her to the next store. When she came out of that one, I got up my nerve and went up to her.

"'Hi. My name's Jeff.'

"'Good for you,' she replied, and started to walk away.

"'I'll take that number, if I may?'

"She turned around and just stood there, looking me over. Then she fished a pen and a scrap of paper out of her purse and wrote on it. She handed it to me."

"What was written on it?"

"'One.'"

Ricki, as she liked to be called, was undeniably alluring, and Jack wasn't blind to that . . . but for all her charms, she wasn't Lucy. In Jack's eyes, Lucy's languid, understated beauty couldn't be matched. There was a mysterious, almost indefinable quality about her that had melted him on the spot on that afternoon, four years ago, when he'd pulled her over for running a stop sign. Before letting her go with a warning, he'd memorized the address on her driver's license. Then, in the boldest move he'd ever made in his relations with the opposite sex, he showed up on her doorstep the following evening.

There was very little in this world that frightened Jack Hendricks, but his knees turned to water when Lucy opened the door. He wasn't wearing his uniform, but she recognized him. In obvious consternation, she peered past him, looking for a police car. Seeing her standing in front of him, three feet away, he forgot all the clever lines he had practiced on the drive over.

"Miss Cappelli," he blurted, "I'm sorry. I . . . I'm not here on police business. I'm here because . . ."

"Yes?"

"Because . . . because I'm hoping you'll let me take you to dinner."

He saw those beautiful green eyes get big, just as they had when he'd pulled her over.

His heart sank.

And then, Lucinda Cappelli's face broke into a smile.

Later that evening, as he walked her to her front door, she turned, kissed him on the cheek and asked, with a mischievous grin, "Where have I been all your life?"

Jack and Lucy had never looked back, and he worshipped her.

Jack didn't have much family of his own—at least, accessible family. His dad had died of a heart attack two weeks before Jack enlisted in the Army, which was no loss. His death had freed Elise Hendricks, Jack's mother, from decades of mental abuse—and from the intermittent incidents of physical abuse that Jack had put an end to when, at the age of seventeen, he had laid out his father with a single punch. Before that memorable day, his older sister, Brigitte, had fled the turmoil, married in haste, and was now living, divorced and embittered, somewhere in New Hampshire. He hadn't heard from her in two years. Jocelyn, his younger sister, a fresh-faced strawberry blonde with dreams of stardom, had moved to Los Angeles right after high school. Jack and Jossie had always been close, and she still stayed in contact. She'd picked up a few minor roles in TV productions, but mainly she'd become a Hollywood cliché, auditioning by day, waitressing by night. To top it off, while Jack was in the Army, his mother had reconnected with an old high school boyfriend who owned a guesthouse in Kauai. She'd married him and made her escape from the city that held so many traumatizing memories. Jack didn't blame her, but he'd only made it out to Hawaii once since she moved, and his mother had sworn she'd never return to Bayonne, even to see her son.

The bottom line was that Jack was the only member of his small family who had stayed in their hometown, and the only one who actually gave a damn about the place.

Jack and Lucy spent a few days shopping, exploring Coconut Grove, and gaping at the voluptuous spectacles on South Beach. They ended each day being seriously over-served at the

Bronte. Finally, they rented a car and drove the Overseas Highway down to Key West.

When they pulled under the porte cochere of their hotel, Lucy let out a squeal of surprise.

Jack had kept the Avenida Miramar a secret. Built during the Roaring Twenties by New Jersey transportation mogul (and rumored mobster) Gaetano Morelli, the hotel had been a favored retreat of politicians and Hollywood celebrities for decades. Jack hadn't told Lucy that he had booked them into one of the most expensive suites at the most expensive resort in the Florida Keys. She'd been flabbergasted, and thrilled, just as Jack had hoped.

But she'd also been distressed.

On their arrival, they'd been briefly ignored as they stood at the open trunk of their rented Pontiac while a doorman and a parking valet fussed over the occupants of the gleaming Rolls-Royce Phantom parked in front of them. When they finally entered the hotel, and Jack led Lucy through the stunning ship-style brightwork of the massive lobby, her legs went weak. There was a distinct flutter in her voice as she pressed close to him and whispered in fright:

"Jack, look at this place! How can we afford it?"

"We'll be okay. It's off season. And you got a deal."

"I got a deal?"

"Yeah! I couldn't accept it—against regulations—but *you* could. So I accepted on your behalf. The reservation's in your name. Go ahead . . . sign us in."

In fact, Lucy had gotten a hell of a deal. In front desk lingo, their one-week stay had been "comped" for them by a crime victim who just happened to work for the head of the New York investment firm that had recently bought the hotel. One evening several months earlier, Jack and Lucy had been on their way to see *The Da Vinci Code* when Jack had interrupted a violent mugging in an alley. He'd spotted the commotion from the sidewalk and sprinted to the victim's aid. Two men were in the process of dragging their young female victim deeper into the blackness, and it was obvious that their intentions involved more than just the theft of a purse. In one of the few firsthand examples of Jack's professional skills that Lucy had ever witnessed, he disarmed both men in seconds, dislocating one thug's shoulder in the process, and knocked both of them unconscious. While Jack stood guard over the pair, Lucy helped the woman to their car, staunched the bleeding from her badly split lip, and comforted her until the police and ambulance arrived.

Yes, Jack had been offered a very good deal on their hotel stay, but when the bellman swung open the door to their breathtaking honeymoon suite, he wasn't sure Lucy believed him. At that moment, he didn't care. He tipped the bellman, latched the door, swept his matchless, irreplaceable wife into his arms, and carried her to the broad bed overlooking the Straits of Florida.

It was only after the essential opening act of their romantic getaway had been taken care of, and Lucy was lying in his arms, that he told her about the phone call he'd received from the grateful woman he had saved that night. The call had come a few days after her two assailants had bowed to the inevitable, pleaded guilty, and received long prison sentences. The woman told him that her boss had agreed to offer him and his wife a free week at any of their company's dozen or so luxury hotels in Canada, the U.S., and Mexico. Jack had thanked her, but responded that a BPD regulation prohibited him from accepting any benefit for services performed in the line of duty, no matter how long after the events took place.

Apparently, his reply had been expected, because the woman continued, "We understand that. But my employer, Mr. Gennaro, is extending this offer to *Mrs.* Hendricks. I am deeply grateful for her help that night. I don't have a contact number for her, so I called you. Would you be able to accept on her behalf?"

"I suppose . . ." Jack replied, his mind tugging in two directions. "Good! I'll send you an e-mail with a list of our resorts."

It had taken Jack about three seconds to pick the one Lucy wanted.

Jack knew he should have reported the gift to his bosses, but he was so excited to surprise Lucy that he couldn't face the possibility that he would be ordered to decline the offer. The adjective "idyllic," so overused in resort literature, came nowhere close to describing their week at the Miramar. Diving trips, parasailing, romantic dinners on their private balcony, and making love morning, afternoon, and night—the experience had surpassed Jack's wildest dreams.

Too soon, the week was over. They returned to Miami, and then to Bayonne, and dropped back into what, for days afterward, seemed to Jack the most lackluster of existences. He and Lucy had always experienced post-vacation letdown, and they had joked about it mournfully, but this time was worse. As the final days of August drifted toward fall, Jack reflected that the summer of 2006 had been the best, the most intense, and the most loving he had spent with Lucy since their honeymoon, four years before. Now he faced what seemed like the most cheerless of prospects—solving crime in the six square miles of one of the most densely populated small cities in the Northeast. A city that was the birthplace of Sandra Dee, Frank Langella, Brian Keith . . . and Jack Hendricks.

A city that Jack Hendricks wasn't sure he loved quite as much as he had before.

In mid-October, Tait decided it was his turn to take some time off, so Jack's captain paired him up with another veteran detective. A few days later, he and his temporary partner got drawn into the back end of a bank robbery investigation that had gone badly wrong for the criminals. A sharp-eyed off-duty cop had spotted them entering a branch of the Bayonne Community Bank and called it in. By the time the two gunmen ran out, their getaway driver was in custody and half-a-dozen cold-eyed cops were waiting to relieve them of their weapons and their take.

With the trio in custody, Jack and his partner were assigned to interview one of the gunmen. The prisoner was in his forties, the oldest of the three. And, unfortunately for him, the intersection of his prior criminal record and New Jersey's "three strikes" law meant he was facing a mandatory life sentence.

A few minutes into the interview, Jack's partner was called away. Assessing what he took to be a green rookie sitting in front of him, the prisoner decided to try him on.

"What did you say your name was?"

"I didn't."

"Aren't you supposed to identify yourself to a prisoner?"

"That's right. You can call me Detective."

"Okay, Detective. And just how long have you been one?"

"The way it goes in here, Mr."—Jack glanced at the folder in front of him—"Mulvaney, is like this: We ask the questions. So we'll just wait here until my partner gets back and then you'll have your chance to answer a few."

"I was just wondering if you knew any of the old cops on the detective bureau."

"Some."

"Know a guy named Cal Parrish?"

Jack hadn't forgotten his suspicions about Parrish—or about Tait, for that matter—but they weren't occupying space in his thoughts at that particular moment. In fact, his mind was on something else: last night's carefully planned lovemaking with Lucy, and whether maybe, just maybe, they had started a family.

The prisoner noticed his change of expression.

"Thought you might know him. Friend of yours?"

Jack thought: *This guy doesn't know Parrish is dead.*

He played along.

"Not really. We work different shifts."

"This three strikes thing . . . what are the chances of a deal?"

"No chance."

"What if I gave you guys something on Parrish? Something that could get him arrested."

"How old?"

"How old is he?"

"No. How old is this something that could get him arrested?"

"Not old. Year and a half, maybe."

"So, let me get this straight. You want to trade information about Detective Cal Parrish in return for some kind of a break on a third-strike sentence."

"That's right. And I'll give you a hint: The guy's connected."

Jack let a few seconds pass while he pretended to ponder the prisoner's revelation. When he replied, he spoke slowly. "Okay. Two things: One—I don't make deals. I leave that to the lawyers. Second—Parrish is dead, so no one's interested."

The look on Mulvaney's face was priceless.

        Tait was Jack's partner, and it was obvious he was hiding something. For his own protection, Jack decided he had to act.

He started working on his own time, quietly putting stray pieces together. Months ago, mainly out of curiosity, he'd searched the Internet and read the press reports on Parrish's murder. He burrowed through those reports again, searching for any unusual fact or allegation prefixed by journalism's old formulaic standby: *informed sources have revealed* . . . He didn't find anything of note. Next, he logged into the department's database and read everything he could find relating to the murder investigation. He found an early draft of Ernie Tait's formal statement that had never been deleted. According to Tait, he and Parrish had decided to return to the scene of a recent break-in at a warehouse on Hobart Avenue. Although the building showed every sign of being abandoned—every window and all but one loading door was shuttered with panels of corrugated iron—in fact, a sealed-off section on the second floor was used by a nearby brand-name clothing distribution facility to store unsorted returns. A week earlier, thieves had bypassed the inadequate security system and made off with clothing and footwear worth thousands of dollars. Tait and Parrish were aware that the covered loading bay behind the building was frequented at night by druggies and their suppliers. They were hoping to collar a couple and squeeze them for information.

The warehouse stretched for nearly five hundred feet along Hobart Avenue. Tait had dropped Parrish at the southwest corner. The plan was for him to hold off until Tait could drive up to East Fifth, cut east, and then drive into the compound from the north. Then they could move on the druggies from two directions. In his statement, Tait said the layout was perfect, with an eight-foot cinder block wall on the west side of the loading bay and a pair of rusting containers and a chain-link fence blocking escape to the east. The crime scene photos confirmed that. He said he'd just left the car when he heard two gunshots in quick succession. He ran to the loading area, thought he saw a figure disappearing south toward the waterfront, and found Parrish lying in the wind-blown litter next to an electrical transformer enclosure. He called it in and stayed with Parrish until the ambulance and back-up arrived. He stated that Parrish had no pulse, and he was certain he was already dead when he found him. The M.E. later confirmed that the detective had been shot twice, once in the chest and once in the head, and must have died instantly.

The area was sealed off, and within minutes one of the crime scene guys found a handgun in a dump skid next to the loading area. The Baikal-Makarov .380 was lying in plain view, as if it had been deliberately left there to be found. It was clean of prints, but within an hour of completion of the autopsy, ballistics had matched it to the crime.

The weapon was registered to a New York jewelry salesman who had reported the gun stolen three years earlier. He was visibly shaken when NYC detectives told him his gun had been used to kill a police officer. He said he made frequent trips to Connecticut and New Jersey on business, often carrying valuable samples. He had valid permits to transport and carry concealed in the tristate area. In early 2002, he'd attended a series of business meetings in Trenton, New Jersey. Because his own vehicle was in for repairs, he'd rented a Mercedes to make the trip. The Mercedes had a "smart key" system. He'd locked the weapon in the trunk, along with his luggage. While he was checking in at his hotel, the car was stolen. He had no idea how the thief had done it, since he'd had the smart key with him at the hotel desk. Supposedly the engine couldn't be started unless the key fob was inside the car. The police theorized that he'd been the victim of something they called a "signal relay attack."

Every detail of the man's story had checked out.

Over three nights, Jack stayed late after his shift ended. Each evening, he visited the archive room in the basement. He had downloaded a list of Parrish's old file numbers, going back to January 1998. He'd picked that month because Tait had said they were partners for "seven years, eight months, ten days." He didn't know if his list was complete because it was hard to know how careful or thorough the data input had been during the department's sporadic transition to computers. At least the case files were easy to find. Each file had been placed in a large manila envelope, or series of envelopes, and stored in clearly marked cabinets and boxes. He didn't know what he was looking for, but his interest was aroused when he came across a thick folder that had been tucked into the back of a closed file relating to a bank fraud complaint. The folder was filled with photocopies of NCIC stolen vehicle reports. Flipping through them, Jack noticed that the reports were from different departments all over the state, with a few from neighboring states.

There were 114 printouts, and every one of them related to a stolen car.

He started checking, using the NCIC system and, in a few cases, by calling the police departments involved. He'd track down a records clerk, ask about a certain file number, and ask if the case had ever been cleared. After a few weeks of this, he had determined one startling fact: Not a single one of the stolen vehicles had ever been recovered.

He began compiling a spreadsheet, listing every detail relating to the stolen vehicles.

Had Parrish been corrupt? It looked that way. It looked like he'd been involved with a car theft ring. Jack began to suspect that he'd been killed to shut him up. Mulvaney had said he was "connected." That meant organized crime. That meant . . . the Mob. Jack knew all the stories about the "Five Families," but in recent decades, words like "Mob" and "Mafia" and "connected" had come to mean organized criminal enterprises of every ethnicity. Not just the Italians, but also the Irish, the Chinese, the Puerto Ricans, the Russians . . .

The Russian-made murder weapon didn't necessarily mean anything. It had been stolen from a legitimate citizen. It could have just been happenstance.

Using it, and leaving it to be found, might have been a crude attempt at misdirection.

So, "connected" to what? Or, to whom?

Jack wondered if his own life could be in danger. Should he tell Lucy? Their marriage was rooted in honesty—always had been, and always would be. He loved her, he trusted her, and he told her everything.

Well, almost everything.

His first and primary instinct was to protect her. Maybe that was some dumb male thing. Maybe women's lib would disapprove. But some aspects of his work on the streets were too disturbing, too oppressive, and sometimes just too soul-destroying to inflict on the sweet-natured girl who was the love of his life.

So he decided to keep silent.

He kept silent to Lucy, but he decided the time had come to speak to Tait.

It was Veteran's Day and they were on their way back to the office after investigating an explosion on a cabin cruiser at the Elco Boat Basin. As soon as the fire department confirmed that the explosion had been caused by a propane leak, and no incinerated bodies were found aboard, they'd departed the scene. They were rolling through a leafy section of Avenue A when Jack decided to test the waters.

"Ernie, I've been looking into a few things."

"Things?"

"Things about Cal Parrish."

Tait's expression darkened. "Are we going to have that problem again?"

"Look, I hate to say it, but I think your partner was on the take."

Tait braked and pulled to the curb. He twisted in his seat. "Let it rest, Jack! The man's dead."

"Yeah, but don't we have an obligation?"

"If Cal was alive . . . maybe . . . probably. I admit I had my suspicions, but this is a man who saved my life. More than once! So I didn't follow up. And now, a year after he was killed, you want to get into this? Think about it! Why do this to his wife and kids? Paula's a good woman and she doesn't deserve it. His daughter, Patti, is my goddaughter, for Christ's sake! Don't do this!"

"Don't you want to know who killed him?"

"Of course I do! But not this way. If Cal was corrupt, and we proved it, what would that achieve? We'd just be embarrassing the

Department and destroying a family's memories! What's the point? Let it go." Tait looked into Jack's eyes and used a word he seldom, if ever, used. "Please."

Jack couldn't believe what he was hearing.

It only made him more determined to get to the bottom of Cal Parrish's death.

7

Lucy was certain there were other dreams. Dreams that she couldn't remember. She was certain because, when she first awoke, there would be a fragment of memory. No, not even a fragment—a filament. At times, it would be the dissolving image of a face, or the distant sound of a voice. Or, just the eerie sensation of something unfinished.

And then it would be gone.

There was only one dream that survived in her memory and dogged her through her waking hours. She never knew when it would come. There was no pattern to it—six or seven times in one year, a dozen in the next. But it was always the same. It was of her and Jack, together and laughing and loving, on their final trip to Key West.

The last trip, before he was killed.

Every time the dream came, she woke up crying.

It had been the same this morning. The dream was as vivid as ever. Jack was as real as ever. Their joy in each other, their wonder, their jubilance, was as real as ever. And Lucy's pain and her tears, when she awoke, were as real as ever.

Except, this time, she found Kevin lying next to her in her bed, pressed close . . . and crying.

It had been a wretched day.

Lucy was deeply worried about Kevin.

For five years, she'd ignored every opportunity to form a new relationship with a man. Her son had been the center of her universe—her sole sunbeam of warmth and joy. At three, he'd been like any other boy of his age she'd ever known, overflowing with all the energy, curiosity, laughter, and tears that came with that stage of development. But at four, he had transitioned into a very different child. His style of play changed. He seemed to develop an instinctive perception of the limits of possibility. He displayed innately superior judgment to that of other children his age. In any group of new playmates, he would quickly emerge as leader. As gratifying as that was to his mother, his private behaviors were eerie and unnerving. His long silences, and—most disturbing—his uncanny insights were at times almost frightening.

And now, the incident this morning. The weeping, clinging boy in her bed who kept repeating, "I love you, I love you."

When she'd dropped him off at pre-K this morning, he'd seemed fine. The problem was—as she'd tried to warn his teacher, without mentioning the paranormal aspects of her son's behavior—that could change quickly.

She knew she'd need to get help for Kevin. But she was alone here. No Ricki. No Jeff. No one she trusted. Just a handful of former friends who had smiled and hugged her when she'd first appeared in the school staff room, but exchanged pointed looks when they thought she wasn't looking.

She knew why.

She wondered if she'd made a big mistake by letting Garrett Lindsay talk her into moving back to Bayonne.

Garrett himself had been warmly welcoming. He seemed oblivious to the turgid undercurrents in the staff room. If he was aware of the whispers and the looks, he never showed it. When he was present, often addressing Lucy, asking her opinion on this or that—not particularly singling her out, but really, actually, singling her out—the other teachers were politely attentive and kept their sideways looks to themselves. Garrett's quick intelligence and his open, generous nature seemed to neutralize them.

It was different when he wasn't in the room.

At first, Lucy wondered if there had been an ulterior motive behind Garrett's out-of-the-blue telephone call—a personal one, maybe a romantic interest that he'd been harboring all these years. But it was soon plain that that was not the case. He adored his wife and their two daughters, and he never gave Lucy the slightest indication that his interest in her extended beyond admiration for her professional talents. He'd pulled strings to get her simply because he wanted her on his team.

And, today, Garrett had again demonstrated his generosity by personally covering for her while she completed unpacking the effects she'd left in storage. It was a task she'd put off for nearly a month, while she settled into her new class, prepared lesson plans, and used every spare moment to shop for, buy, and, in some cases, assemble new furniture for her re-occupied home. There were boxes, some full, some partially emptied, all over the house. She'd thrown herself into the task, but it had been a day of high emotion. She sat on the floor slitting boxes open, finding things that brought back vivid memories, finding things that brought her to tears, unpacking more, crying more—reliving the joys and reliving the sorrow.

Now she was in the third bedroom, the room she and Jack had always used as their home office, attacking a half-dozen mismatched grocery and liquor store boxes labeled with a marking pen in her sister's distinctive hand: "B/R3." Since moving back in February, Lucy had found this room oddly different from the rest of the house. It was a room of great light—attributable to the sliding glass doors—but, inexplicably, of little warmth. She hurried to finish the task at hand.

There were two boxes left. She opened one. With a shock, she found herself staring at her old scuba gear—wetsuit, mask, snorkel, BCD vest. She peeled back the flaps of the last box. There was Jack's gear, with his H. Dessault dive knife lying on top. Something brown and stringy protruded from under the guard. She unsheathed the knife and plucked at the object. It came away in her fingers. She looked at it closely.

A withered blade of turtle grass, from their last dive.

Last night, the dream . . .

This morning, her weeping son . . .

Now this.

It was too much.

In a tearful fury, Lucy shoved the boxes into the closet, threw the knife in after them, and slammed the sliding door closed with a bang that echoed through the house.

She'd advertise the gear and sell it . . . or maybe just give it away.

In the meantime, she could not—*would not!*—look at it.

That night, as she toweled Kevin dry after his bath, he said, "Remember when we had baths together?"

"Do *you* remember? You were just a baby then, honey."

"No, Mommy. I mean when I was big."

Disconcerted, Lucy asked, "When you were big?"

"Yeah. And you were my little wifelet."

Lucy was dumbstruck.

She combed through her memory. She couldn't remember mentioning Jack's affectionate nickname in front of Kevin.

Not ever.

8

Hudson County was the smallest in New Jersey in terms of land area, but it was the most densely populated. In fact, it was the sixth most densely populated county in the United States. Despite that dubious distinction, the county prosecutor's satellite office was situated in the last place an uninformed person might expect to find it—behind the heavily shaded windows of a weather-stained, two-story structure in a light industrial area of Jersey City. The building sat on the eastern shore of the Hackensack River, two hundred yards from the long shadow of U.S. Route 1/9's Pulaski Skyway. As one prosecutor had put it to Jack: "Yeah, it's a nondescript dump, but we like it that way."

Jack met with Robert Olivetti in the prosecutor's drab corner office on the second floor. The wall space below the window sills was lined with out-of-date heating units, as if the building's original design had been intended for a military installation in the high Arctic. The dingy panes above the heating units overlooked a tractor trailer repair operation, a mini-bus storage yard, and—across the river—the Kearny Generating Station.

Olivetti was in his mid-thirties, above average height, with dark hair and a relaxed manner. Meeting him away from the office, someone with limited insight might have guessed he worked as a waiter in an upscale eatery.

Bad guess.

Robert Olivetti's current position as lead prosecutor for the Robbery and Homicide Unit was the latest in a series of assignments in which the attorney had consistently distinguished himself. On more than one occasion, he had confounded his police investigators by locating a key piece of evidence himself, or identifying a witness they had overlooked. He had handled a few of Jack's cases over the years, and Jack was fully aware of the formidable intelligence that resided behind that easy smile. That was exactly why he'd deliberately sought him out.

Olivetti waved him into a chair. After a few quick pleasantries, Jack got to the point. He spoke carefully. "I have a sensitive question to ask."

Olivetti chuckled. "This isn't the CIA, Jack. Ask away."

"It's 'sensitive' because it's not my case."

"Understood."

"Do you think your office would be prepared to offer a sweetheart deal to a three-striker in return for information on a possibly corrupt police officer?"

"Depends. What three-striker?"

"His name is Thomas Mulvaney."

Olivetti didn't miss a beat. "The BCB job."

"That's the one. Any chance it's your file?"

"No. But I could make that happen."

"That would be helpful."

"Mulvaney . . . he's the old guy."

"That's right."

Olivetti chewed a lip. "Okay. What cop are we talking about?"

"He's dead—shot behind a derelict warehouse on Hobart Avenue, down near the Point. Case was never solved. This could explain why."

"You're talking about that detective . . . Parrish."

"I am."

"You're saying you have evidence that he was corrupt."

"More than that. Mulvaney says he was connected."

"The Mob."

"That's what he says."

"Who have you told?"

"Just you. My partner was out of the room when Mulvaney came up with this."

"Who was your partner?"

"Don Bolton."

"Bolton's an older guy."

"That's right."

"Let me guess . . . Mulvaney figured the young cop would be more receptive than some old screw waiting for his retirement date."

Jack thought: *This man doesn't miss much.*

"That's my guess, too."

"Any corroboration? Or is it too soon?"

"Some." Jack described his visits to the archive room . . . the folder filled with car theft reports . . . the fact that none of the cases were ever solved. Rather than complicate matters, he left Tait's name out of his explanation. He concluded: "I've been working on an analysis . . . putting it all on a spreadsheet."

His account had clearly engaged Olivetti's attention. The prosecutor was silent for several seconds. Then he said, "If there's any substance to this, I think this office would be *very* interested. But I'd have to hear more before offering a deal to a three-striker, and I'd have to clear it with the boss."

"Understood. I'll see if I can get a statement."

"I've seen this Mulvaney guy's sheet. He's been around the block.

He may balk at signing anything this early in the game. If he drags anchor, get what you can, write it up, and come back to see me."

"I will. Thanks."

"Bolton was in here last week. He had a different partner with him."

Okay, Jack thought. *Here goes . . .*

"I'm partnered with Ernie Tait. He was on leave when the robbery went down, and Bolton's partner had a family emergency. So the boss teamed us up."

"Ernie Tait? Wait a minute—?"

"That's right. He was Parrish's partner when he was killed. He found the body."

"You haven't told him about Mulvaney?"

"No."

"Why?"

"A couple of weeks ago, after I finished in the archive room, I told him I thought Parrish might have been corrupt. I didn't tell him I'd been conducting a serious investigation. I just said I'd been looking at a few things. He didn't even ask 'What things?' He didn't seem to want to know. He just said it would do no good to investigate now. Said it would just embarrass the Department and bring down a lot of pain on Parrish's widow and kids. It sounded like he was very close to the family."

"Embarrass the Department? Upset the widow? Kind of twisted logic."

"That's what I thought."

"Well, obviously, you won't be discussing this with him again."

"Got that right."

Jack rose from his seat.

"Hang on." Olivetti took out a business card and wrote on it. He handed the card to Jack. "My cell number's on the back. Call me when you've got something."

"Will do."

They shook hands and Jack left.

It took Jack a few days to arrange a visit with Mulvaney at the Hudson County Correctional Facility in Kearny. The bank robber hadn't been able to make bail and was awaiting trial or—he clearly hoped—an offer of some kind of deal that would save him from a life sentence.

A prison officer escorted Jack to a tiny interview room and locked him in. The miniscule space stank of mold and body odor, making Jack wonder—as he had on earlier occasions—if the standards in the rest of the facility were as bad as various activists' reports alleged. Mulvaney's opening remark after they were alone meshed perfectly with Jack's impressions.

"Detective! Thank God! Any way you can get me moved out of this shithole?"

"Doubt it."

"These guards are animals! And half the inmates don't even speak English. What's with all the fuckin' foreigners in a county jail? Rastas and ragheads 'n shit? Ain't the Feds got their own jails?"

"They ran out of space."

"Yeah? Well, let me tell you . . . Rikers was paradise compared to this place!"

"Spent time there, did you?"

"You know I did." He leaned forward, rattling the chain restraints that secured him to the table. "Ready to tell me your name, Detective?"

"Hendricks."

"Okay, Hendricks. Last time we were in one of these little rooms, you told me Parrish is dead and nobody cares. So why are you here?"

Jack had already decided he wouldn't tell Mulvaney that he had already spoken with a prosecutor. He'd also decided that he wouldn't ask for a written statement. Instead, when he heard the prisoner escort's key in the door, he'd activated a digital recorder in his jacket pocket.

"I'm here to tell you that, maybe, somebody *does* care. I'm here to see if you've got something that's more than just talk. If you do, I'll speak to the prosecutor. If not," he added, with a level stare, "the drive over here cost less than a buck in gas. Our budget can handle it."

Mulvaney returned Jack's stare.

But he blinked first.

"Major league car theft."

"Major league?"

"Yeah. High-end models . . . Jags, Mercedes, Rolls if they can get 'em. They steal them, then store 'em at different locations until they're sure they don't have tracking devices, and then ship 'em overseas. They make big money selling them to rich guys in Africa 'n Russia 'n places like that."

"How do you know all this?"

"I ran a crew. Got out."

"Why did you get out?"

"Because of Parrish. He kept showing up in my life, pressuring me, asking questions."

"He was a cop. Cops ask questions."

"He was a *Bayonne* cop. What was he doing in Jersey City? Up in Teaneck? Way down in Toms River? We stole cars from different towns and delivered them to different places. Always different places. Sitting in a bar after a delivery, there he was. Stop for a burger after a boost, there he was."

"We cops call it 'investigation.'"

"It weren't that kinda investigation."

"What do you mean?"

"He never interfered. Never showed up at a boost. He just wanted

a name. Wanted to talk to the 'higher-ups,' he called 'em. He said certain people were interested. People who don't take no for an answer.
He squeezed one of my guys to get my name, then started on me. Kept
saying he was just an 'envoy.' Liked that word. 'I'm just the envoy,' he
kept sayin'. 'You don't wanna meet the people who sent me.' I kept my
mouth shut, but he kept coming back. I didn't like the odds, so I made
the healthy choice and moved down south for a while. Seeing that
Parrish got whacked, guess that was the right decision."

"And you're saying his visits . . . this was a Mob thing."

"Had to be."

"Why?"

"The cars we stole were going out in containers. No one could
run an operation like that for long without those guys muscling in.
They control the unions, and the unions control the waterfront."

"What was the name you didn't give him?"

Mulvaney looked up, his eyes scanning the walls, the ceiling.

"Got a piece of paper?"

Jack opened his notebook to a blank page. He passed it across the
table, along with a pen.

Mulvaney scrawled something, his hand at an awkward angle, im-
peded by his handcuffs. Jack retrieved the pad. He studied the name
Mulvaney had written. He took a long, careful breath. He was deeply
shaken, but he kept his expression neutral.

"Okay. Look . . . Tom, is it?"

"Yeah."

"Okay, Tom, I'm sure you know how it works. For this to be of
any use to the prosecutors, you'll have to give us chapter and verse.
Everything you did—every felony, every misdemeanor. Also, anything you were doing down south that might come back to bite. And,
you'll have to give us more than this. You'll have to describe every
contact you had with Parrish, every conversation, every word you can
remember."

"I'll give you everything. But not until you get me a sit-down with a prosecutor who's got the balls and the juice to cut me a deal."

Jack left the lockup and walked slowly back to the visitor parking area. Before he started his car, he opened his notebook. He tore out the page Mulvaney had written on. He folded the page into a small rectangle and slipped it behind his driver's license in his wallet.

That evening, after Lucy left for her yoga class, Jack went to the desk in their home office and started up the laptop. He attached a flash drive. The menu listed a single folder entitled "PARRISH." It consisted of two documents: a 950 kb pdf entitled "NICB" and "SS," the ever-expanding spreadsheet based on his late-night research visits to the BPD archive room. He set about adding the digital recording of his interview with Thomas Mulvaney. When the download was complete, he checked it to be sure the entire file had been copied. Satisfied, he erased the conversation from the recorder.

After running a quick search to ensure that the audio file had not been replicated anywhere in the laptop's drives, he ejected the flash drive.

He swiveled his chair and looked around the room.

9

Lucy's days were full.

Five days a week she was in the shower by six in the morning, making breakfast for herself and Kevin, dropping him at pre-K (situated, thankfully, right on campus at the Oresko School), grabbing a large coffee from the staff room, and hitting the classroom by at least seven-thirty, sooner if she could manage it. Then came the real morning race. The hour or so before her students arrived wasn't an oasis of quiet time to review the day's lesson plans—she'd done that work the night before, after Kevin was asleep. No . . . that hour was spent photocopying handouts, clearing up leftover messes from yesterday's classes, and lately, because of the current flu epidemic, wiping down every student desktop with disinfectant.

And then there were the parents. It wasn't just replying to the flurry of e-mails that routinely awaited her—it was dealing with the parents, mostly mothers, who deified their children. Mothers who had actually scheduled their pregnancies to mesh with school enrollment dates so their offspring could begin school at an optimum age. Mothers who had populated their children's formative years with therapists and "play-date

tutors." Mothers who (in the words of one shrewd education professional) mistook cell phones for umbilical cords, and were so obsessed
with enriching their children's lives that a few of them had become a
plague on Lucy's.

Somehow, she handled them.

She taught Language Arts and Social Studies and she had a solid
routine for her classes. But after working with students for over six hours,
with at best thirty minutes for lunch, her working day wasn't close to being over. Now came the balancing act: She needed to collect Kevin and
walk him to the nearby daycare that was costing her a small fortune, but
she also needed to be available for pupils who asked for extra help. So
she'd set appointment times, deliver Kevin into the custody of Geraldine
Taunton, the sharp-featured woman who ran the daycare, and then spend
the rest of the afternoon helping students, answering the day's crop of
e-mails, dealing with clockwork visits from Helicopter Moms; grading
tests, sometimes attending staff meetings, and, twice a week without
fail, working out at a gym. Even staying fit took a bit of organization.
Luckily, one of her male colleagues—married, with kids, and monumen-
tally unimpressed by staff room gossip—was quite happy for Lucy to
drop off Kevin two evenings a week for playtime with his children.

During the week, the only "quality time" (she detested that worn-
out phrase) she had with Kevin was from around six in the evening, when
she finally left the school, until bedtime at eight or a bit later on days
when he'd had a nap at daycare. It was a grind for Lucy and it was a grind
for Kevin, but, from the outset, the boy had displayed uncanny maturity
about the whole routine. He seldom complained. In fact, his docility was
worrying.

In one respect, the demands of her job, and the antisocial hours they
imposed, suited Lucy well. It made it easy to avoid happy hour bar crowds
and the singles scene. Her logical mind instructed that, after five years,
a new relationship might offer some long-missed comfort, but she still
could not accept the idea.

There was no one . . . *no one* . . . like Jack. And there never would be again.

And there was another factor.

It did not take long for Lucy to notice that some of her fellow teachers kept their distance, even though they had been friendly in the past, in the old days before Jack's death. She easily guessed the reason: The swirl of media coverage after Jack's murder had included rumors—published in brazen disregard of either the facts or the feelings of his young widow—of his alleged connection to organized crime. While the frequency of those articles had eventually dwindled, it hadn't helped that shortly after her return to Bayonne, yet another story had run in the Newark *Star Ledger*. The headline, "Murdered cop's widow resumes teaching post," had clearly just been an excuse to recycle the old speculations about Jack. One male teacher, new in the community, who had initially showed interest in Lucy and seemed to be angling to ask her out, backed off after reading the story.

Lucy had never been a combative personality—far from it—but this was the limit. While she would not have accepted her potential suitor's offer of a date, her anger was roused by his craven demonstration of rumor-driven backpedaling. She consulted an attorney recommended by Garrett Lindsay. Floyd Jackson worked at a boutique law firm in Newark, where he specialized in personal injury work. Lucy told him she wanted to sue the newspaper—not only for once again smearing Jack's memory without a shred of evidence to support the allegations, but also for using the outdated press coverage as a means to defame her personally.

"That article has lowered me in the estimation of my fellow teachers and, more important, in the eyes of all my students' parents!"

Jackson replied with a surprised smile, "You've been doing some legal research, Mrs. Hendricks."

"Call me Lucy, and yes, I have. I'm sick of this, and I want it to end! If the only way to achieve that is to take them to court, then that's what I want to do."

Jackson was an old friend of Garrett's and he seemed genuinely interested in trying to help. He studied the news article that Lucy brought with her, and listened intently as she outlined the background. He asked her to come back to see him on the following day. He said he wanted to do a bit of research himself, and he promised he wouldn't charge her for his time.

When she returned, the news wasn't good. Jackson had run an Internet search of all media websites for the tristate area, as well as those of the wire services. He'd printed off every archived story he could find. After reviewing them all, he concluded that any defamatory statements in the most recent article—most of which he was unsure would actually meet the legal test for libel—were not about Lucy, but exclusively about Jack.

"Your husband is a deceased person. He died over five years ago. For a defamation action to be sustainable after death, the defamation must have occurred during the life of the victim. That didn't happen here. Even if it had—even if Jack had been defamed in this way during his lifetime— New Jersey has what we lawyers call the 'Survival Statute.' That law requires that executors or administrators of a decedent's estate file an action within two years of the claimant's death."

"What about me?"

"I was getting to that. The journalist who wrote this latest article was either very smart, or his editor took legal advice before they ran the story. The paper cleverly avoided any innuendo—*innuendo* is a legal concept that I will explain in a moment—suggesting that you either knew of your husband's alleged activities or participated in them in any way. In defamation law, the word 'innuendo' means a statement which shows the defendant's true intended meaning by reference to antecedent matter. In your case, that would require a statement such as this: 'Detective Hendricks and his wife, although supporting themselves on the salaries of a low-ranking police detective and an elementary school teacher, owned a waterfront home at Bergen Point and are known to have made several trips to Florida during their marriage. Just four months before his death, Hendricks and his wife spent a week in a luxury suite at the Avenida Miramar Resort in Key West, a reputed Mob hangout, where even the most modestly priced rooms go for six hundred dollars a night.'"

Lucy was startled. "How do you know all that?"

"By lifting passages from various press articles, and adding a few things Garrett told me."

"Garrett?"

"I called him. I'm sorry. I wanted to have some facts so I could make it clear how innuendo works. So, do you see what I mean?"

"I do. And there *was* a story about us staying at the Miramar."

"I read it. It was published in 2007. You're past the limitation period for suing on it. What the newspaper did in this recent story was use the rather unremarkable fact that you've returned to Bayonne as a pretext to recycle old material. It's reprehensible, Lucy, it's detestable, but I don't believe we can base a successful lawsuit on what they've done."

Reflecting on it, Lucy had to admit to herself that Jackson's analysis made a kind of sense, but the effect of the entire episode was to cause her to draw even more into herself. Apart from her students, most of whom—with the exception of a few smart-asses—she was coming to enjoy, and Garrett Lindsay, she determined to keep the rest of the world at arm's length and just get on with doing her job and raising her son.

Raising her son . . .

That normally quotidian undertaking was becoming more and more perplexing.

She'd always known that Kevin was different. In his first weeks of life, she'd wondered if he was damaged in some way. *Cognitively challenged,* as the zealots of political correctness delicately phrased it. But she'd quickly realized he wasn't. She'd been there every minute—for his first smile, his first tooth, his first word, his first step . . . his first moment of understanding the purpose of the alphabet. Her son had hit most of his development milestones early.

There was just this strangely alert maturity about the boy.

With increasing frequency, Lucy would notice him standing or sitting in one spot—as if some deeply profound thought or sensation had arrested him mid-action. After several seconds, he would come out of his trance and resume his play as if nothing had happened. She had asked him about his behavior, about what was happening, what he was thinking, but the only time she managed to get a response, it was confusing.

"It's the man."

"What man, sweetheart?"

"The man . . . from before."

Lucy felt like she'd crossed into another dimension.

She questioned Kevin's teacher and the daycare supervisor, but neither had noticed similar behavior. Both described him as well behaved, and his teacher added that he was "remarkably serious-minded" for a child of his age. Lucy had a catalog of reasons for concurring with that assessment, but she kept them to herself.

One evening, while Lucy was working in the kitchen, The Police's old hit, "Every Breath You Take," came on the radio. An odd feeling came over her. She turned. Kevin was standing in the dining area, watching her with eerie intensity, and mouthing the words of the song. It had been one of Jack's favorite songs.

At the end of May, as she was about to read him a bedtime story, Kevin said: "Can I tell you a story, Mommy?"

"Of course, sweetheart."

He looked up at her. For a fleeting second, she felt a wash of recognition.

Jack . . .

"Do you know about following cars?"

"What do you mean?"

"You know, like a spy?"

Lucy didn't recall ever letting him watch a spy movie.

"Where did you see a spy movie?"

"I don't know. They got movies at Gerry's."

Gerry was Geraldine, his daycare supervisor. As far as Lucy knew, all she showed the children were kids' cartoons. With rising uneasiness, she asked, "What about following cars?"

"If there's this big highway, 'n lots and lots of cars, all you need is a screw thing."

No . . . !

"Screw thing, Kevin?"

"Yeah." He made a twisting motion with his fist. "One of them things."

"Do you mean a screwdriver?"

"Yeah. You make a hole."

"Where do you make a hole?" Her voice was a whisper.

"In the red thing, you know, on the car."

Lucy felt the hairs stand up on the back of her neck. Her throat constricted. She struggled to control a rising tide of shock.

Years ago, Jack had told her a police anecdote. He'd accumulated a large collection of them, although she knew he kept the grislier ones to himself. He told her he'd heard this one from a retired British policeman. The man had worked on some secret unit that targeted the IRA. He told Jack that they sometimes needed to tail vehicles being driven by suspected IRA bombers. At night, it was almost impossible to keep track of these cars on a busy freeway ("motorway," as the Brits called them). This was in the days before electronic tracking devices. So, before the operation started, an officer would use a Phillips head screwdriver to punch a small hole in a rear light lens of the target vehicle. That way, they would have no trouble picking out the vehicle from the sea of cars on the roadway ahead—the only one with a bright white dot in the center of one of its red taillights.

Lucy had never repeated that story to anyone—certainly not to her little boy. And it was far too sophisticated an account to expect any young child to understand, or to relate.

Lucy was beginning to believe that, against all reason, her beloved Jack had left something behind.

His memories . . .

Either that, or the impossible conversation she had just engaged in with her four-year-old son had never taken place, and Lucinda Arianna Hendricks, née Cappelli, had finally, terminally, and incurably . . . lost her sanity.

Either way, she could never reveal what she had just heard.

Sobbing uncontrollably, Lucy hugged the bewildered boy to her breast.

10

Jersey City was the so-called "sixth borough" of New York City—the back office community that most people passed through on their way to the real Gotham. It was also the home to a few dozen multi-story parking garages and, at this moment, Jack was prowling through a four-story monstrosity near the Newport Centre. He was searching for a particular vehicle. He had watched it enter the parkade. He just needed a private moment with it before settling in for the next step in his investigation into the sub rosa activities of Detective Cal Parrish, lately deceased.

He completed his survey of the first floor. Rather than take the stairs, he hiked up the curving vehicle ramp to the next level. Nearing the top, he heard an engine start. He quickened his pace. As he rounded the last turn, he noticed a black Ford Explorer backing out of a space on his left.

It was the vehicle he was looking for!

His eyes swept the area, looking for a place to step out of sight.

The Explorer's engine suddenly roared and the vehicle reversed toward him, tires shrieking on the sealed concrete of the garage floor.

Stunned into action, Jack dodged to one side.

Too late.

The left rear corner of the big SUV drove him into the concrete wall and pinned him there, upright and in shock.

The engine kept revving and the rear wheels kept spinning. Seven thousand pounds of Dearborn steel demolished Jack Hendricks's right shoulder, pulverized the right side of his pelvic girdle, and destroyed his hip. His screams of agony were drowned out by the redlining rpm's as the big V-8 crushed muscle and bone and cartilage into mush.

As suddenly as it had started, the rpm's dropped, the transmission thunked into gear, and the Ford pulled forward five feet.

Jack's broken body dropped like a sack.

The passenger door of the vehicle swung open. Footsteps approached. A form appeared above Jack's gasping form. Mangled and in shock, he tried to free his weapon, but his right arm wouldn't move.

The figure looming above him held a silenced Ruger .22. The gun fired once . . . twice. The first slug entered Jack's chest, and the second blasted through the middle of his forehead.

The last thing Jack's dying senses detected before his body went still was the smell.

The driver's door opened and another figure joined the assassin. He kneeled and quickly searched Jack's pockets. He found a screwdriver, and set it aside. He went through Jack's wallet. He found a slip of paper tucked behind his driver's license. He unfolded it, read what was inscribed there, and pocketed it. He replaced the wallet. When he finished frisking the body, he pried Jack's mouth open and used two fingers to jam an object deep into his throat.

Seconds later, the vehicle drove away.

It was 9:45 P.M. on Friday, December 1, 2006.

Twenty-five minutes later, a trio of happy-hour revelers found Jack Hendricks's body.

11

The doorbell rang at seven minutes and sixteen seconds after midnight.

Lucy would always remember the exact time, because she'd been lying in bed, trying to read, but mostly watching Jack's Big Ben alarm clock with the sweep second hand.

She'd been watching it because Jack was late.

Really late.

Really late because after he'd left for work, she'd checked his roster. He wasn't scheduled to work that night. He'd mentioned something a few days ago about a surveillance operation, but he hadn't said anything about it tonight. She didn't suspect for a moment that he was on a personal mission. That he was hiding something from her. That he was seeing another woman, for example. In her entire romantic life as an adult, brief though it had been, she'd never felt more certain about the unconditional love of a man.

When the knock came, she'd been about to break their agreement and call Jack on his cell. The routine was that he would phone her if he was going to be late, unless he was in the thick of something and couldn't make the call. He'd always been reliable about that. So she'd tried not to worry, but now, at this time of night . . .

And then the doorbell rang.

Lucy pulled on her housecoat. She descended the stairs, her bare feet chilled on the polished steps. She heard the doorbell again, followed by insistent knocking on the door. She put her eye to the peephole and saw Ernie Tait standing there, wearing some kind of sweat suit instead of his usual jacket and tie. At his side was a uniformed female officer she didn't recognize.

She opened the door with a thump in her chest and a knot in her stomach.

She saw the expression on Ernie's face, and she plunged into the darkness that would never leave her. The last wisp of memory she had of that night was of Ernie carrying her in his strong arms to the couch, and of a young, stricken policewoman holding her hand.

After that . . . only blackness and despair.

What Lucy didn't learn until days later was that it had taken from 10:10 P.M., when Jack's body was found, until 12:07:16 A.M. for the Jersey City cops to get word to the Bayonne Police; for a supervisor to send someone to the scene to confirm that the deceased was Detective Jack Hendricks; for that officer to confirm that Jack was definitely, positively, dead; for the BPD's deputy chief to contact Ernie; for Ernie to find a policewoman to accompany him; and for the two of them to drive to Jack and Lucy's home to deliver the devastating news.

What Lucy kept turning over and over in her mind—what kept her stomach roiling for months afterward—was that while she sat on their couch that evening watching *Law & Order*, Jack was already dead.

While she brushed her teeth and got ready for bed, Jack was already dead.

While she lay under the covers, vainly trying to concentrate on John Grisham's *The Innocent Man*, Jack was already dead.

•   •   •

The following week turned into one of unrelenting torment.

The chief of police placed an honor guard outside the entry way of the funeral home, and stationed officers at each end of Jack's casket. Lucy's early private viewing had been something she'd both craved and dreaded, and it almost destroyed her. The sight of her once vibrant, laughing, loving, gorgeous husband, now an embalmed waxwork, was cold steel through her heart. An ambulance had to be called, and her sister and brother-in-law, newly arrived from Florida, had rushed to the hospital to be with her.

Unknown to Lucy, who was in no state to make her wishes known, the chief had sent out a NCIC All Points Broadcast, announcing the line-of-duty funeral of his fallen officer. On the day of the service, a flood of uniforms from departments across the Northeast, the South, the Midwest, and as far away as Washington State descended on tiny Bayonne, New Jersey. The chief ordered Avenue C closed from Twenty-seventh Street to Thirty-first Street to provide space for the visiting officers to muster. Dozens of volunteers from the Hudson County Sheriff's Department, the Port Authority Police, and the New Jersey State Police pitched in to perform traffic control and security duties.

Despite the chief's good intentions, for Lucy the day of Jack's funeral was an impenetrable brume of prayers, hymns, eulogies, marching uniforms, bagpipes, and motorcycle escorts. The drive to the cemetery wound slowly past shops and residences decked out for Christmas. In the dark world of her despair, Lucy couldn't fathom why anyone would dare to display festive decorations when her Jack was dead. She couldn't understand why cars and pedestrians still filled the streets, why planes flew overhead, why TVs flickered and children laughed. She couldn't understand how life could just go on, as if nothing had happened.

At the graveside she sat between Ricki and Jeff on one side, and Jack's mother and younger sister on the other. After three seasons on a popular TV show, Jossie had attracted a pack of annoying paparazzi, whose presence along with press photographers only served to exacerbate the ordeal and deepen the insult to Jack's memory. Lucy was wavering on the brink of collapse until the final rituals were completed. When the police chief approached and respectfully offered her the folded flag, she flinched so violently that Ricki had to intervene to accept it.

Lucy Hendricks couldn't imagine a more horrifying week than the one she had just endured, but the following weeks, then months, almost proved her wrong.

Somehow, through the fog of her grief, she noticed she had acquired a heightened sense of smell. This condition was brought home to her a few days after the funeral, when the smell of the spoiled milk in her neglected fridge sent her retching to the sink. As more days passed, her sensitivity sharpened to the point where even the smell of day-old leftovers began to revolt her.

She knew her period was overdue, but she had put that down to stress.

Now . . . she began to wonder.

She was trying to suppress the intrusive train of thought when her phone rang.

"Mrs. Hendricks?"

"Yes."

"This is Detective Eric Trousdale. I'm with the Jersey City PD."

Lucy's stomach tightened. "Have you made an arrest?"

"No, ma'am. I'm just touching base. I want you to know that your husband's murder is our top priority. Our chief has promised all the resources we need, and we're working closely with the Bayonne PD. We're determined to get to the bottom of this."

Lucy's eyes filled. "Thank you, Detective."

"Call me Eric. My partner and I will come to see you in a day or two. We'll call first."

"Thank you."

Two nights before Christmas, Ernie Tait came to the house.

Big, quiet, and respectful, he asked, "Did Jack mention anything he was working on?"

"Wouldn't *you* know what he was working on?"

"No one knows why he was in that garage. Your statement says he left for work at five o'clock on that day, and that he'd mentioned a surveillance job. That doesn't match anything we were doing together, and anyway, we weren't on shift. The bosses want to know what he was working on."

"I don't know. He told me a few days earlier that he would be on surveillance and might be working extra hours."

"Did he mention a target?"

"No. He didn't like to bother me with his work."

Tait looked incredulous. "He never discussed our cases?"

"Once in a while, but not usually. He didn't want to upset me."

"Kinda old-fashioned for a young guy."

"He was, and I loved him for it!" Lucy was beginning to lose it. "He didn't tell me what he was working on, Ernie! I can't help you."

Tait changed gears. "Maybe he kept something here—a notebook, a file?"

"He never brought files home."

"Do you mind if I look?"

"What? Yes, I mind!"

"Lucy, I'm just trying to help. There's . . . talk around the station."

"What kind of talk?"

"That Jack was . . . I'm sorry. That he was mixed up in something. Maybe . . ." He swallowed.

"What?"

"Maybe, on the take."

Lucy exploded. *"That's insane!"*

"He was seen drinking with a guy . . ."

"So?"

"This particular guy has Mob connections."

"This is New Jersey! Soprano-land, remember? Every second guy on the street is related to a Mob guy, knows a Mob guy, or went to school with a Mob guy's kid! How can that mean anything?"

"We're not talking about some random mope, Lucy! This guy's in deep!"

"For God's sake! They gave Jack an honor guard funeral!"

"They were committed to it before doubts were raised. If they'd canceled, it would have led to questions."

Deeply insulted, Lucy ordered him to leave.

"I'm sorry, Lucy, I really am! But you know, they won't let go of this."

After he was gone, Lucy crawled into bed and cried herself to sleep.

The next morning, bleary-eyed and nauseous with dread, she opened a package that had been sitting on her bathroom counter for the past several days. With trembling hands, she peeled the wrapping off a small plastic baton and tested her urine.

Three minutes later, the device confirmed she was pregnant.

In her heart of hearts, she'd already known. But at the sight of the positive reading, her head swam, her knees gave out, and she woke up on the bathroom floor.

12

The cops left Lucy alone for a week. Apparently, as she later decided, even the most callous among them wasn't brave enough to intrude upon a newly widowed bride's lonely Christmas.

When Jack was killed, he and Lucy hadn't even begun to turn their minds to the holiday, so there was no tree and no decorations. If there had been, Lucy would have trashed them. Ricki and Jeff tried to persuade her to fly down to Coral Gables to spend a week or two with them, but she hadn't wanted to impose her sorrowful existence on their three-year-old daughter's Christmas. And, in truth, she hadn't been able to muster the energy to book a ticket.

Her bereavement leave from work ran into the school vacation, but Lucy warned her principal, Garrett Lindsay, that she wasn't sure when she'd be able to resume her duties. She told him in a phone call that he should consider replacing her. He showed up at her house later the same day and tried to persuade her to join him—or any one of a number of teachers who had offered—for a family Christmas, but she wasn't responsive.

She spent most of the holiday in bed.

On December 29, Detective Trousdale called and arranged to visit on the following day. He arrived at her door accompanied by a compact, hard-looking woman carrying a thin leather case . . . and by Ernie Tait.

Trousdale introduced himself. "This is my partner, Carla Scarlatti. And of course you know Ernie."

Lucy let them in. They followed her into the living room. She offered them coffee. They all declined. Lucy sank onto the couch. The others found seats nearby. Trousdale removed his winter coat; Scarlatti kept hers on.

Tait led off. "Lucy, I'm not involved in this investigation. This is Jersey City's case. And anyway, indirectly, I'm a witness. But the chief asked me to be here today."

His expression reminded her of the night he'd brought her the news of Jack's death. She felt suddenly frightened.

"Why?"

"So you'd have a familiar face in the room."

Lucy glanced from face to face. "Why is that important?"

"Because this is going to be very difficult for you," Ernie replied.

Trousdale took over. "Mrs. Hendricks, I believe you've been told how your husband died?"

"Just that he was run down by a car and then . . . shot."

"From his injuries, and from the tire marks, we think a vehicle backed into him. Because of the pattern of his injuries, the M.E. thinks it must have been an SUV or a van. The bullets—" He stopped when he saw Lucy's pained expression. "I'm sorry."

Lucy took a deep breath and steeled herself. "Please go on."

"The bullets that were removed from Jack's body were .22 caliber. Our ballistics people say they bore certain distinctive marks, called 'scrubbing.' That suggests that the weapon was equipped with a silencer. That, plus the wound pattern, leads us to believe this was a professional hit."

"Wouldn't that mean—?" Lucy turned to look straight at Ernie Tait. "Wouldn't that mean you have to go back over your old cases?"

"Other than the odd guy who was a Mob associate—which means not a made man—Jack and I never had a case that involved the Mafia."

"That Mob thing again, Ernie?"

Trousdale looked at Tait. "What does she mean?"

"I visited her before Christmas. Told her about Jack being seen with a Mob guy."

Trousdale and Scarlatti exchanged a look. Scarlatti opened her leather case. Distractedly, Lucy noticed the woman had reddened, scaly patches on the backs of her hands. She handed Lucy a plastic evidence bag. It contained what looked like a man's silver bracelet. It bore a bizarre insignia consisting of three human legs, bent at the knee, radiating in a symmetrical pattern from a woman's head. Her hair looked like a tangle of intertwined, golden serpents.

"Have you seen that before?"

"I recognize the insignia, but not the bracelet."

The woman cop seemed surprised. "You recognize that insignia?"

"Yes. It's called a trinacria. It's on the flag of Sicily."

"How would you know that?"

"My father owns a bar in Florida. There's a Sicilian flag on the wall. What's this got to do with Jack?"

Scarlatti ignored the question. She pressed Lucy. "Why would your father have a Sicilian flag in his bar?"

"Because he was born there!" Lucy was getting angry. She leaned forward. "Answer me, please! What's this got to do with my husband?"

Scarlatti looked at her partner.

"That bracelet you're holding was found by the medical examiner," Trousdale replied. "It was stuck in your husband's throat."

Lucy's hand went to her own throat. Her eyes filled with tears. "They choked him?"

"No." His tone was gentle. "He was already dead when it was placed there."

"I—I don't understand."

Tait interjected. "Lucy, in the old days, when the Mafia got rid of someone who'd been talking too much, they'd sometimes leave a dead canary in their victim's mouth. It was a warning—a warning to anyone else who was giving away their secrets, talking too much, maybe thinking about making a deal with the FBI. Things like that."

"A canary?"

"Yes," Scarlatti answered. "In this case, according to our intelligence people, that bracelet is a known calling card of the Lanza crime family." There was no gentleness in the woman cop's tone when she added, "We believe it was left deliberately, as a warning to others. Your husband wasn't working on any investigations related to Mob activities. Both Detective Tait and the Captain in charge of the Bayonne Detective Bureau have confirmed that. And, just to be sure he wasn't working off the books with federal law enforcement, we checked with the FBI, the Department of Justice, Treasury—everyone we could think of. They don't know him. There was no reason for the Mob to kill him because of his police work. So that leaves only one other logical conclusion. He must have been on the Lanza payroll, and he screwed up with them somehow."

Lucy sat in stunned silence.

Involuntarily, she combed her memory for any comment, any sign, any unexplained flush of wealth—*anything!*—that Jack had ever said or done or shown her that could support this cop's sickening allegation.

There was nothing.

She stood up.

"Out! All of you!"

"Lucy . . . !" Tait, who had been sitting beside her, reached for her arm. She pulled away. Blood boiling, she turned on him.

"You were Jack's partner! You come here, into his house, and lie to me about him! You, of all people! How could you be part of this?"

"Mrs. Hendricks," Trousdale began. "Please let us just—!"

"No!" Lucy's voice rose to a screech. *"Get out of my house!"*

They left.

They returned in force, on the following day, armed with a search warrant. Tait stood by with Lucy, looking thoroughly embarrassed, vainly trying to comfort her, while a team of Bayonne Internal Affairs cops, accompanied by Trousdale and Scarlatti, turned her house upside down. They found nothing, a point Lucy had emphatically predicted when they arrived. She had the puny satisfaction of spitting that prediction back in Scarlatti's face at the end of the search, only to have her rage reignited when the bitch told her they were taking her laptop. It was returned to her three weeks later. Although the officer who brought it back said nothing, it was obvious to Lucy that they hadn't found a shred of evidence on the hard drive to support their ridiculous suspicions.

By March, Lucy had still not returned to work, and Garrett Lindsay had finally been forced to "release" her from her position. She hadn't objected. She knew she was incapable of effective teaching. She met with Garrett at his office one evening, received the paperwork, allowed him a farewell hug, and walked away.

She was now four months pregnant, still tormented by grief and, with every passing day, plagued by the hysterical thought that her child would look so much like Jack that she'd be incapable of caring for it.

She was stressed, frightened, and increasingly isolated.

Still struggling with the petty obsessions of the pension board bureaucrats, and without her teaching salary, she was relying on savings and some money from her father and Ricki to meet her expenses. Someone in the Jersey City PD or Bayonne Police had leaked information to the press about the investigation into Jack's death and suspected activities, forcing her to screen calls from pestering reporters. When she began to suspect she was being followed, she called Ernie Tait. He was concerned and responsive. He promised to make a "confidential inquiry," as he called it, and he was as good as his word.

When he phoned her back, he said, "It's not the police, Lucy. It's the press."

"How do you know?"

"Do you have a copy of today's paper?"

"Which one?"

"The *Star Ledger.*"

"No."

"You're on page three. Looks like you're coming out of a drug store."

When she picked up a copy of the paper, she realized the photo had been taken three days earlier after she'd picked up a prescription. It appeared with a regurgitated story about the continuing investigation into Jack's murder. The headline read:

DEAD COP MAY HAVE BEEN INVOLVED WITH ORGANIZED CRIME

The last straw came with the break-in at her house, and the indifferent attitude of the cops who responded.

The following night, after she hung up from her regular call with Lucy, Ricki had persuaded Jeff to help her mount a rescue operation. Jeff called an old classmate who practiced with a firm in Trenton and hired him to take over Lucy's fight with the pension board. By the time he got off the phone, Ricki had packed a bag and was ready to drive north.

By the middle of April, Lucy was living in Coral Gables.

But even then, the torment didn't stop.

Unable to stop herself from picking at the scab, Lucy began each day by obsessively checking New Jersey media websites. Articles kept appearing. One suggested that authorities were "worried that Detective Hendricks had compromised significant investigations"—without naming one. But it was a later story in May that plunged her into the deepest despair. Someone at an obscure small-market weekly paper in southern New Jersey—a journalist wannabe who gloried in the byline "Fred Tantrum, Investigative Reporter"—tried to burnish his CV with a story asking how it was that Jack and Lucy Hendricks, lowly wage earners that they were, had been able to afford "a pampered week in the Presidential Suite of a luxurious Mob-built hotel in sun-bathed Key West, Florida."

PART
II

FORZA

13

Speed equals smarts. Modern life, it was said, was a fast-paced blur of information and communication, of aggression and retreat, of beating that clock, outwitting that competitor, exposing that fraud, filing that patent . . . that story . . . that lawsuit . . .

Therefore, the most valuable citizens must be the quick-witted, the quick thinkers, the quick studies. It stood to reason: The people making the fastest connections must be the smartest ones.

Wrong.

Making fast connections didn't mean making the right connections. It had been shown, time and again, that quick thinkers made more wrong decisions than deliberative ones. And if intelligence was directly related to reaction time, the modern world was in deep trouble, because a Swedish university study had shown that average human reaction times had declined steadily between 1884 and 2004.

If reaction time truly equated to intelligence, then the average IQ of today's population was thirteen points lower than it was during the Victorian Age.

IQ had nothing to do with making fast connections. It had everything to do with making the right connections.

Lucy was about to experience a live demonstration of her own intelligence.

In May, with the weather becoming warmer and the days longer, she began alternating her gym workouts with a five-mile run around and through Stephen Gregg Park. One evening, late in the month, she was pounding south along her usual route on the waterside leg of Park Road. As she passed the first baseball diamond, she noticed a silver-colored car.

It caught her attention because it was approaching too fast, well above the park's fifteen-mile-per-hour speed limit.

And, because it was traveling in the wrong direction on a one-way road.

Abruptly, the vehicle's nose dipped. Tires yowling, it swerved, climbed the curb, and came to a shuddering stop, blocking Lucy's path. Doors flew open and two men jumped out, one from behind the wheel and the other from the rear seat.

Lucy's instincts kicked in. The bleachers to her left prevented her escape in that direction, so she pivoted right and darted into the roadway, sprinting for the opposite curb. Beyond it lay a low, grassy ridge, a thin curtain of scrub and gnarly white pines, and then the Newark Bay walkway, frequented by cyclists.

The rear-seat man had anticipated Lucy's move and was already moving to cut her off. He was obviously fit because he moved with blinding speed. In a second, he had her wrapped in powerful arms. He lifted her off her feet and carried her toward the car. Her frantic attempts to kick free were neutralized when the driver rushed over and seized her legs. Before she could scream, or even catch her breath, she found herself face-down on the floor in the rear compartment. The first assailant piled in after and pinned her there. The other man jumped behind the wheel. With a bone-jarring bump, the car reversed into the road and squealed away, back in the direction from which it had come.

Five years of grief and depression hadn't prepared Lucy for the cata-clysm of mind-numbing terror that engulfed her in the few seconds it had taken to abduct her off the street.

But five years of brooding introspection had.

Five years remembering Jack's imperturbable confidence.

Five years remembering his loving protectiveness.

And five years remembering the strict lesson he had drummed into her: *"Curb your fear. If you don't, you won't be able to think. Your physical strength might not save you. Your brain will."*

She stamped down on the fear and gave herself an order:

Think!

She could tell by the car's initial maneuver that it was traveling south.

It didn't make sense. These men must have known her running route, but instead of rolling up on her from behind and snatching her off the sidewalk, they'd taken the risk of speeding north on Park Drive, against the warning signs.

Either they hadn't noticed the signs, meaning they didn't know the park . . . or, they were stupid.

"What are you doing?" Lucy gasped. "What do you want with me?"

"Shut up!" her rear-seat captor rasped. Then he added, in a more moderate tone, "Please."

"Please? You want me to *please* shut up while you kidnap me? Who the hell are you?"

"This is just a delivery. We won't hurt you."

"You're already hurting me!"

"Sorry, ma'am." He adjusted his body, loosening the pressure on her back and neck.

Please?

Sorry, ma'am?

Delivery?

While Lucy processed their baffling verbal exchange, she felt the car make a sharp left. She waited for the sharp right that she knew would eventually lead to the park's southeast exit.

It didn't come. The car rolled straight on.

Straight on signified one of two possibilities: Either these two goons were heading into the dead-end tangle of footpaths next to the basketball courts to "deliver" her to someone waiting there, or they really were just plain stupid.

Considering that it was still light outside, and there would probably be local guys shooting baskets on the courts at the end of this road, Lucy went with stupid.

When they'd started out, the man in the back had been half-sitting, half-lying on the seat, holding Lucy to the floor with a rough hand on the back of her neck and a knee on her lower back. When he'd eased the pressure on her, she'd noticed a cylinder lying under the front seat a few inches from her nose. It was a pressure can. She could just make out the lettering on the label:

Prestone Windshield De-Icer

The business end of the container was a combined nozzle and ice scraper.

She moved her left arm, pretending to try to get more comfortable.

"Don't move."

"My arm's going to sleep!"

"Sorry."

He released her for a few seconds while she pretended to get more comfortable.

The car kept going.

Lucy knew they were rolling deeper into the cul-de-sac.

Her minder must have noticed they were running out of road. He jerked upright, releasing his grip on her neck. He pounded on the back of the driver's seat.

"Idiot! You missed a turn back there! This is a dead end!"

The driver cursed. The car slowed to a stop, then started to move forward again.

Lucy slid her left hand under the seat. She gripped the spray can. By flexing her wrist, she could tell it wasn't empty. She adjusted it in her fingers so the nozzle was in the right position.

"You can't go up there!" her captor barked. "It's a walking path!"

"Shut up! I'm just getting turned around!"

Lucy felt the car stop, then go into reverse.

She made her move.

She twisted around, almost wrenching her spine in the process.

She caught her distracted abductor by surprise.

"What are you doing? Stay put!"

As he reached for her, she sprayed a blast of de-icer directly into his eyes. He let out a bellow of pain and lurched backward.

The car rocked to a stop. The driver craned to see what caused the commotion. Lucy clawed her way upright. "Thanks for the ride!" she hissed. She swung with all her strength, stabbing him in the face with the blade of ice scraper, yanked on the door latch behind her, and threw herself backward out the car.

She picked herself up off the pavement and got her bearings. To her right was the broad stone stairway leading up to the park overlook. She'd often seen Bayonne PD cruisers parked up there, engines running, with officers in discussion. It seemed to be a meeting point.

She ran.

Fifty feet from the car, she could still hear the screaming from the man in the back.

Seventy-five feet from the car, she heard a squeal of tires. She checked over her shoulder. The vehicle wasn't pursuing her. It was speeding back the way it had come.

Lucy flew up the stairs. She'd run them enough times to know there were forty-four shallow steps. She caught herself counting as she surged toward the top. Before she crested the last flight, she was craning to see if there were any police cars in sight.

There were none.

But there was an older man near the flagpole. He had a German shepherd on a leash and they were walking in her direction. She rushed toward him. He froze in place, taking in the sight of what Lucy later realized must have looked like a madwoman. She came to a gasping halt just beyond the reach of the man's now alert and growling dog.

"Do you have a cell phone, sir? I've just got away from some men who tried to kidnap me!"

A BPD patrol car arrived within minutes. As soon as the lead officer had the gist of Lucy's story, he interrupted her to get a description of the men and the vehicle. He told his younger partner to relay the details on his radio.

"The man in the backseat got a good shot of de-icer in his eyes," Lucy added. "The other one's going to need stitches. They might go to a hospital."

The officer nodded to his partner, who got back on the radio. "That was damned quick thinking, ma'am," the officer remarked, in an admiring tone.

Lucy didn't answer. It hadn't felt very quick to her.

The officers took the dog walker's name, and Lucy completed her narrative as she led them down the stairs to the scene of her escape. It wasn't difficult to locate—the spray can was still lying on the spot where she'd bailed out of the car. After they'd photographed and bagged it, and Lucy had assured them she didn't need any medical treatment, they drove her to the police office to record a formal statement.

The older officer, whose name was McQuarrie, conducted her interview with sympathy and careful attention to detail. Lucy sensed that he had recognized her name. If so, he was polite enough not to mention it until they reached a certain point in the interview.

"He said you were a 'delivery'? He used that word?"

"Yes."

"Can you help me with that? It sounds like someone hired these men to grab you."

"I know. But I don't understand it. I'm a schoolteacher! I don't have any enemies like that. As far as I know, I don't have any enemies at all."

"I apologize for bringing this up, but . . . have you thought this might be related to your late husband?"

Lucy bristled. "I was waiting for this."

"I'm sorry. But it can't be ignored."

"So, are you another one?"

"Another one what?"

"Another one who believes the myth."

"As I understand it, there were unanswered questions."

"Yes, there are unanswered questions. Like what my husband was investigating that got him killed! And why someone tried to make that good man look bad! No one has ever answered those questions . . . I suspect because they don't want them answered." Lucy stood. "Are we finished?"

McQuarrie sighed. "For now."

He offered to ask his supervisor for Lucy to be provided with police protection until they caught the two men. The thought of being followed everywhere by a BPD officer appalled her. She declined, but accepted his alternate suggestion. He said he could arrange for patrol officers to make regular passes at her house.

The next morning's paper was entirely unabashed about identifying Lucy. The police hadn't released her name, but a reporter had interviewed the dog walker. The paper featured a short account of her ordeal at the bottom of page one, and then used the report as an excuse to remind inattentive readers that the victim . . .

. . . a local schoolteacher, is the widow of Bayonne PD Detective Jack Hendricks, whose activities were the subject of a lengthy police probe after his December 2006 murder in a Jersey City parking garage. His killing remains unsolved.

When Lucy saw the article, she threw the newspaper across the room. That afternoon, she enrolled in a self-defense course.

14

The knock on her door startled her out of her doze.

It had been another long day, and it had taken longer than usual to get Kevin settled down and into bed. As tired as she was, she hadn't really minded. She treasured her time with her son.

But the strains of the day had taken their toll.

On top of her teaching duties, there'd been the anxious questions from Garrett about her abduction in the park. Then there'd been the questions from her fellow staff members, some of whom, until now, had remained mostly aloof. Their new and somewhat dubious expressions of concern grated on her. There had even been questions from her class. The questioners were two of her more mature female students; apparently the boys didn't have the nerve to ask.

And then . . . more questions from a detective who'd been assigned to her case. John Boyd was a cop she'd never met and never heard of before today. He appeared in the back of her classroom at the end of her last teaching block. She'd made him wait there while she delivered Kevin to daycare.

Their subsequent interview was bizarre. The man had a weird habit of talking fast, changing subjects, jumping back and forth, and not finishing sentences. It was like being interviewed by someone on speed. On top of that, he kept leaning forward, examining her as if she were a museum exhibit.

The police had had no luck tracing the silver car or identifying the two men who had grabbed Lucy. Wearily, in fits and starts punctuated by the detective's staccato questions, she repeated the story she'd told Officer McQuarrie. By the end of the interview, as far as she could tell, she had added nothing to her original statement. The detective went away.

There was still a call to make—she needed to tell Ricki before she and their father learned of her abduction by other means. She'd been putting that off until Kevin was asleep. Except now she'd almost fallen asleep herself. At least tomorrow was Saturday. Maybe she'd just get an early night and call Ricki in the morning.

Another knock. Three sharp, confident raps. Whoever it was had no use for doorbells.

Maybe it was a BPD officer, checking on her.

When she stood up, the book she hadn't been reading slid off her lap to the floor. She left it there.

She'd left the porch light on, but the foyer was dark. That was deliberate. Without backlighting, no one on the porch would know if she was checking the peephole.

Her visitor looked to be in his sixties. A grave and orderly man in a three-piece suit. A hard-lined face that still hinted at the strikingly attractive younger man who had preceded it.

He stood waiting, staring straight at the peephole.

Staring straight back at Lucy.

This was no police officer.

She called through the door. "Yes?"

"Lucinda Cappelli."

It wasn't a question.

Instantly wary, she replied, "Sorry. Wrong house!"

"Lucinda! My name is Dominic Lanza. I would like to speak with you."

Lanza! The name pulsed through her like an electric shock.

"Please leave, or I'll call the police!"

"That's the last thing you should to do."

"Please go!" Lucy pleaded. "If anyone sees you here, it will just confirm all those rumors about my husband!"

It happened without warning.

There was a rustle of cloth, and a thick hand covered her mouth. In a precisely executed action, an arm reached past her, unlocked the door, then encircled her torso and moved her effortlessly aside. The door swung open and Lanza stepped in. He closed and locked the door behind him.

Abruptly, Lucy was released.

A tall man with a pallid, heavy face and a receding hairline appeared from behind to her. "You should have checked your patio door," he said, with unexpected politeness.

"This is my friend Carlo," Lanza said. "He won't hurt you, and neither will I. May we sit down?"

"The police have orders to check on me! They'll be here any minute!"

Lanza was unfazed. "This won't take long. Please lead the way."

Trembling with fright, Lucy led them to the living room.

Lanza pointed at the near end of the couch. "After you."

Lucy sat.

Lanza settled on a soft chair across from her, while the tall man positioned himself near the front window.

"First," Lanza began, "I want to apologize for those fools who abused you last night."

Lucy's eyes widened. "*You* sent those men?"

"Yes, and no. They overheard me saying I wanted to meet you. They thought to impress their employer. They acted stupidly and without my authority, and for that I am sorry." He paused. "De-icer. That was fast thinking."

Lucy wasn't interested in his assessment of her thinking. "Are you saying those men grabbed me just so you could *meet me?*"

"They've been severely dealt with, I assure you."

Lucy felt a chill. "What does that mean—'severely'?"

"Normally, I would say you don't want to know. In this case, after we got them patched up, I sent them away. To one of our . . . branch offices."

"So they're alive?"

"Yes."

"That man I sprayed. Did I blind him?"

Lanza looked amused. "Do you care?"

"No. Well, yes. I mean, he roughed me up, but he didn't hurt me. I wouldn't want—"

"You are a strange lady. No, he's not blind. There was a bottle of water in the car. He rinsed out most of the chemical in time. He'll be wearing sunglasses for a while. But his companion didn't do so well."

"I didn't spray the driver."

"Maybe not, but our doctor had to sew a piece of his nose back on."

The man at the window let out a bark of laughter.

"I'm sorry . . . this is funny?"

"Of course not. I make no excuse for what my men did to you. But the fact that they were completely outwitted by a schoolteacher . . . well, perhaps you can guess the entertainment value."

Lucy started to relax. The conversation was bizarre, but it was becoming apparent that Lanza wasn't here to harm her.

So, why was he here?

Lanza had stopped talking. He shifted back in his chair and just sat there. Watching her.

Unblinking.

"Are you afraid of me?" he asked.

His tone had changed. Now his voice was quiet. And menacing.

Feeling suddenly ill, she realized she had relaxed too soon.

"Yes." She clasped her hands to stop them from trembling.

"You should be. If you know something about your husband, now is the time to tell me."

"There's nothing to tell!"

"Someone may have been paying him off. Someone with a motive to eliminate him and make trouble for me at the same time. You will know something."

"I don't, because no one was paying my husband. I would have known. I would have seen the signs. But Jack was an honest man, and it never happened."

Lanza said nothing, his eyes boring into her. Finally: "We didn't kill him, Lucinda. Do you believe that?"

Her jaw tightened. "I don't know if I believe that! I don't know what to believe!" In a flash, anger overcame fear. "But if you did, Mr. Lanza, one day, somehow, you will pay!"

Out of the corner of her eye, she saw Carlo turn away from the window. Lanza held up a hand and the man turned back to his vigil.

"Thank you, Lucinda."

"For what?"

"For confirming that your husband was not corrupt."

He's been playing you, Lucy . . .

"I'm not sure I'm ready to thank you yet," she said firmly.

"Thank me for what?"

"For not killing my husband."

Lanza's jaw dropped, and then he roared with laughter. For a woozy second, Lucy wondered if she'd been dropped into an alternate universe.

She waited.

The mobster's laughter ended as abruptly as it had begun. "I came tonight because I wanted to be sure about you," he said. He reached inside his jacket.

Lucy tensed—wondering if she'd read the situation wrong, wondering if she was about to die, disbelieving it *because it made no damned sense!*—until she saw what was in his hand.

He leaned across the space between them and handed her a small, black Nokia cell phone.

She stared at it, relieved, but bewildered.

"It's a pay-as-you-go," Lanza explained. "Consider it my business card. When you're ready to talk, check 'draft messages' and call the number you find there. It will ring—after a few intervening call-forwards—on the one I'm carrying." He removed a similar phone from another pocket and showed it to her.

"You're giving me a burner?"

"You know the term?"

"I watch TV."

"Of course." He smiled. "Cost of doing business. Certain federal agencies would love to monitor my calls. It's not just a burner. When you call, it connects to a VOI system and goes through a couple of untraceable links before it reaches me."

"How very high tech."

"We move with the times."

"You said, 'when I'm ready to talk.' Talk about what?"

"The press would like the world to believe that people like me have scores of crooked cops on the payroll. The fact is, there aren't that many corrupt ones, and we stay clear of most of them. Your husband never had any contact with my organization."

"I know that! I've always known that. But you haven't answered my question—talk about what?"

"We may be able to help each other."

"Me, help *you*? I'm sorry, but why would I help . . . ?" The word died in her throat.

"A Mob boss? A Godfather?"

Lucy didn't reply.

Lanza sighed. "I really hate those movies." His woeful, offended look was almost comically human. "Listen, young lady. I'm not Vito Corleone, all unsmiling, talking in parables. And I don't own a waste disposal company. So get over it."

Lucy pressed on. "And, why would you trust me? Aren't you worried I'll report all this to the police?"

Judging from his expression, he'd expected her question.

"Lucinda . . . did you love your husband?"

She felt a rush of the old pain. She replied through gritted teeth. "Yes!"

"Are you satisfied with the investigation of his murder?"

"No."

"Do you believe me when I swear we had nothing to do with his death?"

He had her. In spite of his sinister reputation, and in spite of his invasion of her home, she realized that she did believe him.

"Yes."

"Someone murdered your husband and tried to make it look like I did it. That I ordered it. The police investigation went nowhere because it had nowhere to go. That was five years ago, but the media won't leave it alone. It's as if someone was deliberately trying to keep the story alive. I don't like that."

"Why would that be a worry?" Lucy picked her words carefully. "I mean, to you. As you said, the investigation went nowhere."

"Let's just call it a matter of principle. But it affects you, too. Do you want to keep reading these press stories?"

"No! I just want the killer caught, and Jack's name cleared!"

"Good. As I said, maybe we can help each other. Don't answer me now. Think about it." He turned to the man at the window. "Carlo?"

Carlo thumbed his phone, then waited. It beeped.

"It's clear."

Dominic Lanza rose to his feet.

"Thank you for your time, Lucinda. We'll let ourselves out."

Lucy waited until she heard her front door click shut. Only then did she get up, go to the door, and lock it. Then she headed for the rear of the house.

Kevin was sitting on the stairs.

"Honey? What's wrong?"

"I woked up."

She went to him. "What woke you, sweetheart?" She was about to lift him into her arms, but changed her mind. She was still wobbly after her encounter with Lanza, and Kevin was already topping forty pounds.

"That man," he replied. He shook off her guiding hand and started climbing the steps himself.

Man, not *men*? Lucy thought.

She followed her son up the stairs and back to his bedroom. As she tucked him in, she asked, in an off-handed tone, "Were you listening to that man?"

He lay there, looking up at her with those disturbing adult eyes she'd noticed lately. He blinked once, and then shocked her with his reply.

"Lucy, be careful."

"Kevin? What do you mean?"

But as quickly as the spooky moment had come, it was gone. The little boy rolled on his side, drew up his knees, reached for his teddy bear, and closed his eyes.

Lucy was particularly cautious with each step as she made her way back downstairs. If anything, her legs were more unsteady than they had been going up.

She checked the sliding doors that led to the rear patio from the dining room and the office. She couldn't tell which one Lanza's man Carlo had used to enter because both were now locked.

Polite kidnappers . . .

Considerate burglars . . .

A warning from a five-year-old . . .

What am I missing?

She telephoned her sister.

"Tell me what Dad did before he bought the Bronte!"

"He worked in a mine in Sicily. He hated the life, so he and Mom emigrated."

"That was always the story, but you know there was more to it than that."

"I thought we agreed we wouldn't talk about it."

"I want to talk about it now!"

"Why?"

"Because I just met a Mafia don, and he knew my maiden name!"

Ricki took a breath. "Lucy, how did you get mixed up with the Mafia?"

"I'm not mixed up with anything!" she fibbed. "I'll tell you about it some other time. I just want to know what really happened, before we were born. Do you know?"

There was a long pause.

"I don't know the whole story."

"What *do* you know?"

"I just know what I overheard one night. You were just a baby. I was in the hallway and Mom and Dad were talking in their bedroom."

"What about?"

"Something about how Dad got the Bronte. But they were speaking Italian! I was only about seven, and you know my Italian wasn't that great. Mom wanted me to learn English, so she—"

"I know, I know. Just tell me what you remember!"

"It sounded like somebody gave him the bar."

"*Gave* it to him? I thought he bought it!"

"I'm just telling you what I think I heard. And Mom was saying something about 'those people,' that they never let go, that he'll never be free, that they'd be coming to him one day, wanting something . . . a favor, something bad."

Lucy remembered the men . . .

The well-dressed men who showed up at the Bronte once every few years and kissed her father on both cheeks. Who sat with him at his corner table, drinking *grappa*. Who sometimes followed him into his office behind the bar.

The men who never came to their house.

Ricki was still talking. "Mom kept saying, 'We have the girls, Joseph! Think of the girls!' And Dad, he said, 'Giulia, how many times do I tell you? It was a settlement.'"

"A settlement?"

"Like, a reward. He called it *un debito d'onore*."

"A debt of honor."

"Yeah. He said, 'They helped us come here, and they bought us the bar, and they will never ask us for anything in return.' I remember he told her, '*Mettiamoci una pietra sopra. Il debito è saldato.*'"

"'Put a stone on it,'" Lucy translated. "'The debt is paid.'"

"Those were his exact words."

Lucy went quiet, trying to process what she had just heard.

"Lucy?"

"I'm here."

"There was something else . . ."

"What?"

"I never said anything, because I didn't want to upset—"

"Ricki! What?"

"Cappelli's not our real name."

Ricki waited while Lucy silently grappled with that.

"What is our name?"

"I don't know."

•   •   •

After that unnerving conversation, Lucy went to her computer. She ran a search phrase: *Lanza crime family.*

The boast at the top of the screen was startling—*About 184,000 results (0.27 seconds)*—but the phrasing of the links directly below startled her more:

San Francisco crime family . . .

California Connection: the Lanza crime family . . .

James "Jimmy the Hat" Lanza, San Francisco crime boss . . .

She opened the James Lanza link, and discovered that the man had died in 2006.

"James Lanza was the last godfather of this crime family, which is now extinct."

Extinct?

Lucy clicked to the next page. More San Francisco Mob articles. She amended her search term: *Dominic Lanza.*

The first hit solved the mystery:

The East Coast Lanzas are not to be confused with a small San Francisco crime syndicate that once bore the same name. That family became dormant with the death of its last godfather in 2006. The two families were distantly related, and law enforcement agencies suspect that the Bay Area group subsidized the rise of the New Jersey branch during the 1950s, but no hard evidence of that connection has ever been uncovered.

The East Coast Lanzas' reach covers New Jersey, New York, and South Florida. Florham Park, NJ, businessman Dominic Lanza, 67, is rumored to be the current head of the family. His paternal uncle, Tommaso Lanza, who died in 1991, was said to be the driving force behind the family's phenomenal growth after the Second World War. Journalist Edgar Leech, the author of two books on the Watergate scandal, has suggested that the elder Lanza had close ties with Peter Brennan, president of New York City's Mafia-linked Building and Construction Trades Council. Brennan served as secretary of labor in President Richard Nixon's short-lived second administration. The connection between the two men came to light during a 1972 Army investigation instigated by General Alexander Haig, Nixon's chief of staff. If true, this tends to support unproven allegations about the Lanza family's influence over certain construction industry unions.

The Lanzas are the least known of the so-called "Cosa Nostra" crime families, due mainly to the family's CIA-like obsession with secrecy. Most associates and soldiers, and even some capo regimes, don't know the names of their counterparts, making it extremely difficult for local police and federal law enforcement to cultivate valuable informants. (This paranoid approach may be a legacy from the San Francisco family, which never grew larger than twenty-five to thirty members due to a strict policy of restricting the admission of new "made men." While this may have protected the West Coast family from being infiltrated by informants, an aging membership eventually led to its extinction.)

Sources within the FBI, who spoke to Edgar Leech on condition of anonymity, view the family with a mixture of frustration and admiration. Only one member of the extended family has ever attracted wide public notice, and even that came long after his death. Ironically, this notoriety was not due to the man's numerous crimes, but because of his public service. Joseph "Socks" Lanza, a distant cousin of Dominic's father, was a vicious *Mafioso* who controlled the Fulton Fish Market and, through his connections, much of the New York waterfront. During World War II, he placed his entire organization at the disposal of U.S. Naval Intelligence in an ongoing effort to identify Axis saboteurs and sympathizers among the thousands of fishermen, seamen, and longshoremen who worked out of the hundreds of piers and warehouses in Manhattan, Queens, New Jersey, and Brooklyn. Only in recent years has his invaluable assistance to the war effort come to light.

Lanza's contribution did not, however, deter law enforcement authorities from arresting him for extortion and conspiracy in 1943 and sending him to prison.

Since 1945, only two of the family's alleged members have ever been convicted of a serious crime. In 1985, a long-time soldier named Alphonso Jovinelli was sentenced to twenty years for extortion. Four years into his sentence, he died of brain cancer. Two decades later, Aldo Gianotti, an enforcer who was said to be closely connected to the family's top leadership, was convicted of murdering the leader of a Jersey City street gang. He was sentenced to life in prison, but on November 11, 2006, he vanished from the New Jersey State Prison at Trenton after serving only fifteen months of his sentence. Prison authorities were dumbfounded by his escape. In the words of the warden's spokesman: "At seven-forty last night, the prison's entire electronic surveillance system went dark. The blackout lasted exactly six minutes. We still don't know how that happened. Shortly after the system came back online, our officers determined that inmate Gianotti was missing. As far as we can determine, the prisoner simply walked out the front gate and someone drove him away. We are conducting a thorough investigation."

The results of that investigation have never been made public, and Aldo Gianotti remains at large. He is rumored to have been involved in the murder of a Bayonne police officer a few weeks after his escape.

The final sentence riveted Lucy's attention. There was a footnote reference link. With trembling fingers, she clicked on it. It led her to an article she'd never seen before. It was dated June 23, 2007, nearly seven months after Jack's death. It summed up what she already knew about the rumors of Jack's involvement with organized crime, but with one addition:

> Based on certain physical evidence found at the scene, unnamed sources within the investigation are saying the killing may have been the work of a Lanza crime family enforcer who had escaped from prison just a few weeks earlier.

She had already seen one piece of physical evidence that allegedly connected the Lanza family to the murder—a trinacria bracelet. Detective Carla Scarlatti had shown it to her a month after Jack's murder. The sight of that bracelet, and Detective Trousdale's description of where it was found, were seared into her memory.

But was there other "physical evidence" she hadn't been told about?

Other physical evidence linking the crime to the escaped Lanza enforcer?

Evidence like . . . DNA?

Lucy was overcome with confusion and suspicion.

15

Over the next several days, Lucy was in a turmoil.

She debated with herself about whether she should track down Scarlatti and Trousdale and tell them about Lanza's visit. Or, visit Jack's now-retired partner, Ernie Tait, to ask for some off-the-record advice. Or, take the bait, call Lanza, and find out exactly what he could do for her, and what he wanted her to do for him. Or, *pretend* to take the bait, meet with Lanza, and then track down Scarlatti, or Trousdale, or Tait, or visit the nearest FBI office.

Or, take a few days off and fly down to Florida to confront her father about his past. Ask him who gave him the Bronte, the bar and grill he had owned for Lucy's entire life. Ask him why it was a gift. Ask him why he and Mom had used a phony surname all these years.

Ask him what the hell their real name was, because Ricki said she didn't know.

But while all this was driving her crazy, her daily routine plodded on. The tumult in her mind made her feel like a visitor in her own life, but she had to keep on teaching, keep on walking Kevin to daycare, keep on meeting with students after hours, keep on reading Kevin his favorite bedtime stories, and keep on paying the bills.

The next turning point came while she was doing just that: paying the bills.

Ever since Lanza's visit, Kevin had developed an odd obsession with one particular corner in Lucy's office. Whether she was in the room or not, he would stand stiffly erect in the corner calling, "Mommy! Mommy!" until Lucy finally came to him. She would cuddle him, humor him, do whatever it took to distract him, and the episode would end.

But Kevin kept returning to the corner.

The penultimate incident took place on Sunday afternoon. She was in the kitchen when she heard his calls. When she reached the office, she froze. Her little boy looked almost spectral, awash in the brash sunlight that streamed into the room, glinted off the golden hairs on his bare arms, and shimmered off his face. Adult eyes watched her. In a flash of panic that she was completely unable to explain to herself later, she rushed over to him, scooped him up into her arms, and ran out of the room.

She set him back on his feet in the kitchen, kneeled in front of him, and held him by the shoulders. "Tell Mommy why you keep going in that room!"

He burst into tears.

Instantly regretting her sharp tone, she hugged him and held him close.

But he never answered her question.

Two evenings later, Lucy was wrapped in a shawl, sitting at the desk in the office, calculator in hand, wrestling with her household accounts. It was the same desk she and Jack had used together, and she hadn't been able to bring herself to part with it, so she'd kept it in storage while she lived down south.

She had left Kevin sitting on the living room floor with his new Animalogic game. Once she'd shown him the basics, he'd taken immediately to the idea of solving the puzzles and helping the animals to cross the river. When she left the room, he was totally absorbed.

She nearly jumped out of her skin when she heard his voice behind her.

"Mom!"

She spun her chair.

The boy was back in the same corner of the room. But this time he wasn't standing at attention. He was on his knees, head down, peering through the grating of the forced air heating vent.

He looked up at her.

Those eyes again . . .

"Luce, you gotta look!"

Thoroughly shaken by her son's tone, and his unprecedented use of another of Jack's nicknames for her, she crossed the room and kneeled beside him. He was trying to push his fingers through a gap in the grate's metal scroll work. Lucy gently removed his hand.

"What's wrong, honey? Did you lose one of your animals?"

"Down there."

She attempted to pry up the grate with her fingers, but it was wedged too tightly into the ductwork.

"Mommy will be right back."

Jack's old toolbox was in the closet by the front door. She fetched a screwdriver and used it to pry up the grate. Almost immediately she spotted a white triangle peeking past the first elbow in the ductwork, several inches below floor level. It appeared to be the corner of a piece of paper. She reached down. Her fingers detected something odd. It felt like an envelope. It was held in place by tape.

She ripped it from its moorings and pulled it out of the vent.

The sealed envelope was the size normally used for a birthday or Christmas card. Not big, but big enough to block the free flow of warm air through the heating duct.

No wonder this room always seemed so cold.

Lucy could feel something inside the envelope—something rectangular and flat. She tore it open.

The object was a USB flash drive.

Dumbfounded, she held it up to Kevin. He blinked at it, and then ran from the room. After spending several seconds trying to make sense of what had just happened, Lucy went looking for her son. She found him on the living room floor, fiddling with his AnimaLogic game as if nothing had happened.

She went back to the office and resumed her seat at the desk.

Beyond anything she had experienced since Dominic Lanza's mysterious visit, the jumble of thoughts and emotions now tumbling through her mind and tensing her body made her wonder if she was truly losing her mind. Kevin's increasingly bizarre behavior since last Christmas, his use of pet names only Jack had used, his retelling of the "car following" technique Jack had once described, his sudden swings between childhood spontaneity and brooding maturity . . .

And now this.

It was all too much to process.

Exercising pure will, she crammed all the wild and distracting speculations into a back corner of her consciousness and focused her attention on the small digital appliance in her hand. Only one person could have hidden the USB drive in that vent.

Jack.

Her stomach churned at the thought of what might be on it.

Evidence that all the rumors were right—that Jack had been corrupt?

Evidence that he'd been on the Mob payroll?

"We may be able to help each other . . ."

Was this what Lanza was after?

Was she holding evidence Lanza already knew existed? Evidence that he suspected Jack had left behind? Evidence that he and Lucy, for their separate reasons, would each want destroyed?

She inserted the device into the port on the side of her laptop.

Heart racing, she opened the drive.

There were three icons on the menu: a pdf file, a data file, and an audio file.

The pdf was titled "NICB." She opened it first. It was a copy of a National Insurance Crime Bureau report. The title read: "Vehicle Thefts in the United States." She scrolled quickly through the document.

1.24 million vehicles stolen . . . thousands shipped intact to other countries . . . buyers pay a fraction of legitimate cost . . . NY, NJ, PA are high incidence areas . . . organized crime heavily involved . . .

No! Jack, please not this!

She quickly closed the file.

The data file bore a simple identifier: "SS"

She opened it.

It was a spreadsheet, eighteen pages long. Lucy's heart sank as she realized it listed vehicles—dozens and dozens of vehicles. Scanning the entries, and judging by the fancy letters and numbers embellishing their names, they seemed to be mainly high-end foreign models. Page after page recorded Mercedes CL65s, BMW X5s, Infiniti Q45s, Lexus LFAs, Jaguar X350s, and even one Maybach 57. She had never heard of a Maybach, but when she later ran an online search, she discovered that a new one sold for close to $400,000.

She had no trouble understanding most of the column headings on the spreadsheet. They listed year, make, color, VIN, state, tag number, owner's name and address, and "blue book" value.

The total value at the bottom of the last column, on the last page, read: "$7,822,380."

Below the figure, across the bottom of the page, a string of odd names appeared: *Orcone, Dorilla, Oronte, Doraspe* . . . and others she didn't recognize.

Feeling suddenly ill, Lucy clicked on the last file.

The audio file.

What she heard almost stopped her heart, but in the end, it rescued her from her fears.

With a sudden chill, she recognized her dead husband's voice.

"It's Hendricks."

"Okay, Hendricks. Last time we were in one of these little rooms, you told me Parrish is dead and nobody cares. So why are you here?"

"I'm here to tell you that, maybe, somebody does care. I'm here to see if you've got something that's more than just talk. If you do, I'll speak to the prosecutor . . ."

As she listened, she realized that the topic of discussion was an auto theft ring. The content, and certain background noises on the tape, made her think the recording was made somewhere in or near a police lockup area, or maybe in a prison. Jack and the other man were discussing someone named Parrish. Lucy vaguely recollected that Ernie Tait's former partner was named Parrish. She also recalled Jack saying that Parrish had been murdered and the case had never been solved.

With a surge of relief, she realized that Jack had not been part of the theft ring. He'd been investigating it. On his own.

Was that because he didn't trust his own police department?

"And you're saying his visits . . . this was a Mob thing."

"Had to be."

"Why?"

"The cars we stole were going out in containers. No one could run an operation like that for long without those guys muscling in. They control the unions, and the unions control the waterfront."

There it was.

The Mob connection.

But not Jack's Mob connection.

Lucy was tortured with questions. Jack had sometimes discussed his investigations with her—in fact, more often than she had admitted to Ernie Tait. Why had he never mentioned this one? Why hide the USB drive? What was he involved in? Was this the reason he was killed?

It must be.

Lanza had told the truth. Jack wasn't on his payroll. But maybe Lanza had lied about the main question. Maybe he lied when he swore he had nothing to do with Jack's death.

Lucy sat very still in her chair. Minutes became an hour; an hour stretched toward two. Over and over, she weighed taking her discovery to the BPD. She no longer knew anyone in the Department. A few officers, maybe. Some of the older ones. Faces but not names.

She couldn't ask Ernie Tait for advice—not now that she knew the man's deceased ex-partner had been at the center of Jack's investigation.

Jack had always been a bit standoffish when it came to fellow cops. He'd never been big on drinking with the boys. He would join them for the occasional celebration—a court victory, a promotion party—but he'd frankly preferred his wife's company. Over the years he had taken more than his share of ribbing about that from fellow officers. Lucy had heard some of the wisecracks. Rightly or wrongly, Jack had tried to protect her from the grittier elements of his life in law enforcement, and, as a couple, they had tended to socialize with some of her fellow teachers, and with a handful of friends from outside their professions.

But they had spent most of their spare time with each other, running in the park, working in the garden, going to movies, drinking wine, and playing cribbage—Jack had learned the game from his grandfather, a retired Navy submariner, who had left him his prized scrimshaw pegging board. Yes, they had had their disagreements, but the thing about their relationship was that neither of them had a default position that automatically put the other one in the wrong.

They had been truly, genuinely, *compatible*.

They had been loners—but loners together.

Always together.

She knew that was the reason Jack's death had almost destroyed her.

The result of it all, five years on, was that Lucy Hendricks didn't know any of the detectives at the Bureau. But even if she had, she questioned whether any of them could be trusted. They had seemed all too ready to suspect Jack of corruption—especially after they learned that he'd failed to report the offer of a free week's stay at a "reputed Mob hangout" hotel in Key West.

The hotel chain executive and his secretary (and lover, Lucy suspected) had both given statements insisting that the offer had been made to Lucy, not to Jack. That explanation had left Detective Carla Scarlatti unmoved. Lucy's later statement to Scarlatti—that Jack's simple motivation had been the chance to surprise her, and for them to spend an uninterrupted week in a romantic setting while trying to start a family—was something the stone-faced investigator seemed incapable of imagining. She had flatly told Lucy that she suspected Benjamin Gennaro, the hotel executive, was himself somehow Mob-connected.

" '*Connected!*' " Lucy had thought violently, just before she ordered the woman out of her house. "*Why is everyone in New Jersey obsessed with that fucking word?*"

Kevin appeared next to her chair.

"Mommy?"

There was the little face she loved, the one with the child's eyes.

"What is it, dear?"

"When's dinner?"

Startled, Lucy checked the time. It was well past six o'clock. She'd completely lost track of time. She'd lost track of everything.

"Oh, darn!"

"What's wrong, Mommy?"

"Mommy forgot to make dinner." She gave him a big smile. "Whatever-will-we-do?"

Kevin loved those code words. A big grin spread across his face. "Pizza!" he cried, and gave his mom a high five.

Oh God, how I love this little man . . .

Yes, Lucy loved her little man. She lived for his care, and she lived for his happiness.

But he was beginning to frighten her.

Who was she going to tell?

Who would take her seriously when she announced, "I've got a problem with Kevin."

"What problem?" she would be asked.

"Well, I'm convinced he's inherited Jack's memories."

"Say that again."

"It's as if Jack has been reborn in Kevin."

"Really? Have you considered psychiatric help?"

"For Kevin?"

"No. For you."

That night, after Kevin was asleep, Lucy returned to her computer and ran a search sequence: *childhood memory past life.*

The report that appeared at the top of her screen astounded her— *About 4,900,000 results (0.36 seconds)*—but the first tier of links was even more unsettling:

Case studies—children's reports of past-life memories . . .

Two-year-old remembers being his own grandfather . . .

Past life memories not uncommon, say psychiatrists . . .

Child recalls life as a World War II pilot—recounts details he could not have known—aircraft found . . .

As she clicked with increasing amazement through screen after screen of academic papers, news articles, and blogs, the name that kept popping up was that of Professor Jim Tucker of the University of Virginia. She discovered that he had published a book about the scientific investigation of children's memories of past lives. After further searching, she located an article he had written for an online journal back in 2008.

Arresting phrases leaped out at her.

. . . forty-five years of case studies . . . over 2,500 cases . . . subjects tend to be young children . . . typically begin describing past life memories at age two or three . . . usually stop by six or seven . . . some children have birthmarks or birth defects that appear to match wounds, usually fatal ones, suffered by the previous personality . . .

The last passage hit Lucy with a jolt. *Kevin's limp*, she thought. *That weak right arm!* She knew Jack had suffered crushing injuries to his right side.

The sliding door near her desk was partly open, and the evening air was cool, but Lucy's brow was beaded with perspiration by the time she worked her way to the website of the UVA Medical School's Division of Perceptual Studies, where Dr. Tucker had spent over a decade studying these cases.

What she learned in the next two hours filled her with inexplicable hope, and at the same time . . . with paralyzing dread.

The next morning, while Kevin ate his cereal, she topped up her coffee mug and parked herself at the breakfast table. She just sat there, looking at him. Lucy usually gulped down her morning coffee while she tidied the kitchen or emptied the dishwasher, so her change of routine must have made the boy feel uneasy.

"What'd I do?"

"What's your name?"

"Silly, you know my name!"

"Tell me."

"Kevin!"

Advice to parents of children who are spontaneously recalling past life memories . . .

"I thought your name was Jack."

He put down his spoon. "That's my Daddy's name!"

Avoid asking a lot of pointed questions . . .

"Do you remember being big?"

"You mean big like you?"

This could be upsetting to the child and . . . could lead the child to make up answers . . .

"Bigger. Big like Daddy was."

Kevin's eyes held hers. As she watched, they seemed to age.

Parents are sometimes more upset by the statements than their child is . . .

Kevin pushed back from the table and stood up.

"I'm not big anymore, Luce. But I'll protect you."

He turned and limped away, leaving his mother stunned.

16

"Mrs. Hendricks?"

Lucy looked up with a start. She'd been nervously flipping through a magazine, seeing nothing. The man who stood before her appeared to be in his early forties. She took in pomaded dark hair, dark eyes, and a pleasing face wearing a slightly quizzical expression.

"Yes." She rose to her feet.

"Mrs. Lucy Hendricks?" The emphasis was on *Lucy*.

Hell! Not another one . . .

"That's right," she replied stiffly.

The man smiled warmly and extended a hand. "It's very good to meet you. I'm Robert Olivetti. Would you like to come to my office?"

Lucy was taken off guard. She managed a thankful nod.

He escorted her down a short corridor to an office door. A sign on the wall announced his ponderous title:

Deputy First Assistant Prosecutor Robert Olivetti

They entered a corner office furnished in soulless institutional style—a small desk that looked like it belonged in a child's bedroom, mismatched bookshelves lined with binders and loose papers, and a pair of stiff-backed guest chairs. Olivetti noticed Lucy's reaction. "The boss's office isn't much better. Comes with the job."

"I'm more surprised by the location." Lucy nodded at the industrial scene outside the windows behind his desk.

"This is actually a satellite office. Most of the prosecutors work in our offices at the courthouse on Newark Avenue. We run specialized units out of this building. It helps us keep a low profile."

"Does one of those units investigate homicide?"

"Every homicide investigation in the county is run out of this building." He gestured toward a guest chair. She sat. He asked, "Would you like some water, or coffee?"

"No, I'm fine, thank you."

Instead of moving behind his desk, he settled on the other guest chair. "First off, Mrs. Hendricks, I want you to know—"

"Lucy's fine."

"Thanks. I'm Robert. Lucy, I knew your husband. I prosecuted some of his cases. I know what's been said about him, so let me try to clear the air right now. I considered Jack Hendricks to be a fine detective. Period."

Lucy felt the tension drain from her body. Finally, someone in law enforcement who hadn't passed judgment. And Robert Olivetti wasn't just *anybody* in law enforcement. He was a senior member of the Prosecutor's Office.

"Thank you."

"You're welcome."

"Maybe I'll have that coffee, after all."

"How do you take it?"

"Black, no sugar."

"Coming right up." He got up and left the room.

Lucy had started the day by phoning the Jersey City Police. She'd been hoping to track down Detective Trousdale. Despite the deep pain he and Carla Scarlatti had visited upon her during their investigation into Jack's murder, Trousdale had left her with a lingering impression of being an open-minded cop—a quality that had seemed singularly lacking in his partner.

She was put through to the Detective Bureau, where a disembodied male voice informed her that Trousdale had left the Department two years earlier.

"Oh? Is he still a police officer?"

"Yes, ma'am," the voice responded.

"Can you tell me how to reach him?"

"That might be difficult, ma'am. You'll have to call the Army."

"The Army?"

"Yes. He joined the military police. And, we heard a few months ago that he'd been deployed."

She didn't bother to ask for Detective Scarlatti. She thanked the officer and hung up.

After a few moments of thought, she decided she had only one option left. She called the Hudson County Prosecutor's Office and asked to make an appointment with the county prosecutor.

"Relating to which case, ma'am?" the receptionist asked, in an impertinent tone.

"Relating to the false accusations against my husband, Detective Jack Hendricks."

"Are you referring to—?"

"Yes. The detective who was murdered back in 2006."

"May I have your name, please?"

"Lucy Hendricks."

"Please hold."

After an interminable wait, the receptionist came back on the line. "Mr. Van Camp is currently on sick leave. If you would like to meet with one of his deputies, Mr. Olivetti will see you. I can slot you in for late this afternoon."

"What time?"

"He can see you at four-thirty."

"Thank you. I'll be there."

Lucy set down her mug.

The coffee was surprisingly good, considering it came from a government lunchroom. Robert's mug sat untouched. For the past several minutes, he'd been frozen in his chair, listening with rapt attention as Lucy had taken him, step by step, through the aftermath of Jack's murder.

She'd told him about Tait bringing her the news of Jack's death, about his pre-Christmas visit to tell her about the brewing suspicions about his activities, and about the post-Christmas visit from Trousdale and Scarlatti with even more allegations. She gave him a succinct overview of the past five years of her life—the poorly investigated break-in at her house a few months after Jack's murder, her move to Florida, Kevin's birth, and the break-in at her storage unit. She told him about Garrett Lindsay's phone call and her return to Bayonne. After she described the foiled attempt to abduct her in Stephen Gregg Park—he'd heard about it and, predictably, offered admiring compliments for her quick thinking—she jumped straight to the main point of her visit. She told Olivetti that Jack had been quietly investigating an extensive car theft operation, and she believed that was what had gotten him killed. She also mentioned what she'd read about Aldo Gianotti, the alleged Lanza family enforcer who had escaped from prison.

"I don't know what 'physical evidence' they were talking about in that article," she continued, with rising emotion, "unless it was just that bracelet the coroner found in Jack's throat. Either the Lanza family had Jack killed, or someone tried to make it look like they did. All I know is that my husband was conducting a legitimate investigation, and that he was definitely not corrupt!"

For reasons Lucy couldn't even explain to herself, she stopped short of disclosing Dominic Lanza's visit to her home.

"And you have evidence of this? Evidence of Jack's investigation?"

"Yes. I found this hidden in our house." Lucy opened her purse and retrieved the flash drive. "It was inside a heating register." There was no way on earth she was going to reveal how Kevin's preternatural behavior had led her to the object.

"What's on it?"

"Proof that I'm right."

"You found it in a heating duct?" He sounded slightly incredulous.

"I was doing some serious housecleaning," she lied. "It was in an envelope taped under the register. At first I thought it was something left by one of my tenants."

"May I look?"

She handed him the drive. They went to his computer, and she led him through the files. Then they started to listen to the audio file.

"Cal Parrish!" Olivetti exclaimed. He paused the playback.

"What about him?"

"Your husband came to see me about him! Before he was killed."

"Why did he come to see you?"

"A prisoner had told him he had information about Parrish. The man wanted to make a deal. Jack wanted authorization to discuss a deal with him." He told her about Jack's visit to his office. "The man he was talking to on that tape must be that prisoner. I don't remember all the details, but I'm pretty sure it was a robbery case. I'll get the file pulled."

They listened to the rest of the recording.

"It sounds like the guy wrote down a name. Did you ever find a notebook among Jack's things?"

"No. If there'd been one, the police would have taken it when they searched. All I remember them taking was my laptop." She pointed at the flash drive. "What about that? Doesn't it need to be preserved? Marked as an exhibit or something?"

"This office has a property and evidence unit. It's run by three police officers. The supervisor is a Bayonne PD lieutenant. Do you want to get the police involved now?"

"What's your advice?"

"I can understand that you want to move as quickly as possible to clear your husband's name. You've been living under this cloud for too many years. But think about it, Lucy. Cal Parrish was a respected Bayonne detective. He was killed a year or so before your husband. No one ever suggested that Parrish was corrupt, but as you know, a lot of Bayonne cops now believe that Jack was. It looks like he was investigating Parrish's possibly illegal activities, and perhaps his murder as well, but I just think we need to know more before we tell the Bayonne police that they've got it all backwards. Does that make sense?"

Put in those terms, Lucy had to agree. "I see what you mean."

"Good. Let me do a bit of digging on this myself before we decide the next move. What I suggest is this: I'll get a new, unused USB drive from our stock room. I'll copy the contents of this one onto it, in your presence. That will give me a working copy. Then we'll seal this one in an exhibit envelope, we'll both initial the label, and I'll lock it in my safe." He opened a door in the right-hand pedestal of his desk, revealing a hotel-style room safe with a combination touchpad. "Is that acceptable?"

Lucy found the man's straightforward manner comforting. She didn't hesitate.

"Yes."

She stood next to him as he went through each step of the process he had suggested. He uploaded the contents of Jack's USB onto his desktop, downloaded it onto the new drive, and then deleted the copy from his desktop and emptied the recycle bin. He dropped the original USB drive in an exhibit envelope, sealed it, and they both signed across the seal. She watched him lock it in his safe.

"When will I hear from you?"

"Soon." He wrote a number on the back of his business card. "That's my cell. Don't bother with the switchboard, just call me on that number. Just a sec . . ." He flipped through a diary on his desk. "I'm clear next Friday. Call me on Thursday afternoon and we can arrange to meet."

He walked her to the entrance. Before they parted, he casually asked, "By the way, did you make a copy of that flash drive for yourself?"

"Yes."

He cocked his head. "And, don't tell me! You hid it in a heating duct."

Despite herself, Lucy laughed. "No! It's on my laptop."

His quick grin turned serious. "Is it password protected?"

"No."

"Do that when you get home."

"Okay."

"At this point, you don't know who you can trust. So I suggest you keep all this to yourself."

"I will. Thanks."

They said their goodbyes, and she left the building.

As Lucy walked to her car, she caught herself smiling. Deputy First Assistant Prosecutor Robert Olivetti was an attractive man.

It had been a long time since a thought like that had crossed her mind.

Olivetti was as good as his word. When she called him late on Thursday, he asked her to come to his office at four o'clock the next day.

"How long will we be? I'll need to pick up my son by six."

"We have a few things to discuss. Can you make other arrangements?"

"I may be able to get his daycare teacher to keep him for an extra hour or so."

"Okay. If we need more time, maybe we can get together on the weekend."

After she hung up, Lucy wondered if Robert Olivetti had just maneuvered her into something vaguely resembling a date.

When she arrived at his office on the following afternoon, the receptionist told her to go right in. "He's waiting for you," the woman said.

When she appeared in his doorway, Olivetti smiled, got up, and came around his desk to greet her. He gestured at two document boxes on the floor behind his desk.

"That's the Jersey City PD file on Jack's murder," he said. "I've been reviewing it."

"I thought you didn't want the police involved."

"The file was in storage at our facility in Secaucus. I used a back channel to get it, so there wouldn't be any paperwork." He paused, then continued. "The fact that it was in storage up there was interesting in itself."

"Why?"

"Because the file should have been stored here. An unsolved case involving the murder of a cop shouldn't have been archived. Even after five years."

They sat down, and Olivetti changed subjects. "I have some bad news." Anticipating Lucy's reaction, he quickly added, "Not about Jack's activities—about that prisoner he was interviewing. The one who claimed to have information about Parrish. I remembered the man was a three-striker, but I couldn't remember his name. Do you know what 'three-striker' means?"

Lucy nodded.

"His name was Thomas Mulvaney. Did Jack ever mention that name?"

"I don't think so."

"Back in '06, Mulvaney was awaiting trial for armed robbery. He hadn't made bail, so he was sitting in custody. After Jack was killed, I told the investigators about his visit to my office. I gave them Mulvaney's name. A day or so later, they went to the jail to interview him. When they arrived, an ambulance was just leaving. Mulvaney had been stabbed in the exercise yard. He died on the way to the hospital. As usual, the other inmates all claimed they were tying their shoelaces and didn't see a thing. The prison staff couldn't even find the weapon—a corrupt guard was probably paid to make it disappear."

"You think he was killed to shut him up?"

"Likely, but not necessarily because he'd been talking to Jack. Mulvaney was being represented in the robbery case by a lawyer from the Public Defender's Office. He was in the process of negotiating a plea deal that would have required him to testify against his co-defendants."

"Were any of those co-defendants in the prison yard when it happened?"

"One was, but there was no evidence to pin the killing on him. As I said, there was no evidence to charge anyone. When the yard was being cleared at the end of the exercise period, a guard noticed that Mulvaney wasn't moving. He was sitting with his back against a wall, as if he was just taking a nap."

"If he was going to testify against the others, why wasn't he kept separate from them? Why was that other man in the yard?"

"A no-contact request had been submitted that same morning. The prison just didn't act on it quickly enough."

"If he was killed because he was going to testify, then there must have been a leak."

"Not from this office. On the other hand, the Public Defender's Office isn't exactly the gold standard when it comes to security."

"So you don't know for sure why Mulvaney was killed."

"No. Either he was killed by his co-accused—or by someone on their behalf—or he was killed because someone found out that he'd been talking to Jack about Cal Parrish. The Jersey City detectives couldn't eliminate either possibility."

"It's pretty clear to me that they picked the first one."

"You're talking about their allegations about Jack being seen drinking with a Mob member, and the bracelet evidence suggesting that he was murdered by the Lanza family."

"Yes. I got the impression from Detective Scarlatti that she was only looking for evidence that confirmed what she already believed."

"Confirmation bias. Cops and prosecutors call it tunnel vision. But did they mention anything else? Any other evidence against Jack?"

"Not that I remember."

"You're sure?"

"Yes! Why?"

Olivetti chewed on his lip, obviously conflicted by what he was about to say.

"What is it, Robert? Tell me!"

"Did they tell you that Jack had been running searches on the police database for information that would be useful to organized crime?"

Lucy was so shocked she could barely find her voice. "No!"

"The detectives ran an analysis of Jack's log-ins. A lot of his searches didn't look right."

"Probably because of his investigation of Cal Parrish!"

"It wasn't that kind of information. He was searching task force operations. At that time, there were a couple of federal-state joint operations targeting organized crime." He looked Lucy in the eye. "How would you describe Jack's computer skills?"

"Not great. He was always asking me to show him how to do something. Why?"

"Not all police officers have access to every layer of the system. Detectives do, but even they aren't permitted access to protected files without special authorization. Whoever ran these searches was walking right in."

"Then it couldn't have been Jack! Someone was using his password."

"Did you know his password?"

"No."

"Did he have a favorite song?"

Lucy was puzzled. "He had a lot of favorite songs. I don't understand what—?"

"Was one of them 'Every Breath You Take'?"

Lucy felt the bottom drop out of her stomach.

"Yes."

"His password was the third line of the song: *Everybondyoubreak*, followed by the numbers *1979*."

"The year I was born."

"The detectives figured that out."

"What's your point?"

"From what you say, it's not a password that he would need to write down. It would be easy to remember and difficult for someone to steal."

"But not impossible. He could have given it to someone in a work situation, and then forgot to change it. Anyway, you said detectives needed special authorization to get into certain files. So his password wouldn't have been enough."

"That's right. He'd have to know a certain key-code. Unfortunately, those codes weren't as secure as they should have been. The evidence is that two weeks before he was killed, someone using Jack's password was pulling up reports from a special investigation team that was targeting the Lanza family's influence over a certain Local of the Amalgamated Transit Union."

Lanza!

Lucy felt her throat tighten.

"It was an FBI–State Police joint operation. The team had evidence that the Local's vice president was taking bribes from the owners of bus companies in return for guarantees of labor peace. The investigators were after bigger fish, so instead of making an arrest, they confronted the guy and managed to turn him. Because he was now being used as a confidential informant, their file referred to him by the code name 'Source 43,' but anyone reading earlier reports would have no trouble figuring out who he was. Jack, or someone pretending to be him, downloaded all the reports. Two days later, the informant answered his front door and some-one shot him through the head in front of his wife and daughter. Twelve days after that, Jack was murdered."

"Jack would never have been involved!"

"Your detective friends Trousdale and Scarlatti thought otherwise. When they applied for that warrant to search your house, they got court approval to tap your phone. They also had you followed whenever you left the house."

Lucy's face flushed. "How long did that go on?"

"A few months. They were hoping you'd lead them to a contact, or a bank account, or maybe a safe-deposit box—something confirming that you knew what Jack was up to. Then they would have pulled you in for a hardball interview. When nothing turned up, the surveillance was lifted, but it's clear from the file that they still believed Jack had been involved with the Lanza family, and that you must have known."

By now, Lucy was perched at the edge of her chair and her entire body was trembling. "Even assuming Jack was corrupt—which I can't believe!—how did the cops explain to themselves why a crooked police detective, who would obviously be highly valuable to the Mob, would be killed twelve days after he did them a big favor?"

"Their theory was that he knew too much—that if he was caught, or suddenly got a conscience, he might lead the police straight to the Mob contact he'd passed the task force reports to. And there was another thing . . ."

"What thing?"

"There were two union informants. Neither of them knew about the other one. When the vice president was killed, the FBI took the other informant—a woman—into protective custody. She happened to be the deputy treasurer, and she'd collected enough evidence to take down most of the Local's top officers."

"So the Jersey City detectives decided that Jack had been killed because he didn't give the Lanzas *both* names?"

"Something like that."

"Then why leave a calling card? Why the bracelet? Why leave bla-tant evidence that they'd killed him?"

"I know. It doesn't make a whole lot of sense."

Lucy launched herself off the chair and strode to the window. She stood there, grim and trembling, staring out at the gray world beyond. Olivetti waited in silence. After a moment, she turned. She looked at him bleakly.

"Robert, will this ever end? I have a son. For his sake, I need to clear his father's name."

"I understand that. I do. I can help, but, Lucy . . ."

"What?"

"I can't change the evidence."

"I'm not asking you to. I'm grateful for your help. If it turns out that . . ." She heaved a sigh. She couldn't bear to finish the thought.

"Lucy?"

"Mmm?"

"Why don't we call it a day? Would you like to go for a drink?"

His cautious question took Lucy off guard. She tried to process the concept—the idea of, well, a *date* with a man. She couldn't come up with a quick excuse to decline.

Do it!

"Not tonight. Tomorrow?"

"Okay."

"On one condition."

"Being?"

"That you meet me here tomorrow afternoon and let me read that file." She pointed at the boxes on the floor.

"Are you sure you want to do that?"

"Yes."

"There are photographs," he said, with a look of concern. "Taken at the scene . . . and at the post-mortem."

For a long second, his words hung like smoke in the air.

"I want to see everything."

"All right. But it's going to take you a few hours. How about we meet here around two?"

There were two thick coil-bound photograph booklets in the Jersey City investigation file. When it came to the crunch, Lucy skipped the autopsy pictures. The scene photos were hard enough to stomach. She realized that the sight of Jack's naked body being dissected on an autopsy table might push her over the edge. She wasn't ready to break down and impose all her sick anguish on her new friend Robert, so she set the post-mortem booklet aside.

She speed-read the reports, pausing from time to time to ponder odd facts, but found little that pointed to Jack's private investigation of Cal Parrish. Most of the investigation seemed focused on proving the theory the detectives had already arrived at—an approach she remembered Jack had once referred to as "the kiss of death" when it came to police investigations.

Late in the afternoon, she discovered that a Phillips screwdriver had been found lying next to Jack's body. That tiny fact, casually noted in an inventory of his clothing and pocket contents, focused her mind. Gritting her teeth, she forced herself to return to the close-up photos taken in the garage. There it was, lying behind his left shoulder.

Then she saw something in a later sequence of scene photos. They showed Jack's car, parked two blocks from the parkade. The investigators had located the vehicle a few hours after his body was discovered. Most of the photos had been taken at night, but two had been taken during daylight on the following morning.

In a photo of the rear of his car, she made out a small hole in the lens of the left taillight.

She felt the blood drain from her face.

She hadn't mentioned to Robert what Jack had told her about using a screwdriver to make it easier to follow someone, and she certainly hadn't told him that Kevin had repeated the rudiments of the same story. Now she told Robert about Jack's original anecdote. "It looks to me," she finished, "like someone was using Jack's low-tech method *on him*."

"And that maybe Jack was planning to use the screwdriver on a particular vehicle in that garage."

"He was a cop! Why wouldn't he use one of those electronic tracking devices you read about? It was only six years ago. They must have had them then."

"They've been around since the eighties. But I'm not sure the Bayonne PD were using them, or that they even had any. And then there's the whole issue about whether he'd need a warrant. That's still being fought over in the courts. If he really was running an off-the-books investigation, he probably wouldn't want to draw his bosses' attention to his activities."

"Okay, then the question is: Who was parked in that garage that night? What car was he looking for?"

"It's a multi-level public parkade—there's no way to know."

"What about surveillance cameras?"

"The only camera was at the exit."

"Didn't the investigators review it?"

"Yes, but nothing had been recorded after eight that night. The lens had been sprayed with foam."

"So his murder was carefully planned."

"It looks like it."

"What about the parking lot attendant?"

"There was no on-site attendant. It was ticket-in, pay at a machine when you're leaving, and ticket-out. If there's a problem, there was a phone number to call. Everything was done remotely. Probably by some guy in a call center in India," he added sardonically.

Lucy was thoughtful. "Something else I learned from that file. Remember that article about Gianotti, the Lanza soldier who escaped from prison a few weeks before Jack was killed?"

"Yes."

"The author of that article claimed he got his information from 'sources within the investigation,' who told him physical evidence found at the scene appeared to link Gianotti to Jack's murder. But the only evidence they found was the bracelet. There was nothing in the file connecting it directly to Gianotti."

"Devastator ammunition."

"What?

"Jack was shot with .22 devastator rounds. The slug has a sort of explosive tip that causes extra damage when it hits the body. They're unreliable, and in Jack's case they didn't detonate, but Gianotti used the same kind of ammo in the hit that originally sent him to jail."

"I didn't see anything about a ballistics match."

"That's because there wasn't one. Different weapons."

"So, the bracelet and explosive bullets—that's all they had to connect Jack's murder to the Lanza family."

"Correct."

Lucy was frustrated. She looked at her watch.

"Robert . . ."

"Yes?"

"I think I'm ready for that drink."

He grinned. "There's this bar down at Bergen Point—it's called The Starting Point. Old style. Blue-collar hangout. It's pretty quiet, so it's actually possible to have a conversation."

Lucy knew the place. It was less than half a mile from her house. She didn't mention that.

Lucy was ready to admit that she found Robert Olivetti attractive. During the afternoon in his office, she'd even allowed herself a fleeting fantasy of something more—intimacy, sex, diverting pillow talk—all experiences long absent from her life. But such thoughts were quickly dismissed. The thought of taking a relationship beyond an hour or so of superficial conversation just didn't sit well. She planned to confine herself to a single drink and let it go at that.

The Starting Point Bar & Grill occupied a featureless one-story concrete block building. From the outside, it looked about as inviting as a commercial storage unit. But behind the broken steps and narrow door of the entrance lay a warm sanctuary of polished tables, dark corners, and nonstop oldies played at a respectfully low volume. They took a table in the back corner. Behind their heads, both walls were lined with LP album covers from the glorious days of vinyl: The Beach Boys, Fleetwood Mac, Ted Nugent, The Doors . . .

Despite her earlier determination, Lucy stayed for two drinks. Olivetti was amiable, and not at all pushy, and soon she felt able to relax. He disarmed her with gentle questions. He listened attentively to her account of life since Jack and showed sympathy at exactly the right moments. He was quite ready to answer her questions about his own background: raised by a single mother in Utica, New York, graduated from Rutgers Law, married at twenty-seven and divorced five years later, no children, something of a workaholic.

Inevitably the conversation led to their Italian heritage—a subject they stumbled into somewhat obliquely.

"Your maiden name . . . you mentioned it was Cappelli?"

"No, I didn't."

"Oh?" He looked puzzled. "Sorry. Why did I think that?"

"It was mentioned in one of Detective Scarlatti's reports. She must have thought my Italian background somehow supported her suspicions about Jack."

"Could be right. So, are you first generation?"

"My sister and I were born here, but our parents came from Sicily."

His interest visibly sharpened. "Sicily?"

"Yes," she responded, with a careful smile, "but without the sinister implication Scarlatti was fixated on. My father was a miner, not a mobster."

"Well, we have something in common."

"Your father was a miner?"

"No, but according to my mother, he was Sicilian. That was unusual, because my mother was a northerner, and traditionally northern Italians tended to scorn the people from the south. They certainly didn't want their daughters marrying southerners."

"But your mother did."

"She always had a mind of her own—probably the main reason why I made it through school." He made a wry face. "She rode me pretty hard."

"Did you ever know your father?"

"He died when I was four. I only have a few memories."

"What happened?"

"Drowned in some kind of freak accident. He was fishing with a few friends on Lago d'Iseo. It's one of those lakes near Milan."

Lucy could tell from the man's expression that he didn't want to take the subject any further. The conversation moved to other topics, and they parted with his promise to call her after he'd done some digging into the file on Cal Parrish's murder.

Lucy had come very close to asking him back to the house for a coffee.

The Starting Point . . .

She began to wonder if he'd picked the place because of its name.

17

Trust.

It was always an issue with Lucy.

It was why she didn't tell Robert Olivetti that she'd been arranging a parallel investigation of her own. She had first met National Insurance Crime Bureau investigator Brandon Kimball through a series of e-mails and, later, on a thirty-minute telephone call. He had persuaded her to send him a copy of Jack's spreadsheet. Her final assessment of Kimball's unusual qualities was based on a face-to-face meeting at Lucy's home, where he spent an afternoon impressing her with his quick and incisive mind. He was ex-NYPD, a thin man whose salt-and-pepper goatee and ponytail might have led inattentive observers to misjudge him—to their serious detriment, Lucy suspected. He had flown out to Newark from Des Plaines, Illinois, for the sole purpose of meeting with her. She played him the recording of Jack's conversation with Mulvaney, and took him on a narrative tour of the events since his murder, just as she had for Olivetti. She explained why she didn't trust anyone in the police after the smear campaign against Jack, and he accepted that. He agreed to work with her confidentially, in exchange for her agreement that she would report to him anything that Olivetti turned up.

"Good, or bad," he said, looking her in the eye.

"You have my word."

As with Olivetti, Lucy didn't mention Dominic Lanza's visit. She didn't want to plant immediate seeds of doubt in the investigator's mind . . . and somehow, behind it all and barely admitted to herself, she wanted to hold that perilous connection in reserve.

Meanwhile, despite her lingering resistance, the relationship with Olivetti was moving in a direction she hadn't prepared for. He called her a few nights after Brandon Kimball's visit and, getting right to the point, he asked her to dinner. On an impulse, she accepted. It helped that she'd finally found a reliable babysitter—the teenaged daughter of a couple who lived a few doors down. Tracy Galvez was an only child, mature beyond her sixteen years, and had come highly recommended by two other couples living on the street. It also helped that, after a few test runs, Tracy had made a point of telling her that Kevin was the best behaved little boy she had ever looked after.

They met at Café Bello. It was packed and a bit noisy, but the food was good and the evening was, well, actually great fun. By unspoken agreement, they refrained from discussing the case, and, by the end of the evening, Lucy felt comfortable enough to give him a parting hug.

Over the next few weeks, in her quiet moments, she continually questioned herself and made resolutions to draw a line in the relationship. Her rising interest in Robert felt like betrayal. Then he would call, and her resolve would evaporate. She found herself rebelling against herself—rebelling against her reserve, against her reticence, and against all the baggage she knew she'd been dragging around for far too long.

Against all odds, and against every woven fiber of Jack's memory, a relationship began to blossom. So far, they had only met at restaurants in Bayonne, and once for a quiet evening at a Portuguese place on Ferry

Street in Newark. Robert had never been to Lucy's home, nor had he invited her to his, but the natural trajectory of events was inching in that direction.

Meanwhile, Kevin had been exhibiting increasingly frequent episodes of odd behavior. Occasionally he limped, favoring his right leg. He sometimes talked about things he couldn't possibly know—events in Lucy's past life, or in Jack's. Events she had never mentioned. Things a boy of his age shouldn't even understand.

She had kept all this to herself.

But then the boy spoke French.

They were in the car, approaching a church. A man wielding an extension pole was just adding the final letter to a motto on a marquee sign next to the road.

"What does that man's sign say, Mommy?"

"It says, 'Feed your faith, not your fear.'"

The spillover effects of 9/11 are everywhere, she was thinking—just before her son almost caused her to lose control of her car.

"*Qui perd sa langue, perd sa foi*," the boy said.

Lucy felt suddenly light-headed. She braked so hard the car behind nearly rear-ended her. Angry horns blared. She swung to the curb.

Jack's mother, Elise, had been born Elise Ouellette in northern Maine. Her parents had come from Quebec. For decades, French Canadians living in the New England states had been discriminated against. In the 1920s, the largest Ku Klux Klan chapter outside the South was headquartered in Maine, and their primary target was the French Canadian minority. Elise had been beaten in school for speaking French. Jack had related his mother's family history to Lucy, and he had occasionally repeated one of her sayings: *Qui perd sa langue, perd sa foi*. Who loses his language, loses his faith.

Lucy leaned toward Kevin. "Jack," she whispered, "is that you?"

"I was," the boy replied. "But I'm gone."

Then Kevin was back, and the moment was gone as well.

Lucy almost broke down. Then and there she decided she needed to talk to someone. And the only person she could think of was Robert Olivetti.

They were back at The Starting Point, sitting in the same back corner.

"Try the meatloaf," the middle-aged lady said as she dropped two menus on the table. "We're famous for it." She was the same woman who'd been working behind the bar on their last visit. If she remembered them, she gave no sign of it.

"She's right, Robert. It's amazing."

He raised an eyebrow. "And you know this because . . . ?"

"I live just down the street."

He cocked his head. "So, our first visit here wasn't *your* first visit here."

"Not exactly. Try the meatloaf! You're going to need some serious sustenance to get you through today's conversation."

"That sounds ominous." He turned to their server. "I guess it's the meatloaf."

"It comes with mashed potatoes, gravy, and candy-glazed carrots. Is that okay?"

Olivetti managed a strained grin. "Bring it on."

"And for the lady?"

"The same. Thank you."

The woman retrieved their menus and headed for the kitchen.

"You're acting very mysterious, Lucy. Why today, and why here?"

Today was Sunday, and Lucy had roused him at seven this morning just to ask him to meet her for lunch at The Starting Point.

"*Today,* because something happened yesterday that I want to tell you about, and *here,* because it's close to my house." While Robert pondered that enigmatic reply, Lucy took a long pull on her beer. Her hand trembled as she set the glass down. "You're going to think I'm crazy."

"I guess I'll have to be the judge of that. Why don't you start by telling me what happened yesterday?"

"Yesterday was just the latest . . . incident. You need to hear this from the beginning."

"How far back is the beginning?"

"Last Christmas."

He took a deep breath. "Okay. When you're ready."

Lucy started talking. She began slowly, describing Kevin's opening act on Christmas Day in Florida, his rising obsession with going home . . . home to Bayonne, a city he had never seen, in a state he had left while still a fetus. She picked her words carefully, watching Robert's face, waiting for the first sign of skepticism, the first signs of dismissal. But soon, at full sail, running downwind through her memories, all restraint was forgotten. Her words and her fears and her speculations just tumbled out as she described her son's episodes of limping, their side trip to Jack's childhood home, the boy's use of pet names for her that only Jack had used, his unnerving lip-sync serenade of "Every Breath You Take," and the whole screwdriver-in-the-taillight business.

"—and, then, yesterday topped it off."

"What did he do?"

Lucy had been watching for any telltale sign, a narrowed gaze, a disbelieving curve of the mouth—any hint of the effect of her words—but Robert's expression had remained steadfastly neutral throughout.

"He spoke to me in French." She explained the significance of the phrase Kevin had quoted, and the child's unsettling response when she asked, "Jack, is that you?"

The sudden arrival of their meal interrupted Lucy's narrative. She hadn't yet told Robert the truth about how she found the USB drive. She was saving that for last.

Robert examined the plate in front of him. It was heaped with food—thick cut carrots, dense slabs of meatloaf, and a Matterhorn of mashed potatoes, all swimming in thick, dark gravy.

"I think," he ventured slowly, "that you and I could have shared an order."

"You're right. I'd forgotten."

"Well, might as well make the best of it." He picked up his knife and fork and dug in.

They ate in silence, mainly because Robert seemed distracted, as if he was turning everything over in his mind, and Lucy was reluctant to interrupt.

"Have you asked Kevin who shot him?"

The question came out of the blue. Lucy's expression darkened. She set down her fork. She felt her body shift away from him.

"Are you mocking me, Robert?"

He looked suddenly alarmed. He reached a hand across and gently covered one of hers. "No! Not at all. I'm sorry if it sounded like that. I'm trying to do what we all do when we read a novel that slips outside life's norms, or, say, when we watch one of those sci-fi channels. I'm suspending disbelief. I'm accepting, for the sake of discussion, that everything you have told me happened, and that one possible explanation for those events is that, somehow, by some means we don't understand, some of Jack's memories have been replicated in Kevin."

Lucy's shoulders relaxed. "Okay. I guess that's all I can ask."

"So I'm saying—assuming all of the above—the one thing we most need to know . . ." His voice trailed off.

She waited.

"Forgive me for putting this so bluntly. We need to know if Kevin is carrying any memory of the last seconds of Jack's life."

"In other words, does he remember the face of the man who shot him?"

"Yes."

A second passed, and then Lucy said, "Why don't we ask him?"

Robert tilted his head.

"*We?*"

"You're thinking: 'Kevin has never met me. Why would he tell me anything?'"

"That's exactly what I'm thinking."

"He probably won't say anything . . . at first. You'd have to earn his trust."

Robert regarded her carefully. "Have I just passed some kind of test?"

"As a matter of fact . . ."

"And if I had failed?"

"Then, today's visit to The Starting Point would have been *The Ending Point* in our relationship."

"Does that mean . . . we have a relationship?"

Moment of truth, Lucy . . .

"I think we do."

18

"Have you spoken to anyone else about this . . . this thing with Kevin?"

Lucy unlocked the front door to her house.

"No. Just you." She swung the door open and called out, "Tracy? I'm home!"

No reply.

"Tracy?"

"In here!" came the answer.

They found Tracy and Kevin sitting at the kitchen table. Playing cards. Jack's old scrimshaw cribbage board lay on the table between them.

As they entered, Tracy looked up and blurted, "Kevin's amazing! He taught me to play this cool game!"

Kevin was sitting across from the teenager, straight-backed and serious. He stared at Olivetti. He laid down his cards. "Mommy, I know that man," he announced.

A second passed as the comment sunk in. Olivetti turned to Lucy. "Did you orchestrate this?"

"I've never mentioned you to him."

Olivetti went pale.

Tracy looked from face to face, clearly puzzled by the exchange. She pushed back her chair. "Guess I should go." She circled the table and gave Kevin a hug. Lucy walked the girl to the door.

As she was leaving, Tracy turned in the doorway and said, "You know, I saw that deck of cards in the kitchen drawer and I asked Kevin if he'd like to play Go Fish and he said, 'No, wait,' and ran upstairs and came back with that ivory scoreboard."

"He must have seen it in my bedside table. It belonged to my husband."

"But he's so young! How did he learn to count cards like that?"

"Kevin's pretty smart."

"He sure is! I mean, most of the time he's just a little boy, but then all of a sudden he acts all grown up."

"He spends a lot of time with adults," Lucy replied, dissembling. "He's probably growing up a bit too fast."

"He's a cool kid! I'll totally babysit him anytime."

"Thanks, Tracy." Lucy smiled. "That totally makes me glad."

When Lucy returned to the kitchen, she found Robert sitting in Tracy's place at the table.

"And what's my last name?" The question was directed to Kevin, but his eyes were on Lucy.

"Olly."

"Olly what?"

"Olly . . . vetty."

"Did you—?" Lucy began.

"I didn't tell him anything. When you were out of the room, he asked me if I would play cards. He addressed me by my first name." Robert turned to the boy. "Kevin, do you remember where we met?"

Lucy watched her son's face. She saw his eyes widen . . . and then she saw the blink. She knew what was coming next. Kevin jumped off his chair and scuttled over to her. She kneeled down.

"Mommy . . ."

"What is it, honey?"

"I'm tired."

"I know." She hugged him tight. Over the boy's shoulder, she said, "Sometimes, it all just wears him out." She rose to her feet and took his hand. "I'll be right back."

As she led Kevin away, Olivetti just sat and stared.

Robert Olivetti stayed for the afternoon, for dinner, and into the evening.

After Kevin awoke from his nap, and until Lucy finally put the boy to bed for the night, there were no more paranormal moments. Kevin remained firmly fixed in his five-year-old persona, and Robert, suppressing every sign of his earlier discomfiture, maintained a relaxed and friendly mien, assuming a sort of uncle role. Despite this, at times it seemed to Lucy that man and boy were circling each other, each taking the other's measure. It was a peculiar dynamic, one that Lucy eventually put down more to her own overactive imagination than to any basis in reality.

Eventually, they had the inevitable conversation.

The one about Kevin's memories, and Jack's murder.

They were sitting on the couch. "Has there ever been an episode when you could have asked him?" Robert chose his words carefully. "I mean, a moment when he seemed to remember that parking garage?"

"No."

"Anything at all relating to his investigation?"

Lucy was quiet. "There was one thing."

"What?"

"I was waiting for the right time to tell you."

"Lucy! You brought me into this! Please don't hold back now."

She sighed. "It was that flash drive."

"The one you brought to my office?"

"Yes. Kevin showed me where it was."

"*Showed* you?"

Lucy related the background, explaining how Kevin had led to her discovery of the USB drive.

For a few seconds, Robert was silent. "Okay, I guess I can understand why you didn't tell me that story when we first met. But why not today, when we were at lunch?"

"I wanted you to see something first."

"*See* something. Like Kevin recognizing me, and knowing my name?"

"I didn't expect that, but, yes."

"You did talk about me earning Kevin's trust."

"Yes."

"But I had to earn yours first."

"That's right."

"You know, I won't . . . I can't be here all the time. I mean, I'm not going to be with you and Kevin every time he zones out and starts being Jack. More likely, only you will see it. More important, the chances are only you would understand the significance of whatever he says."

"You being here all the time . . . that's a different conversation."

His hand covered hers. "I know."

Lucy settled her body against his. "Do you want to have that conversation now?"

"Do you?" An inviting smile hovered on his lips.

She leaned in and kissed those lips.

Robert kissed her back . . .

And kissed her . . .

And kissed her . . .

Lucy's head swam, and all reticence fled.

All resistance fled.

All doubt fled.

She loved Jack, and she would always love him, but it had been so very, very long . . .

She took Robert Olivetti's hand and led him up the stairs.

19

The doorbell rang at exactly six o'clock. That had been the agreed time, and Lucy felt reassured by the man's punctuality.

But people with OCD were usually punctual, and the man had seemed a bit weird on the phone. Weird in an OCD way. While they talked, she could hear a tapping sound in the background, as if he was tapping out the cadence of their conversation on his desk.

And he had kept repeating "Mmm, yes . . . mmm yes," while she was speaking.

But, bottom line, the man was an assistant professor in the Psychology Department at Rutgers University who just happened to be involved in a research project that resembled the one run by Professor Tucker at the University of Virginia.

She opened the door to a short man wearing a beat-up cross-strap reporter bag and a straw fedora.

"Mmm, yes, Mrs. Hendricks? Neil Clooney here. Neil Clooney."

"Hello. Thank you for coming, Professor." She stepped to one side. "Please . . ."

"Thank you." He snatched the fedora off his head as he stepped in.

"Clooney's the name. Mmm, yes. No relation to George," he added. "People ask."

Lucy eyed the dumpy little man standing in front of her and thought: *Really?*

Lucy had already thoroughly briefed the academic during their telephone discussion, in time with the background score of his rhythmic tapping, so she expected he would want to meet Kevin as soon as he arrived.

"I'll call Kevin," she said as she led him into the living room.

"No, no! Pre-meeting, Mrs. Hendricks. Pre-meeting. Very important."

They took their seats. He set down his man bag, and then launched into a briefing that sounded very much like a playback loop, embedded in his brain from countless previous encounters with concerned parents. His verbal tics were distracting, but Lucy soon found that her mind was able to edit them out so she could focus on what he was saying.

He was explaining investigative protocols.

"The most important thing is for you, the parent, to make careful notes of what your child has been saying . . . yes? The accounts given by the child should then be followed up by independent investigators to determine if anything the child related was true, and to ensure that anything he or she said could not have been known to the child from a contemporary source. It is vitally important to demonstrate that there was no way the child could have picked up the information from an overheard conversation or some other medium. Only after those preliminary steps have been completed should the child be transported to any location or confronted by any person—if any living person can be identified—that relate to his alleged previous life."

"At this stage, I don't think there are any locations he needs to be taken to."

"From what you told me yesterday, there may be a crime scene. The scene of his—"

Lucy cut him off. "I don't want to expose him to that kind of trauma."

Clooney seemed oblivious to such alien concepts as emotional sensitivity. Or, to be fair, maybe he was just following protocol.

"Mmm, yes. Probably right. Early days. Early days."

He sounded disappointed.

Lucy offered him a sop. "I have been making notes, but I didn't do that from the beginning. I only started recently, when things got so strange, so a lot of what I've written is based on my memory."

"And the more recent entries . . . they were written immediately after the episode?"

"As soon as I could. If we were here, then right away, but if we were in the car, then as soon as we got home."

"May I see the notes?"

"Of course." Lucy went to her purse and retrieved a small, red notebook. "Would you like some coffee, or tea?"

"Mmm, yes. Tea would be nice, thank you. Just black, no sugar."

When she returned with their cups, he was absorbed in her notes. He finally looked up, noticed the cup in front of him, took a sip, and said, "I would like to borrow these, to make copies. I will return them."

"Of course."

He slipped the notebook into his bag. "What about birthmarks? Does Kevin have any unusual birthmarks?"

"No, but as I told you, he sometimes limps, and the doctors couldn't find any reason for it."

"Tell me again, in as much detail as you can, about your husband's physical injuries at the time of death."

There was that protocol, again, but an answer was unavoidable. Lucy took a deep breath, and recited every detail she could remember from reading the autopsy report.

"There have been cases," Clooney said, "some of which I have personally investigated, where birthmarks or unexplained physical problems have exactly matched injuries suffered at the time of the previous personality's death."

"I'm aware of that."

"You've done some reading on this subject?"

"Just on the Internet."

"Are you also aware of the research program at the University of Virginia?"

"Yes. I read that they have a department that investigates cases like Kevin's. Cases of children who remember past lives."

"Mmm, yes. What do you think about that?"

"If you'd asked me a year ago, I'd have said the whole idea is ridiculous. That universities have better things to spend their money on."

"The UVA's Division of Perceptual Studies is supported by a very generous private grant. Professor Neil Clooney, on the other hand, is an unfunded one-man show. So, depending on my findings, I may want to invite Professor Tucker and his colleagues to look into your son's case. Are you okay with that?"

"Maybe. Probably. But because all of this is tied in with an unsolved murder—*my husband's* unsolved murder—I want to leave that for a later decision. Yesterday you agreed that your investigation will remain confidential until I say otherwise. Is that still our agreement?"

"You have my word. I just wanted you to be aware that my facilities are limited."

Finally, Lucy fetched Kevin from his bedroom, where he had been engrossed in the task of assembling a barely identifiable "castle" using Scotch tape and a collection of cardboard paper towel and toilet rolls.

Right from the start, Kevin was wary of Clooney. He was more interested in the man's straw hat than his strange questions. Finally, the boy got frustrated and turned to his mother.

"Can I go back to my room? I'm working on stuff."

Lucy flashed on an idea.

"Kevin . . . *Qui perd sa langue, perd sa foi.*"

Kevin's eyes blinked. Blinked again. "That's what my mother said." The boy's voice was changed. It was huskier. Gruffer. Older.

Clooney had already skimmed through Lucy's notes, so he caught on quickly. He jumped in.

"Detective Hendricks? I'd like a word with you, sir."

"I don't want to talk to you."

"I need to ask you about one of your cases."

"I don't discuss my cases with civilian personnel."

"I'm a special consultant who works for the police. I need your help."

"Then meet me at my office. I don't bring my work home. It upsets my wife."

Choosing his words, Clooney planted a seed. "I understand you have an office here . . . in the building."

"Yes."

Clooney shot a questioning look to Lucy. She replied by darting her eyes toward the rear of the house.

"Your office is here on the ground floor?"

"Yes."

"Could I make an appointment to meet you there?"

"I suppose."

"Perhaps this evening?"

"I'm sorry. I'm very busy."

"I understand." Clooney checked his watch. "Shall we say this time tomorrow—seven o'clock?"

"All right."

"Here at your office?"

The boy nodded.

"Thank you, sir." Clooney held out a hand. "Until then." He and Kevin shook on it. The boy turned, limped to the stairs, and climbed slowly.

"This is genuine progress, Mrs. Hendricks!" Clooney exclaimed, after Kevin was lost from view. His face wore a hugely gratified expression. "I will return tomorrow at exactly seven o'clock. Perhaps you could arrange for Kevin to be waiting in his office at that time."

Lucy couldn't find her voice. Pale with shock and disbelief, she managed a nod.

Clooney scooped up his bag. She followed him to the door.

"Tomorrow, then . . ."

"Yes," Lucy responded, her voice barely above a whisper.

"The best approach is for you to say nothing to Kevin about what just happened. He may volunteer something—perhaps later, when you put him to bed. I noticed in your notes that he tends to bring things up at bedtime. But please don't encourage him."

She recalled the advice on Dr. Tucker's website: *Avoid asking a lot of pointed questions* . . .

"I understand."

Professor Clooney gave a little bow and left.

Watching him, Lucy thought she detected a definite spring in the academic's step as he made his way down the walkway to the street.

20

"Lucy Hendricks?"

The tall man standing in front of Lucy when she opened the front door was wearing a sports jacket, slacks, and an open-necked dress shirt. He looked exactly like a police detective, and the shield visible on his belt confirmed Lucy's instant impression. His partner was similarly dressed.

"I'm Detective Geary. This is my partner—"

Carla Scarlatti!

"I know who your partner is! What's the Jersey City police doing on my doorstep?"

"I'm with the Hudson County Sheriff's Department. Detective Scarlatti is assisting me."

With the Scarlatti woman standing on her doorstep, barely hiding a smirk, Lucy was in no mood to be polite. "Assisting you with what?" she snapped. "More harassment over my husband's murder?"

"No. We're investigating the murder of a university professor named Neil Clooney."

To the detectives, the shocked expression on Lucy's face must have spoken volumes.

"Clooney?"

"May we come in?"

Lucy backed away from the door, leaving it open. The officers followed her into the house. Even in her distress, Lucy couldn't bear the thought of Carla Scarlatti assuming the same position, in the same living room chair, as she had on her first visit. She led them to the dining room table and sat down. Geary took a chair opposite her. Scarlatti remained standing.

"Obviously, you knew Dr. Clooney," Geary began. "What was your relationship?"

Lucy ignored the question. "You said he was murdered?"

"Yes."

"When?"

"Sometime last night."

Lucy let out a long breath.

Geary tilted his head. "Mrs. Hendricks, when did you last see Dr. Clooney?"

"Last night."

Two sets of eyebrows notched up.

Scarlatti spoke up for the first time. "Where?"

"Here."

"What time did he leave?"

"A few minutes past seven." Lucy looked at Geary, then at Scarlatti. "I only met him yesterday. He came here at six, left at seven. How did you know to come here?"

"Two reasons," Geary replied. "The campus police found your name and address on a notepad on his desk. Can you explain that?"

"Dr. Clooney's a psychologist. He was here to help me with my son, Kevin."

"Help you, how?"

"Kevin has some behavioral problems."

"What behavioral problems?" Scarlatti asked.

Lucy wasn't having it from her. "That's not relevant." She turned to Geary. "You said two reasons."

Scarlatti answered for him. "His body was found at eleven-thirty last night . . . in a parkade at the Newport Centre."

Suddenly, Lucy felt like she was having an out-of-body experience.

"What parkade?" She heard herself ask the question, but the look on Carla Scarlatti's face had already told her the answer.

"The same one where your husband was killed. Clooney's body was found on the same spot, with his head and feet oriented in the same position. So, I'm sorry, Mrs. Hendricks, but I have to ask you this: Where were you between seven o'clock, when you say he left your house, and eleven-thirty?"

Lucy's eyes locked on Scarlatti's. "What?"

At that very moment, Robert Olivetti walked into the room.

"The door was open. I saw the cruiser . . ." He took in the scene. "Geary . . . Scarlatti . . ."

"Counselor . . ." Geary responded, startled.

Robert's gaze came to rest on Lucy, looking pale and stricken. "What's going on here?" he demanded.

Olivetti had been outside with the cops for the past twenty minutes. When he came back in the house, Lucy was still sitting at the dining room table.

"Are they gone?"

"Not yet." Olivetti pulled out the chair next to her and sat down. "I had to pretend I knew you had arranged for Clooney to consult on Kevin. 'Behavioral problems'? Why didn't you tell me?"

"Just an idea I had. I found him through a blog on the Internet. I didn't think I needed to consult you first."

"I'm sorry. Of course you didn't." He glanced around. "Where is Kevin, anyway?"

"Swimming lessons. Tracy's with him. I wasn't feeling well, so she agreed to take him."

"What's wrong?"

"Just time of the month. But I was feeling even worse after they left."

"Why?"

"Those cops showed up."

"They didn't want to tell you this, but . . ." Robert grimaced.

"But what?"

"Clooney was tortured before he was killed."

"Oh, God, no! Oh, Robert. How?"

"You don't want to know." He took her hand. "What did Kevin tell Clooney? Did he get anywhere with him?"

"No. Well . . . yes, sort of. At first, Kevin was suspicious of him. He wasn't responding to the questions. It was like they were circling each other. Then I recited that French phrase and Kevin did that thing, that zone-out thing. Clooney immediately started talking to him as if he were Jack. He made an appointment with him to discuss a case. To discuss *the* case. Jack's murder. He was going to come back tonight, for their appointment. It was pretty spooky."

"Okay. I doubt these cops will be smart enough to ask about Kevin's behavior, but—"

"Scarlatti already has."

"Hmm. Well, obviously you didn't say anything about . . ."

"No, of course not."

"It might be wise to avoid any of the details. I mean . . . credibility and all that."

"Credibility?"

"I do have to work with these people."

"Aah . . ."

"You can imagine how fast the word would spread that I was involved in some kind of paranormal inquiry."

"I get it."

"Thanks."

Lucy suddenly remembered something. "Oh, damn! My notebook!"

"What notebook?"

"I've been keeping notes of things Kevin says. Jack things. Clooney took it with him to make a copy. He was carrying this beaten-up old leather bag. He put it in there."

Robert looked disturbed. After a pause, he said, "I'm not going to ask them about the bag. They'll want to know what's in it. I'll use another channel to get an inventory of what was found at the crime scene."

The detectives came back into the house, asked a few more questions, and Geary made an appointment with Lucy to provide a formal statement.

As they were leaving, Lucy felt a sudden boil of anger toward Carla Scarlatti. Before Olivetti could stop her, she stepped in front of the woman and grabbed her by the arm.

"I won't forget that question you asked, Scarlatti! 'Where was I between seven and eleven-thirty?' *Are you for fucking real?*"

Scarlatti pulled her arm away. "The question had to be asked."

"I remember that parking garage! It has a security camera. Did it occur to you to check it?"

"It now has cameras on every level, but the lenses were covered with spray paint."

Lucy stared at her. "Just like last time."

Geary interjected. "Not exactly. Last time it was foam. And since then, the owner has had tamper detection installed. The software program set off an alarm as soon as the first lens went black. But the security response was too late. All they found was the body."

"Then you've narrowed the time window," Olivetti suggested.

"Right, but that just tells us when he was dumped. The M.E. says he was killed somewhere else."

The cops left just as Tracy was returning with Kevin from his swimming lesson, red-eyed from the pool chlorine and bubbling with excitement over his official graduation from Flounder to Tarpon.

21

Brandon Kimball's second visit to Lucy's home changed every-thing.

"We've been looking at this the wrong way."

"Meaning?"

"Meaning, from what I've dug up, it looks like Parrish was running his own investigation, just as your husband did later. He was only *pretending* to be Mob connected, playing on the fears of the low-level players to get information. None of the street thieves would want to get caught on the losing side in a power struggle between their current bosses and a Mob crew that was trying to muscle in. Word of what he was doing probably found its way up the line to the management level and somebody decided to take him out. And that means whoever killed him probably knew he wasn't connected. Otherwise, I doubt they'd have risked a direct confrontation with an organization as powerful as the Mafia."

"How did you figure all this out?"

"I'm coming to that, because it also proves your husband was inno-cent."

"Tell me!"

"I have a few contacts at the FBI. I asked one of them to run an off-line search. That's a term the NCIC uses for a specialized database search that can bring up lots of information that an online search won't. One of the things it can do is query NCIC transaction logs and provide a printout of every online inquiry that was ever made respecting a particular person, or a particular item of property."

"Such as a vehicle?"

"Exactly. An offline search can even get into purged databases, which means it can go a long way back in time. I asked them to search every vehicle on Jack's spreadsheet." Kimball pulled a fat three-ring binder out of his briefcase. He opened it at random, revealing a scramble of print-out data that filled an entire page. "They were all stolen vehicles, so naturally each one had been entered on the system as soon as their theft was reported. And of course, some of them had been the subject of traffic stops and parking violations before they went missing. But the key thing for us is this: Between October eighteenth and November twenty-first, Jack ran a query on every one of them. The key point is: He knew his searches could be traced."

Lucy stared at Kimball, realization dawning. "But he wouldn't have done that—!"

Kimball nodded. "That's right. He wouldn't have done that if he was doing something wrong."

"And Cal Parrish. Did he do the same?"

"Yes. A little over a year earlier, he ran a similar set of searches. What I can't understand is why nobody bothered to investigate his activities in just the same way as I did, with an offline search. And that raises another question . . ."

"What?"

"Why didn't Trousdale and Scarlatti run an offline search to see if Jack was working on something like this? They could have done that by simply searching his name. For every online search, the first field that has to be filled in on the form, right next to the date, is 'Name of Requester.' And one of the first things that comes up in an offline search result is that law enforcement officer's name." Kimball tapped an index finger on a spot near the top of the page that lay open in front of them.

Lucy bent closer to look.

Jack G. Hendricks (Det.)

Just seeing his name was a blade in her heart.

"You mean, they put me through all that hell for nothing? Because they were incompetent?"

"It looks like it. But that leads me to another question: Mr. Olivetti is supposed to be helping you. Why didn't *he* suggest an offline search?"

"He and I agreed to keep the police out of it until we had something concrete."

"His office could do that search themselves. He has full access."

"Maybe . . . well, he's a prosecutor, not a cop. Maybe he didn't think of it."

"Maybe. But I think you'd better see this." He slipped a thin folder out of his briefcase and passed it to her.

Inside the folder were four five-by-seven photographs. They weren't original prints—they were photographs of prints. Each original had been laid on a flat surface and photographed, in the way someone might do with a smartphone. The backdrop in each of the four originals was instantly recognizable as the New York City skyline. From the angle, the photos had been shot along the Waterfront Walkway on the New Jersey side of the Hudson, somewhere near the Newport-Midtown ferry landing.

Each photo had been taken with a long lens. They looked like surveillance shots. Each one was date-stamped.

07/18/2005 17:08
07/18/2005 17:10
07/18/2005 17:13
07/18/2005 17:17

The subjects of the photographer's interest were a man and a woman. They looked to be in their early thirties. The man was wearing cargo shorts and a T-shirt. The woman was in jeans and a long-sleeved chiffon top. They had their arms around each other in that unmistakable way that said: "What we've got going here is more than just sex."

In the final shot, they were entwined on a bench, kissing passionately.

Struggling to keep her voice calm, Lucy asked, "Where did you get these?"

"From a divorce file in the Family Division at the Hudson County courthouse. They were part of an evidence packet."

"Why do you have them? Why did you do this?"

"Just something I heard. Then I saw you at the Adega Grill in Newark. You were so wrapped up in your conversation with the guy, you didn't notice me sitting at the bar. But I remembered what you'd told me—about the woman cop."

Lucy's throat tightened as she studied the photographs again.

The man was Robert Olivetti.

The woman was Carla Scarlatti.

"You knew the whole story!" Lucy's knuckles were white as she gripped her phone. "For Christ's sake, you *knew* she was one of the investigators, you knew how much I dislike her, and you didn't say a thing!"

"Just a minute . . . you had *me* investigated?"

Lucy ignored the question and plowed on. "You walked into my house and found her standing over me, accusing me of killing Neil Clooney, and both of you pretended you barely knew each other!"

"She wasn't accusing you. She was—"

"Beside the point! Why didn't you tell me from the start?"

"I wanted to tell you but, hell, it ended years ago! Long before Jack's murder. My relationship with her has been purely professional ever since."

"You should have told me! I let you into my life, and I let you into my bed! You know how I am, how all this has affected me! I thought I could trust you! You were the *one* person around here I thought I could trust!"

"I still am!"

"Are you kidding me? *After this?*"

"I just thought . . . why complicate things? Why complicate . . . us? I was going to tell you eventually, when we'd cleared everything up. When I'd be able to look you in the eyes and say, this happened, back in my past, but I never let it influence me. I never let it interfere in our search for the truth."

"Noble words, but you know how they sound? Like—what do you lawyers call it?—ex post facto justification?"

"I guess it does sound like that, but it's not." He sounded utterly chastened. Defeated.

"Was she the reason your marriage fell apart?"

"Yes. But it takes two. We worked a big case together. It was pretty intense. We'd go for a drink once in a while. She made it pretty clear she was . . . available. I didn't have to go there, but I did. It started as a one-nighter. She owns a little house in The Heights, at the top end of Collard, across from the reservoir. It was private. It was supposed to be no strings, but like all these things, it got out of control. Sandra found out. She didn't cause any big scene. She just moved into the spare room and stopped talking. Maybe she'd been waiting for the excuse. I don't know. All I know is I came home one day and she'd moved out."

"Where is she now?"

"Out West. I don't even know where. I haven't heard from her in years and her family won't talk to me." When Lucy didn't respond immediately, he jumped into the silence. "Listen, can we get past this? I mean, can you? Can we start again?"

"I don't know. Really, I don't. I need to think."

"Lucy . . . !"

More than once during the conversation, Lucy had been tempted to just hang up and cut him off in mid-sentence. Instead, she left him with a quiet "Bye, Robert," and ended the call.

22

Sitting dead center on the sideboard in Lucy's dining room was a majolica cachepot from Caltagirone. The baroque *objet d'art* was brilliantly executed in sage green and yellow—the colors of Sicily itself, as Lucy's mother had never failed to explain to interested guests. Lucy had always loved it. After her mother's death, the ceramic was the first thing from his wife's prized possessions that Joseph Cappelli gave to Lucy.

Lucy carefully tipped the heavy ceramic to one side and retrieved a Nokia cell phone from under its broad base. She tried the power button. The tiny screen lit up.

Good thing, she thought, since Lanza had neglected to leave her a battery charger.

She scrolled through the menu to *Drafts*. As the Don had promised, there was a single stored entry. A phone number. The area code was 605. She looked it up.

South Dakota.

Interesting.

He had said there would be some call forwarding involved.

Until now, she had doubted she would ever make this call. But two things had happened:

She'd discovered that Robert Olivetti was not the one-hundred-and-ten-percent trustworthy ally—okay, ally and lover—that she'd believed him to be.

And, this morning's *Jersey Journal* had carried a front-page article that had left her feeling deeply hurt. The headline read:

MURDERED COP'S WIDOW INTERVIEWED IN RUTGERS PROF KILLING

She dialed the number.

A long humming sound . . . a relay click . . . another click . . . silence . . . then . . .

A distant ring.

"Lucinda. How are you?"

"I think you can guess."

"Because you're calling me."

"Yes."

"I'll send a car for you."

"Not here. I'll meet your driver somewhere. But first I need to make arrangements for my son."

"I understand."

Lucy checked the time. 4:10 P.M.

"Would later this evening work for you?"

"I'll make it work. Call me again when you're ready." There was a click, and he was gone.

She remembered what he had told her: "*Certain federal agencies would love to monitor my calls.*"

Their conversation had lasted no more than fifteen seconds. But in that short span of time, Lucy had crossed a very definite line, and she knew it.

Complete loss of trust can make you do that.

She called Tracy. The girl said she was sitting for another neighbor, but just until six. She'd made plans to spend time with her friends that evening. Lucy offered her double pay, and told her she'd spring for pizza. Tracy relented.

"Twenty-nine East Thirtieth. Take the driveway. The brick building in the back used to be a commercial laundry. Now it's a private parking garage. I own it. Your car will be out of sight."

When she pulled into the garage just after seven that evening, Lanza's driver was waiting, standing next to a black Lexus sedan. Even though she had just entered a one-story building, not a multi-story car-park like the one where Jack had been killed, Lucy felt a fleeting sensation of danger.

But for some reason, the feeling didn't frighten her. It just quickened her blood.

She squeezed her car between two others on the rear wall, locked it, and walked toward the man. He had already strolled forward to meet her. He was middle-aged, with a pallid complexion, fatigued eyes, and pursed lips. Apart from the knitted cap on his head, he looked more like a loan manager than a Mafia soldier.

"Mrs. Hendricks?"

"Yes."

"My name is Cowan. Mr. Lanza sent me." He didn't offer to shake hands.

"Let's go then." Lucy moved toward the front passenger door of the Lexus.

"Sorry. Could you sit in the back please?"

"Fair enough. Is there a reason?"

"I'll explain in the car. But first, open your purse."

"What?"

He stood there, waiting. She opened her purse. He peered inside, plunged a hand, felt around, and then withdrew. "Thank you." He opened the rear door for her.

"What were you looking for? A gun?"

"Something like that."

Once they were out of the garage and rolling north on Avenue E, he said, "Please look at the windows in this car. You will notice that the rear window, and the side windows in the back, have a dark tint. We're allowed to do that in New Jersey, but the windshield and the front windows have to be clear."

Cowan definitely had a banker's precise way of speaking.

Maybe loan-sharking has become more genteel.

"What you're saying is that your boss doesn't want anyone to see me in this car."

"What I'm saying is . . . we're heading for Mr. Lanza's place in Florham Park, where he never conducts business. And I'm saying that, when we get to the Short Hills Mall, I will be asking you to lie down on the seat."

Lucy didn't know whether to be comforted or disturbed by such a precaution.

To distract herself from what she was doing—or, as she phrased it more bluntly in her raging thoughts, to keep her mind off *what in the fucking hell* she was actually doing—she changed the subject.

"Cowan doesn't sound Italian."

"Now, now. Do you really believe the stereotype thing?"

"Just saying . . ."

"This is the twenty-first century, Mrs. Hendricks."

"I heard that somewhere."

"Mr. Lanza tries to respect modern values."

"What about 'Family' values?"

"They still govern. But there can be exceptions."

"And in your case . . ."

"In my case, my mother was Italian."

"So, Family values."

"To that extent, I suppose."

"And you're not just his driver, are you?"

"No."

"You're not his driver at all. You're his accountant."

Cowan's head swiveled. He shot her a raised eyebrow, then turned back to the road.

"You're a shrewd lady."

"I'm learning to be."

They rode in silence for the rest of the way.

Contrary to Lucy's preconceptions, Dominic Lanza's house was a large but unprepossessing Cape Cod–style home sitting on a modest half-acre lot at the end of a cul-de-sac.

She didn't actually see much of this when she arrived. She'd been stretched out on the rear seat for the final ten minutes of the ride, and Cowan had insisted she stay there until he'd pulled the Lexus into the garage and the massive door had descended behind them.

"Mr. Lanza is waiting in the den," Cowan told her, as he escorted her through a laundry room into a featureless hallway. They entered a small sitting room at the rear of the house. It had a large bay window, but every curtain was tightly drawn and the only light was provided by a few scattered lamps.

Lanza rose from a soft lounge chair to greet her. "I'm sorry for the security measures, Lucinda. They're for our protection. For us to be seen together would be self-defeating."

"I understand. Thank you."

The Don fluttered a hand in the direction of the shut curtains. "This property backs onto the Brooklake Country Club. A section of woodland separates my rear garden from one of the fairways. From time to time Carlo has come across golfers in those trees who seemed much more interested in this house than the lost balls they were pretending to search for."

"Federal agents?"

"Very likely." He addressed Cowan. "Thank you for driving today, Bert. How are you holding up?"

"Feeling a bit light-headed, boss."

"Get some rest. Carlo will take Mrs. Hendricks back to her car."

"Should I ask Stella to bring some coffee?"

Lanza turned to Lucy. "You're looking a bit stressed, my dear. Maybe you'd prefer a glass of wine?"

"That would be nice."

Cowan started for the door. "I'll tell Stella."

"Thank you, Bert."

"In case you were wondering," Lanza said, after the man had left, "he's on chemo."

Lucy suddenly understood the woolen cap. And the shadows around Cowan's eyes.

"I've given him a room downstairs. A nurse comes once a day to administer the poison." He paused. "I'll miss him."

"It's that bad?"

Lanza nodded. "He doesn't know yet."

An elderly woman entered the room. She didn't look a day under eighty years old. She wore a food-stained frock and a black hair net over a lopsided bun of white hair. She was carrying an opened wine bottle in one hand and a pair of stemmed glasses in the other. Without a word, she set the bottle and glasses on a side table, shot Lucy a curious look, turned, and left.

Lanza noticed Lucy's bemused expression. "Ex-wife's mother," he offered. "She needed the work."

He poured their wine. Lucy received her glass with a thankful smile. She was feeling completely off balance. So far nothing, and no one, had come close to the fraught images of today's meeting that she'd constructed in her head.

•   •   •

"I told you when we met that my organization never had any contact with your husband."

"You also said we could help each other. What did you mean?"

"I'll come to that. But first I need to establish something." He watched her face. "Your husband was a police officer. He worked to uphold the law, and I must assume you not only loved him, but admired him."

"I did." She felt her lower lip tremble. "Jack was a good man."

"Well, Lucinda, as you have probably guessed, there are times when I am not a good man. If you and I are to have a fruitful conversation, I will need to speak plainly. That means I will need to trust you. So the question is: Can I?"

"You can search me if you like."

God, did I just say that?

Lucy couldn't believe the words that had just come out of her mouth, but she soldiered on. She stood up and stepped away from the chair. "I mean it."

"You mean, search you to see if you're wearing a transmitter?"

"Yes."

Lanza smiled. "As tempting as that offer might be, it's not necessary. This house is wired with jamming devices. I already know you're not wired."

Relieved, Lucy dropped back into her seat.

"Let me ask this," Lanza said. "When I visited you in your home, I said we might help each other. You were unconvinced. Now, six weeks later, you're sitting in my home." He leaned forward. "Tell me how you think *you can help me*."

Lucy blinked. She opened her purse and retrieved a USB drive. "With this." She handed it to him.

Lanza looked intrigued. "What's on it?"

"Some files that Jack kept at home, hidden. He was doing an off-the-books investigation and I'm sure that's what got him killed." She explained how she had found the original flash drive—without mentioning Kevin's role—and summarized what the files contained. "The County Prosecutor's Office has the original. I have a copy. That copy is for you." She explained about Olivetti, about how she'd come to give him the original, and about the informal investigation he had agreed to conduct.

"Olivetti . . . we mainly deal with federal prosecutors, but the name's familiar."

"Italian typewriter company?"

He smiled. "Maybe."

"He's not related to them."

"Just as well. I believe they went broke."

"No, they merged with somebody else."

"Merger is sometimes the smartest move."

"But always risky."

"As long as you understand that."

"I do."

"Speaking of risk, by giving me this, you're probably committing a crime."

"What crime?"

"How about obstruction of justice?"

"Mr. Lanza, did you have Jack killed?"

"Call me Dominic."

"Did you?"

"No."

"Is there a current police investigation into Jack's murder?" She answered her own question. "There isn't. There are a few boxes in a prosecutor's office, and he's conducting an unofficial investigation at my request. He has specifically excluded the police from the process."

"Meaning?"

"Meaning, where's the obstruction? Under the New Jersey Code, obstruction requires purposefully impairing or perverting the administration of law, or—in our case—attempting to prevent the police from carrying out an investigation, by intimidation or violence or by some unlawful act. So, where's the obstruction?'"

"You've done your reading."

"I'm a teacher."

Lanza held up the flash drive. "What are you asking me to do with this information?"

"You have resources. You could conduct your own investigation."

Lanza was thoughtful. "We could. But understand . . . our justice system is more quick and efficient than the other one. You might not like the outcome."

"I can't trust the police."

"You have your prosecutor friend."

"I don't trust him either. I mean, now. I'm not talking about our investigation. I . . . I made a mistake." Lucy looked away.

"Tell me."

"I got too close to him."

"And?"

"And, I discovered he'd kept something back from me. That he'd had an affair with a female detective—the one who keeps pushing. The one who is convinced Jack was corrupt."

"When was the affair?"

"Back in '05. Before Jack's murder."

Lanza didn't say anything. He watched her with a gravely inquiring expression.

Waiting.

Lucy felt her face flush. She stumbled on. "The point is, he didn't tell me. He knew how I felt about her. He knew she'd judged the case right from the beginning. Judged Jack! He knew all that, and he knew I despised her, but he never told me that they'd had a relationship. Or that she was the reason his first wife left him."

"You slept with him."

Lucy sighed. "Is it that obvious?"

"Did you tell him about me?"

"No."

The old woman who had brought the wine appeared at the door. "They're ready for you."

"Thank you, Stella," Lanza replied. "Tell them we'll be there in a moment."

The woman disappeared.

"Tell who?" Lucy asked, alarmed. "Ready for what?"

"The caterers. I've arranged a small dinner for us."

"Us?"

"Just you and me, Lucinda. Relax." He paused. "And, as for conducting an investigation, we have already begun."

"What do you mean?"

"In our line of work, we don't own a lot of property. We own people. I didn't own your husband, but I had to be sure that no one else did. Since you and I last met, I have reached out to our brother organizations on this side of the country and checked with our affiliates on the West Coast. We are now certain that your husband had no involvement with any of the other families." He held up a hand before Lucy could reply. "I know, I know . . . you always knew that. But I had to be sure." He rose from his seat. "Now, let's go in to dinner. Leave your glass. They'll have clean ones at the table."

Lanza led Lucy through a large living room, across a broad front foyer and into an enclosed dining room. One end of a long marble-topped table was set for two. An older gentleman, liveried in a cutaway steward's jacket, stood waiting.

"Angelo here is a good friend. He owns a very fine restaurant in Morristown."

Angelo held a chair for Lucy. "*Signora, prego* . . ."

Feeling vaguely off-balance, Lucy took her seat.

When they were settled, a plate of prosciutto-wrapped cantaloupe appeared, their water and wineglasses were filled, and Angelo withdrew.

"Tell me the real reason you called," Lanza said when they were alone. "It wasn't only your issue with the prosecutor."

"You don't miss much."

"A survival skill, Lucinda."

"Have you heard about the professor from Rutgers? The one who was murdered."

"Yes."

"Have you read today's *Journal?*"

"No."

Lucy removed a torn newspaper page from her purse and passed it across the table. She sipped her wine, watching him scan the text. She could tell from his facial expression when he'd reached the pivotal passage. She continued:

"As you see, Professor Clooney was at my house on the night he was murdered, and someone in the police leaked that to the press. I have a pretty good idea who it was, since Carla Scarlatti was one of the cops who came to visit me. The leaked information must have been like catnip to the reporter. Not only was Clooney's body found in exactly the same place Jack's body was found, but he was happy to highlight the fact that the crooked cop's widow is mixed up in it somehow."

"Why was Clooney at your house?"

"That will take a while to explain. I'd rather come back to it."

"If you want my help, you'll have to tell me everything. Everything that's happened since I visited you."

"I will, but I want to tell it in a certain order."

"Fair enough. Begin."

"Do you have a laptop?"

23

Over the *prosciutto e melone aperitivo*, Lucy walked Lanza through Jack's spreadsheet and the NICB report.

Over the *arancini di riso antipasto*, she replayed Jack's interview of Thomas Mulvaney.

Over the Tuscan *malfatti primo*, she detailed her failed attempt to connect with Detective Trousdale, her subsequent alliance with Olivetti, the crime scene details she had gleaned from the police file, and Mulvaney's prison yard murder. She told him about the visit from Detectives Geary and Scarlatti on the day after Clooney's murder, and how Olivetti's last-minute appearance had probably prevented her from being arrested for assaulting Scarlatti. And, because there was now no reason to hide anything, she told him about her blossoming relationship with Olivetti that was now on the rocks.

"This insurance investigator . . . Kimball?"

"Yeah."

"Does he know about our connection?"

"No."

The *secondo* arrived. *"Involtini di pesce spada con gamberi alla griglia,"* Angelo proudly announced. *"Buon appetito!"*

Lucy goggled the plates before her, laden with swordfish roulades and grilled prawns. "I'll never eat all this," she whispered to Lanza after the man withdrew.

"Sample them. That's all that's expected."

They started to eat. After a moment, Lanza said, "You've left one thing out."

"Yes. Clooney."

"Tell me."

How do you tell a Mafia godfather about a paranormal experience?

There was only one answer, Lucy decided. Jump right in.

"My son Kevin was born with Jack's memories."

Dominic Lanza sat back in his chair. He studied her face. He set down his knife and fork.

"I'm listening."

She told him. Everything. He sat there, concentrating on her words, his food getting cold. Not once did he interrupt her.

When she finished, he was silent.

"You think I'm crazy."

"No. My uncle would have, but I don't. I've read about these cases."

"Read about them? Why would you—?"

"Why would a mobster be interested? This mobster," he announced, with just a hint of satisfaction in his voice, "has a psych degree. It sometimes comes in useful."

"Forgive me. I guess I just never pictured a crime lord with a degree."

Lanza grinned. "What *did* you picture—Albert Anastasia?"

"No, but—"

"It's true, the earlier generations arrived here with little education. They were often preyed upon by their own people. It was a constant fight just to survive. But they pulled themselves out of the gutter and made a life for themselves, and their children went to school. And in some cases the older generation hoped their children would *not* follow in their footsteps."

"But not in your case."

"My father didn't want me in the business. Sent me to college."

"You and Michael."

"You need to get that Corleone shit out of your head."

"You're in the business today. Running it."

"My father was killed. Shot by one of his *capos*. The guy had delusions of grandeur. My uncle was *capo bastone* at the time, but he was out of the country. Visiting family in Sicily. Two guys tried to take him out over there at the same time, but he got them first."

"So, you—?"

"I had just started on a master's degree. Got the call from my uncle. Went home and took care of it." He smiled at her quizzical expression. "No, we didn't 'go to the mattresses.' It wasn't that complicated."

"That makes it even more puzzling to me."

"What?"

"You're well educated, you obviously have it in you to be kind to people—there's Cowan, and Stella . . . and me—but look at what you do."

"Do you really want to have this conversation, Lucinda?"

"Maybe we should, since we're . . ."

"Allies?"

"Yes."

"You'll hear some hard truths."

"I can take it."

"I'm sure you can. But that's not what's going on here. You're telling yourself you've made a deal with the devil, and now you're self-mutilating."

"Is that psychologist talk?"

"Perhaps." He hesitated. He seemed to be shaping what he would say next. "First of all, you need to understand that this is not *Cavallieria Rusticana*. If you think my world is all pride and ambition and vengeance and *omertà*, then you're believing the myth. Some families are still caught up in the old ways, but not this one. This is the twenty-first century. The modern world requires a modern approach. To us, 'Mafia' is just a brand, and that brand is based on intimidation. To that we've added another dimension: Instead of oaths and rituals, we have taken a page from the security services. We operate on a 'need to know' basis. It's a very effective business model." He paused, tilting his head. "No, we're not exactly welcome in café society—but you'd be surprised how many of the great and the good come to us for help with their dirty little secrets. We do favors . . . and we collect on them. The ancient Greeks had a saying: 'The best, once corrupted, are the worst.' I run a modern business, Lucinda, with investment advisers and tax specialists, and all the rest, and it's a very successful one."

"With one difference."

"Yes. One difference. The threat of violence."

"Not just the threat."

"Sometimes we use force. But you knew that when you called me, didn't you?"

"I did. But it doesn't make me feel comfortable."

"Life is violent. You know that better than most. In my business, violence is just part of our service sector. Nowadays, we find that it's seldom needed." Lanza leaned forward. "Tell me, what does everyone want in this life?"

Lucy sat very still, pale, and thoughtful. "Love? Respect?"

"Yes, and . . . ?"

"Money, I suppose."

"You suppose! This is America, the hallowed home of the individual. Anyone in America who says he doesn't want all of those—love, respect, *and* money—is lying to himself. Even if a rich man acquired his wealth by swindling the faceless multitudes and ruining lives, as long as he doesn't get caught Americans will admire him."

"It's hard to get love and respect if you're killing people."

"You're sitting here, aren't you?"

Lucy blinked at him. She couldn't think of an answer.

Or you can't face the answer, girl!

"Our approach is supremely practical. Violence is an effective tool for creating power relationships and sustaining them. But as I said, despite the myths and the sensationalism of Hollywood movies, the truth is that, unlike our outdated counterparts in Italy, we seldom resort to violence. All that is required is the threat. It's a rational strategy, and it works."

"How do you deal with guilt? You have families, wives, children . . . you can't all be psychopaths."

"So now you want to have an academic conversation?"

"Might be easier on my nerves."

"Okay . . . First off, we screen out psychopaths. Those people are only loyal to themselves."

"How do you screen them out? Kill them?"

His mouth twisted into a half smile. "Sometimes. Consider it a public service. Does that help your nerves?" He pressed on without waiting for an answer. "Second, yes, guilt is always there. We treat it as a risk-management issue. It's a threat to efficiency, and it can sometimes be a threat to security. But we've learned to deal with it."

"How?"

"Guilt is backward looking, so we deal with it in advance."

"In advance?"

"No action proceeds until every participant fully understands why it is required . . . understands that all other options have been tried and failed, or have been examined and rejected as impractical. Understands that we have no other choice."

"It sounds so callous."

"It is. But it is also the way the rest of the world works. It's the way human nature works. Look at the armed forces. They go into Afghanistan, they go after a target, and they kill people. They have already dealt with guilt. They have already agreed that, faced with opposition, they will eliminate the enemy and they will know they had no choice."

"But they're fighting terrorists!"

"Yes. But the reasoning is no more valid than that of the terrorist. Those guys are saying the same thing—they're saying, 'I had no choice.'"

"This all sounds . . . completely immoral."

"Not immoral, Lucinda—*amoral*. And it's exactly how all of us deal with the bad things we do."

Lucy sat in silence for long seconds, her meal cold, wrestling with herself. Dominic Lanza was unlike anyone she had ever encountered—a man so dense with subterranean knowledge that he was at once both terrifying and deeply attractive.

Despite everything she'd always believed, she was looking at him differently. Almost with affection.

Almost . . . but not quite.

She took a long breath. "Dominic?"

"Yes?"

"Why did you trust me with that?"

"You came to me. You asked for my help, not knowing if you would be indebted to me forever. You made the hardest choice the widow of a murdered police officer could ever make. So I will trust you. And," he added, "because you've never told your friend Olivetti about my visit. The fact that you are sitting at this table tells me everything I need to know."

"I might have told him."

Lanza's expression made it clear he didn't believe she had.

"Okay," she continued, "how do you know I won't tell him now? How do you know I won't tell him everything we've said?"

"Because you respect me. And because there's something else. Something that's been lurking on the fringes of your life that you've never faced."

"What do you mean?"

"You're a *compare*, Lucinda. More trusted than blood."

"What do you mean?"

"You're one of us."

"No! My father was a miner!"

"Yes, he was."

"I don't understand."

"You will."

Carlo drove Lucy back to Bayonne.

Riding behind the big man, with his wide shoulders and thinning black hair touching his collar, she realized that he was the only person she'd met who fit the Mob image.

Her head was swimming. The man she had just dined with was well educated, engaging—even, for all his years, attractive.

But he was a *Mafioso*.

He was the *capo famiglia* of a major crime family.

Lucy had just reached an understanding with a seasoned criminal.

That significant fact should have bothered her. In their conversation, she had consciously attempted to be bothered by it.

Instead, it comforted her.

What's wrong with me?

Her reverie was interrupted by a ringing phone. Carlo took a call. He listened, muttered something in reply, and disconnected. His eyes found Lucy's in the rearview mirror.

"The cops are watching your car."

"How do you know?"

"A friend."

"Did your friend say what cops?"

"Only that they're not Feds."

"What do you want to do?"

"I can't take you to the garage. Some of these county cops know who I work for."

"Drop me on Broadway. I'll walk the rest of the way."

"Why don't I leave you somewhere near your house? You can go home and wait them out."

"No. I'm not playing games. If they're watching my car, they think they've got something. If I don't show up, they'll come looking, and I don't want my son to see that."

"If they arrest you, Mr. Lanza can't help."

"If they arrest me, they'll wish they hadn't."

In the mirror, she thought she saw a hint of respect.

"They could be watching the Broadway intersection."

"Drop me at Walgreens. It's a five-minute walk."

24

When Lucy walked into the parking garage, the first face she saw was Carla Scarlatti's. The woman was leaning against Lucy's car, talking on a cell phone. She was dressed in jeans and a short jacket, her sidearm prominent on her left hip. When she spotted Lucy, she abruptly ended her call, dropped her hand to her weapon, and advanced on Lucy.

Lucy heard footfalls behind her. She glanced back. Geary was entering the garage.

Scarlatti dispensed with all pretense of niceties.

"Where were you, Mrs. Hendricks?"

Lucy had her keys in her hand. She stepped past Scarlatti, keyed the remote to unlock her car, and kept moving.

"Stop right there! We want to ask you some questions."

Lucy swung around. "I've answered all the questions from you I'm going to answer!" she snapped. "You obviously have a personal agenda that has nothing to do with finding the truth about my husband's murder! Five years ago, you were just a tactless bitch who wasted valuable time chasing a ridiculous theory. If anything, you hindered the investigation! Now you're back with more harassment because someone murdered a psychologist who was helping my son." Lucy shifted her gaze straight to Geary and raised her voice as she aimed her next words. "What is it this time, Carla? Are you just upset because your old boyfriend decided to help me? Or is it something else? Something *you're* trying to cover up? Whatever it is, you'd be very wise to back off!"

Scarlatti seemed taken by surprise at the heat of Lucy's verbal assault, and unsettled enough to glance over at Geary before responding.

The man's expression revealed nothing.

"Nice speech, Mrs. Hendricks," Scarlatti shot back with a self-righteous smirk, "but you're still going to have to explain to us why your car is parked in this garage, blocks from any convenient shopping, and why you were seen this afternoon riding away from this location in a vehicle registered to a company owned by a known member of the Lanza crime family. And why, hours later, you appeared miraculously at the intersection of Broadway and Thirtieth and strolled back here."

"I don't have to explain anything to you, Scarlatti!"

"In that case, Mrs. Hendricks, I'm placing you under arrest."

Geary interjected. "Detective . . . !"

"This woman's husband was murdered in circumstances that point directly to Lanza family involvement. We now have evidence that she has been consorting with a member of that same crime family, that she was apparently the last person to see Dr. Clooney alive before he was abducted by his killer or killers, that Clooney was tortured in classic Mob style—obviously to get some kind of information out of him—that he was then murdered, and that his body was dumped on exactly the same spot where Jack Hendricks was found. And we have one other piece of evidence relating to Clooney. Do you know what I'm talking about?"

Geary was thoughtful. "Yes."

"I'm saying all of this means that we have probable cause to believe that Mrs. Hendricks was complicit in her husband's murder."

WHAT?

Lucy could not believe what she was hearing. She stared at Geary, daring the man to agree with this insanity.

Geary took a deep breath, held it, let it out . . . and nodded his head.

Scarlatti whipped out a pair of handcuffs and advanced on Lucy, triumph in her eyes.

Lucy felt her body stiffen.

She felt her mind harden.

She had always detested Carla Scarlatti. Now she felt that loathing transform into quiet, deadly hatred.

But for the woman's spineless partner, she felt only disdain. "Geary!" she called to him, as Scarlatti pulled her arms behind her, snapped on the cuffs, and started droning her Miranda rights.

"What?"

"You're a contemptible coward, and a disgrace to your badge!"

The BPD interview room looked much like the ones Lucy had seen on television—cinderblock walls, scarred wooden table, beat-up chairs, video camera, and the obligatory one-way mirror for outside observers. But if Scarlatti and Geary thought the setting would intimidate Lucy in any way, they were sorely mistaken.

First, because she was angrier than she had ever been in her entire life.

Second, because, once during her marriage, she had sat outside this very room, watching Jack interview a female suspect. He had asked for her help in assessing the credibility of a female teacher who had been accused of sexually abusing a young male student, and his captain had agreed Lucy could attend.

Lucy knew this room.

And, she knew that someone well above these two detectives' pay grade was monitoring her custodial interrogation. A captain, or even a deputy chief, would be standing in that dark space on the other side of the glass, pondering whether Lucy's delivery to a police station in hand-cuffs had been based on no more than bare suspicion; pondering whether these two cops really had probable cause to detain her for complicity in the murder of her husband; and wondering how many heads would roll when it emerged in the resulting lawsuit that neither of the officers who were using this room was even a member of the Bayonne Police Department.

For the past forty minutes, Geary had said little. He just stood in a corner, listening, while Scarlatti tried every transparent trick in the book to get answers from Lucy.

Lucy had just sat there, pale and cold, her eyes burning into Scarlatti, saying nothing.

Until now.

It began with the second phone. The Nokia 100 they'd found in her purse.

Geary had run a fast check on Lucy's late-model smartphone, a Samsung Galaxy. There were no saved e-mails, but he'd quickly reviewed it for texts, recent calls, and contacts. He'd found nothing that connected her to anyone other than her own family in Florida, the school where she taught, her son's daycare . . . and Robert Olivetti.

Meanwhile, Scarlatti had checked the Nokia.

Now she set it in front of Lucy.

"Explain this to me," she said, as she took a small tube out of her pocket, squeezed ointment into her left palm, and idly rubbed it into a scaly patch on the back of her right hand. "Why are you carrying this phone?"

Lucy made a deliberate show of wrinkling her nose at the medicinal smell of the ointment and responded to the question with an icy smile. "It's my son's. He's at home with my sitter. Why don't you arrest him, too? Maybe he was in on the conspiracy."

"A cell phone for a five-year-old?"

"It's a toy. They're practically giving them away these days." Lucy paused. "But then, I'm not surprised that you know nothing about children."

"It's a prepay. A burner! And there's time on it!"

"Really? And how many numbers?" Lucy wasn't worried that they'd found Dominic's contact number. As an extra precaution—one that she was now thankful for—she'd memorized the number and deleted it from both *Drafts* and *Dialed Numbers* before she left the house that day.

"None. Do you know how that looks?"

"I don't really care how it looks. If you'd bother to check, you'd know that a lot of providers give away those phones, with time already loaded on them. It's a sales gimmick." Lucy checked her watch. "And by the way, I know I'm entitled to a phone call. So if you plan to continue this ridiculous interview, I'll need to call my sitter."

Scarlatti ignored her. "Why don't you tell us about Professor Clooney?"

"I've already told you about him."

"So you say, but we have a little problem here."

"Yes, you do. And it's about to get bigger."

Scarlatti brushed aside the implied threat. "The problem—your problem, Mrs. Hendricks—is Dr. Clooney's connection to the Lanza crime family."

For the first time in the interview, Lucy was shaken. She'd been listening to Scarlatti's questions, saying nothing, letting the stupid woman reveal what she had—which was basically nothing. Now, finally, Scarlatti had tipped the "other piece of evidence" she'd mentioned in the garage just before Lucy's arrest.

She steeled herself.

"What connection?"

"Clooney testified for Dominic Lanza in a custody fight. The testimony was heard on camera, so we've never seen a transcript. But, whatever he said, it didn't work, because the ex won the case."

"When was this?"

"Two years ago."

"From what I've read, Lanza's a bit old for a custody fight."

"Second wife. A lot younger than him. Guess she went for the money."

"Interesting, but what has that got to do with me?"

"Let me spell it out for you: 2006 . . . your husband is a BPD cop, but his body is found out of jurisdiction, in Jersey City, with a Lanza family calling card jammed in his throat . . . before he was killed, he'd been accessing police databases he had no business accessing . . . you're the grieving widow, and you claim you know nothing about his activities, even though you'd just enjoyed a luxury, all-expense-paid vacation with him in a Mob-connected hotel in Key West . . . you disappear to Florida . . . five years later, you're back in Bayonne, living in the same house, meeting with Dr. Clooney, another person Lanza may have felt knew too much about some aspect of his life . . . within hours of your meeting, Clooney shows up dead in exactly the same place your husband's body was found. Today you're spotted riding in a vehicle owned by a known affiliate of the Lanza family. Who are the common denominators in all this? You and Dominic Lanza!"

"Dr. Clooney was at my home on a professional consultation. He was visiting my son."

"What's wrong with your son?"

"That is none of your business."

"You're not helping yourself."

"Neither are you." Lucy leaned forward. "I've heard everything you've had to say. The same questions, over and over. I'm not some illiterate perp you can bully. That mishmash of so-called evidence you just recited is nowhere near probable cause. This is called false arrest and unlawful detention! Now, I want to call my sitter, *and* my attorney."

"What attorney?"

"Robert Olivetti!"

"You think having a prosecutor boyfriend is going to save you?"

The door swung open and a male voice spoke: "Actually, it *is* going to save her, Detective."

Robert Olivetti was standing in the doorway, holding Lucy's purse. Behind him stood another man. Lucy recognized the BPD's deputy chief. He wore a look of profound irritation, and his ire clearly wasn't directed at Olivetti.

Olivetti handed Geary a sheaf of papers.

"What's this?"

"Perhaps you've heard of habeas corpus?"

Olivetti helped Lucy out of the chair. As they were leaving, she scooped the Nokia off the table.

"I stuck my neck out on this."

Olivetti was driving her back to her car.

"I realize that."

"Is this going to come back and bite me in the ass?"

Lucy didn't reply.

"Lucy, were you with Lanza today?"

She hesitated. She didn't want to lie to the man who had just freed her from Detective Scarlatti's clutches—from his own ex-lover's clutches—but she'd need to be careful.

"He contacted me," she replied, without specifying exactly when. "He wanted me to know that his organization, as he called it, never did business with Jack, and they had nothing to do with his murder."

"Why call you now? After all these years! *Why now?*"

"That story in the *Journal*. About Professor Clooney's murder. The one that mentioned me. The one your girlfriend must have leaked!" Lucy caught herself. She touched his arm. "I'm sorry, Robert. I shouldn't have said that."

"It's okay."

"I really am grateful for what you did for me today."

"Glad to help." He was silent for a moment. "Do you believe Lanza? Do you believe he had nothing to do with Jack's murder?"

Lucy pretended to consider the question.

"I do."

"Did he say anything about Clooney?"

"Just that it wasn't his doing, and he was sorry I'd been dragged into the story." She paused. "But it does worry me. The connection Scarlatti mentioned."

"There must have been more to the meeting! How did it play out? What did he say?"

The line had been reached. The line Lucy had already drawn in her mind. The one she wouldn't cross.

She deflected.

"I'll tell you sometime. But right now, I'm exhausted. I need to get home, get a night's sleep, and then figure out how I'm going to explain all this to my principal after Carla Scarlatti leaks to the world the fact that I was arrested."

Olivetti sighed. "Okay. But you need to understand something. You're playing a dangerous game having contact with Dominic Lanza."

"You can rest easy. There won't be any more contact."

It was a smooth lie, but one Lucy had planned for. She didn't feel the slightest bit guilty.

A dubious lesson in amorality, learned from a master.

25

Lucy's arrest never did hit the papers.

She figured Floyd Jackson's letter to the Office of Professional Standards in Trenton, with copies served personally on Scarlatti and Geary, had probably dampened Scarlatti's enthusiasm for ruining her life. At first, her attorney had relished the prospect of filing a civil rights case against both officers. But after hearing Lucy's carefully edited narration of events, under the convenient protection of attorney-client privilege, he was alarmed enough to suggest that an Internal Affairs complaint would be deterrent enough. He doubted a jury would understand Lucy's admission that she'd met with a notorious Mob boss not just once, but twice.

Lucy was fine with that, especially since she hadn't bothered to tell the lawyer about her third meeting with Dominic.

The lead-up to the meeting had felt vaguely ridiculous, like being dropped into a third-rate spy novel. On Friday, she'd come out of the school at the end of the day to find a slip of paper tucked under the driver's side windshield wiper of her car. It bore a single hand-printed word:

CALL

She had waited until after ten that night before using the Nokia.

"Lucy. We need to meet."

Lucy?

Apparently her new partner in crime had decided "Lucinda" was too formal for a discussion between trusted allies.

"Do you know what happened to me? After last time?"

"I heard about your ordeal."

"Fortunately, no one else has."

"I'll come to you."

"Where?"

"Your home. Tomorrow night."

"Are you sure? I mean—"

"I understand your concern. We have ways. Turn off all the lights in the rear half of your house and leave a glass door unlocked."

"The door on the left. If you come after nine, Kevin will be asleep."

"I'd like to meet him."

"Are you serious?"

"Yes."

"Is this the Psych major talking?"

"I suppose it is."

"Do you know how surreal that sounds?"

"I suppose it does."

"All right. Come at eight."

"See you then."

Dominic arrived on the dot of eight. He stepped through the curtains into Lucy's office, shut the sliding door behind him, locked it, looked at her and said, "I walked from Avenue A. Carlo has the other phone. We'll use yours to tell him when to pick me up."

"This must be important."

"It is. We can discuss it after Kevin is in bed."

"He's in the living room."

"Don't mention my real name. Kids have good memories."

"He'll remember your voice." Lucy had already told him about finding Kevin sitting on the stairs after his first visit.

"Just say I'm your husband's great uncle, passing through."

"What's your name?"

"How about Nathan?"

"I doubt you'll fool him."

"Why?"

"You'll see."

She led Dominic to the front of the house. Having learned from his example, she'd already closed the blinds and curtains on every window.

Kevin was nestled on the couch in his pajamas, watching a cartoon on his LeapPad.

"Kevin, this is your dad's uncle Nathan. He was passing through and came for a visit."

Dominic held out a hand. "Hello, young man."

Kevin stared up at him. He didn't move. Instead, he said something that brought Lucy's hand to her mouth.

"You're not our uncle." The boy returned his attention to the flickering screen perched on his lap.

"How do you know that, Kevin?" Lucy asked.

"I seen that man before, and you didn't tell me he's our uncle. You woulda told me."

Dominic now looked thoroughly intrigued. He dropped onto the chair he had occupied on his first visit. Lucy sat beside her son.

Kevin muted his cartoon and looked Lanza straight in the eye. "Are you a bad man?"

Lanza didn't miss a beat. "Sometimes I am, Kevin. But not tonight."

"Will you hurt my mom?"

"Never. Do you believe me?"

"I don't know. Do you believe him, Mommy?"

"Yes."

"Did he ever try to hurt my dad?"

"No."

Lanza said, "I never, ever hurt your dad."

Kevin studied Lanza with cool regard. Lucy could see that the Mafioso was intrigued by the boy's unexpected maturity.

Intrigued, yes, and perhaps a bit disturbed.

"It's important that you believe me, Kevin. I didn't hurt your dad."

Kevin's neck muscles tensed. His back straightened. Lucy knew the signs. She had seen Kevin transform enough times before. She thought she was ready for what was coming.

But she wasn't.

The next words out of her son's mouth sent a chill down her spine.

"I am aware of your occupation, Mr. Lanza. But I do believe you. Thank you."

Lanza's eyes narrowed. He looked at Lucy. She shook her head. She had never mentioned his name to Kevin.

Lanza made a decision. He slipped out of his chair and kneeled in front of the boy.

"Jack Hendricks. Do you remember the person who hurt you?"

Lucy held her breath. A second passed. Another. Then:

"I couldn't see."

"What do you remember?" Lanza asked gently. "Anything?"

"The smell."

Lucy was astonished. Kevin had never talked about this. "What smell, honey?"

"Like . . . a hospital lady."

While Lucy processed that puzzling revelation, Lanza held out his hands. "The gun, Kevin. What hand was it in?"

Kevin stared at him, as if in a trance.

Then he touched Lanza's left hand.

A left-handed killer . . . ? A nurse?

Lucy's racing thoughts were instantly derailed when Kevin's calm expression suddenly transformed to pure horror. He looked up at her, eyes bulging with fear, and cried, "Luce! I saw Jack!"

Lucy's skin prickled. "But, Kevin, you *were* Jack!"

"I saw him! Jack! I wanted to live, but I couldn't! I couldn't live another day!" He screamed and then burst into tears.

Lucy held the sobbing boy tight to her breast as tears filled her own eyes and coursed down her face.

Lanza resumed his seat. He looked mystified . . . and deeply affected.

The thought flashed through Lucy's mind that, in that moment, Dominic Lanza seemed more like a worried grandfather than a ruthless crime boss.

"We've been asking questions. Calling in favors. I want you to know what we found."

It was after nine. Kevin was asleep upstairs. Dominic had waited patiently while she dried the boy's tears, readied him for bed, and read him a story. He hadn't questioned Lucy about what he'd seen and heard. He seemed to accept that, somehow, Kevin had inherited scattered, ragged memories from his father's life. When Lucy had expressed her surprise at his equanimity, he had replied softly, "In my business, dear girl, you don't survive unless you have a good nose for deception. You're a very accomplished woman, but I can't believe what I have just witnessed was staged for my benefit."

They were back in their places in the living room, working their way through a bottle of *Primitivo*.

Lucy was sharing a drink with Dominic Lanza, notorious Mafia kingpin.

Her new friend.

She wondered what Detective Carla Scarlatti would think if she walked in right now.

"We have contacts in Boston. Back in '06, they were running a protection racket on the waterfront up there. A couple of their associates got themselves arrested. The Boston cops had them on tape, making threats. The usual. Nothing big. Nothing that couldn't be fixed. But one of the guys didn't follow tradition. He tried to make a deal." Lanza took a swallow of wine. "You've seen the movies. You know where that can lead."

Lucy nodded, marveling at her own composure as she listened to this.

"An order went out, but before anyone could act on it, he turned up dead in his cell. Someone had gotten to him first."

"Who?"

"Someone from down here."

"I don't understand. Why?"

"The guy had offered a sweetener. His lawyer told the prosecutor that if they let him off with a token misdemeanor charge, he'd not only sell out his waterfront bosses, he'd give them a high-end car theft ring in New Jersey. Seems that before he moved to Boston, he'd been part of a crew down here. They'd steal luxury cars and deliver them to a dead drop. Another crew would take them to a salvage yard, where the cars would be rolled into containers, and then shipped overseas as 'used car parts.' Sometimes they'd cut them in half—put half in one container and the other half in another one. They were sending them to places like West Africa and Eastern Europe where demand was high and no questions were asked. They had a few crooked cops running interference for the street crews, and giving cover for the trucks that delivered the containers to the docks. The thing is, we control the unions in the Port of Newark, and we never got wind of this. I'm guessing they had a customs agent on the payroll. There's always a Maersk captain around who will look the other way if a few extra containers get loaded. For a price, of course."

"You said luxury cars . . ." Lucy could see where this was going.

Dominic nodded. "It ties in with your husband's spreadsheet. The evidence the guy gave to the Boston prosecutor mentioned a salvage yard in East Orange. He said he'd never been there, but some of the pickup crews had talked about it. By the time the Boston cops got the Feds involved and put a case together for a search warrant, the scrap yard had closed down and the manager—some guy named Parnell—had disappeared."

"How do you know all this?"

"Our Boston friends have friends."

"Meaning, friends in the police?"

"And . . . other places." He drained his glass, topped up hers, and refilled his own. "Parnell ran the operation, but he wasn't the boss. The cops discovered that the East Orange property was owned by a New York company. When they checked, they learned that that company was owned by a Delaware company, and that company was owned by a Texas company, and so on. They never did figure out who was behind it." He smiled. "We didn't either, but we got further than them."

"Tell me."

"There were eight shell companies registered in seven different jurisdictions, but the trail ended in Delaware. Most people don't know that the most secretive place in the world isn't one of those offshore tax havens like the Cayman Islands or Luxembourg. It's Delaware . . . right here in the self-righteous, holier-than-thou U. S. of A." Dominic produced a folded sheet of paper from his pocket and handed it to Lucy.

It was a copy of the last page of Jack's spreadsheet.

"Look at that string of words across the bottom."

Orcone, Dorilla, Oronte, Doraspe, Policare, Meroe, Tomiri, Tigrane . . .

Lucy remembered them. They had puzzled her from the beginning.

"They're the names of characters in an Italian opera," Dominic said.

Lucy stared at him, confusion written across her face.

"The opera is called *Tigrane*. It was written back in the seventeen hundreds. But what's important about those words is that they're the names of shell companies: Orcone Ltd. is the New York company that owned the East Orange property. Dorilla Inc. is the Delaware company that owned Orcone. Oronte is the company that owned Dorilla, and so on, right down the list. Tigrane Holdings Ltd. was the company in Delaware where the trail ended. Somehow, Jack got his hands on that list. Maybe he researched it. Maybe he figured out who owned that last company." He spoke gently. "Or, maybe he was killed trying."

Lucy was stunned. "Dominic, I need to take this to Robert! Now he has grounds to start a proper investigation!"

"You would need to hide our involvement. You would need to explain how you obtained the information about the Boston investigation." He was thoughtful. "There's a certain private investigator who owes me a favor. I might be able to arrange something."

"Thank you!"

"But I have one reservation."

"What's that?"

"It concerns your Mr. Olivetti. Perhaps it no longer involves him directly, but it needs to be looked at."

He drank some wine.

He looked at her.

"Dominic, please don't leave me hanging!"

"The composer of *Tigrane* was a man named Alessandro Scarlatti."

It took a moment for the implication to sink in. Lucy leapt to her feet.

"THAT BITCH!"

"Stay calm, my girl. Think!"

Lucy started pacing. "Left-handed killer? Scarlatti opera characters? And now, 'hospital lady' smell? That woman has eczema on her hands! She uses an ointment that smells like a hospital! Too many coincidences, Dominic! I'm going after her!"

"Lucy, what did I just say?"

She whirled and faced him. Hot tears ran down her face. "I can't wait on this! It's been too many years! Too much pain!"

"What do you imagine you can do?" Dominic asked calmly.

"Confront her! Get her arrested! Get her ass thrown in jail!"

"Lucy . . ."

"What?"

"What is your evidence?"

Lucy stood immobile, nailed in place by the question, angry and confused. "The . . . the names of those companies. They're completely unique! I bet that composer was some sort of ancestor!"

"We don't know that."

"Easily researched! There are all these genealogy websites. It shouldn't take long."

"Assume you're right," he said quietly. "Assume she's a direct descendant of Alessandro Scarlatti and you can prove she has intimate knowledge of all his operas. What else have you got? What have you got that connects her to this guy Parnell? Or to the operation in East Orange? Or to a single stolen car?"

The questions confounded her.

Dominic pressed his point. "Didn't this Scarlatti woman arrest you? Just a few days ago?"

"Yeah."

"And weren't you the one lecturing her about probable cause? Didn't your Mr. Olivetti get an immediate court order to have you released?"

Lucy didn't reply.

"Do I have your attention?"

"Yes."

"You're very angry."

"Yes."

"Anger is counterproductive. To be useful, it needs to be channeled. *Essa deve diventare la tua forza.*"

"It must become my strength."

"Yes."

"What are you thinking?"

"How determined are you?"

"Try me!"

"What skills do you have?"

"My husband trained me. You might be surprised."

A second passed. Another . . .

"Surprise me."

26

It was a classic late-season storm. It began as a tropical wave, sliding off the African continent on October 11. By the eighteenth, it had crossed the Atlantic, glided past the Windward Islands, and penetrated the Caribbean.

By October 21, it was beginning to show primitive signs of organization. Barometric pressures were falling, and circulation was becoming more well-defined. A day later, deep convection formed near the system's center, creating a tropical depression. It moved slowly west, then southwest. But then an upper-level trough over the northwest Caribbean changed everything. Like a carnivorous animal, the beast turned, first north, then northeast. Within hours, it strengthened to become a tropical storm.

It accelerated, stalking its first prey.

It transitioned into a Category 1 hurricane just south of Kingston, Jamaica, and crossed that country's eastern parishes on October 24. It re-emerged over the deep, warm waters of the Cayman Trench, leaving one person dead and thousands of damaged homes. It strengthened quickly—Category 2, Category 3—and then slammed into Santiago de Cuba with all the fury of a major hurricane. It spent five hours grinding a path across that storied island, leaving eleven dead and 17,000 homeless. It was one of the costliest hurricanes in Cuba's history.

But Hurricane Sandy was far from done.

Haiti, the Dominican Republic, the Bahamas . . . each was assaulted in its turn, leaving death and destruction in its wake.

By October 26, tracking northeast, passing Great Abaco in the Bahamas, it briefly dropped below hurricane strength.

But its span had vastly increased.

By the twenty-seventh, it had regained hurricane strength, now with a radius of maximum winds exceeding one hundred nautical miles.

On Sunday, October 28, the center of Hurricane Sandy— "Frankenstorm" as it would ever after be known—began curving north. Soon it was riding the warm, deadly waters of the Gulf Stream as it churned past North Carolina.

The National Hurricane Center in Miami warned that Sandy was expected to bring life-threatening storm surge flooding to the Mid-Atlantic coast, including Long Island Sound and New York Harbor, with winds expected to be near hurricane force at landfall.

Bayonne's mayor announced that a state of emergency would go into effect at six in the evening on Sunday.

But Lucinda Hendricks wasn't paying attention.

Scarlatti.

Every corporate register associated with the car theft ring led back to that name.

The same theft ring Jack had been investigating.

The people who killed Cal Parrish.

The people who killed Jack.

Jack said he hadn't seen his killer's face.

Jack said the killer was left-handed.

JACK . . . said . . . ?

Lucy wondered if she was going insane.

It was eleven at night and she was sitting in her car, a few doors north of Carla Scarlatti's residence.

Waiting.

It hadn't taken much effort to figure out where the woman lived. During Lucy's big blowup telephone call with Robert, he'd let slip that she lived on Collard Street, in The Heights, across from the reservoir. The north end of Collard terminated next to Reservoir No. 2. There were fewer than a dozen houses on that final stretch of roadway. Last night, Lucy had called the Jersey City Police's main number, pretending to be a witness Scarlatti had been trying to contact, and asked what shift the detective was working. The receptionist told her she'd just started afternoons. So, after that call, Lucy had parked at the east end of Spruce Street and waited. Sure enough, just after eleven thirty, a black SUV had rolled past her and turned north onto Collard. Scarlatti was at the wheel.

Lucy had waited ten minutes and then driven slowly up Collard. It had taken her less than a minute to identify the woman's house.

And it had only taken her ten more seconds to realize the significance of what she had spotted on the rear bumper of Scarlatti's 2005 Ford Explorer.

Now, twenty-hours later, she was back.

She was back, and she was thinking.

She was thinking about how relentlessly this woman had tried to make Jack's murder look like a Mob hit. About how sharply she had questioned Lucy after she innocently identified the trinacria symbol on the bracelet extracted from Jack's throat. About how reliable she had been in ensuring that Lucy's name kept showing up in leaked press reports. About how the woman seemed so determined to implicate Lucy in Neil Clooney's murder.

She was thinking about how the woman carried her service weapon on her left hip.

About how she'd held her pen in her left hand during Lucy's in-custody interview.

And . . . about the faded bumper sticker on Scarlatti's Explorer.

A sticker that featured an image of Hollywood actor Kiefer Sutherland.

Sutherland had played Agent Jack Bauer in *24*, a long-running TV series that Lucy's Jack had always enjoyed.

She was thinking about that bumper sticker on Scarlatti's Explorer because it bore a three-word legend:

Live Another Day

At eleven forty-five, Carla Scarlatti's Ford pulled into the short drive in front of her house. She got out, tugged her jacket collar close against the gusting wind and drizzle, locked the vehicle, and strode to her door. She didn't notice Lucy waiting only a few steps away, in the narrow, dark space between Scarlatti's house and her neighbor's.

As the door opened, Lucy made her move.

Scarlatti must have heard the scrape of Lucy's foot. Her left hand went for her Glock. But by the time her fingers found the holster, the gun was gone and she was pitching headlong onto the tiled floor of her front hallway.

The cop rolled over, and found herself staring into the barrel of her own service weapon.

"My husband taught me a few things," Lucy said calmly.

"You fuckin' little—!"

"SHUT UP!"

Scarlatti shut up.

"Now, get up!"

Scarlatti got to her feet.

"Walk!"

"Where?"

"Kitchen!"

Scarlatti led her to the kitchen.

Lucy glanced around. "Take one of those chairs"—pointing at the dinette set—"and place it in front of the stove."

Scarlatti complied.

"Now, sit!"

Scarlatti sat.

"What do you want?"

"Handcuff your left wrist to the oven door!" Lucy ordered.

"Are you insane?"

"Do it!"

Scarlatti complied.

"Now, what do you want?" she repeated.

"Let's start by you admitting you murdered my husband."

"What? You're crazy!"

"Am I? Let's see . . . you've spent years trying to divert attention from the real reason he was killed. Why? Because his investigation of your little car theft ring was getting too close."

Scarlatti's eyes widened imperceptibly.

Lucy noticed.

"You thought I didn't know? You thought I didn't know you were shipping stolen cars out of the country, and that Jack knew exactly how you were doing it? He had a complete file on every car you'd ever stolen. And he knew that you and your gang killed Cal Parrish."

Scarlatti stared up at her. "That's all lies. Who's been feeding you this shit?"

"Someone I trust."

"Who?"

"My husband."

"Now I know you're insane!"

"There's more. Jack was killed by a left-handed woman."

"How could you possibly know that? There was nothing at the scene to indicate—!"

"*You're* left handed."

"Millions of people are left-handed!"

"Maybe, but only one of them drives your vehicle."

"What are you talking about?"

"That Explorer outside was used in the attack on Jack."

"That's ridiculous! Where's your evidence for that?"

Lucy noticed that a new note of fear had crept into Scarlatti's voice.

"Your bumper sticker gave you away."

Lucy knew she'd struck a nerve. She could see racing thoughts behind the woman's staring eyes. It was time to shake her up a bit more.

"Tigrane," Lucy said.

"What?" Scarlatti looked genuinely startled.

"Orcone, Dorilla, Oronte, Doraspe, Policare, Meroe, Tomiri . . . they all lead to Tigrane Holdings. Your company. The place where you hid all your illegal profits."

"You're talking in riddles!"

"I can see by the look on your face that I'm not."

For long seconds, Scarlatti was silent. Finally, she said:

"You're bluffing."

"You think so? You think when Robert Olivetti sees the evidence, your old relationship's going to do you any good? And it won't just be him! It will be the FBI. They'll be looking at everything you've done, everywhere you've been, and every phone call you've ever made, right back to the day the first car on Jack's list was stolen. They'll be tracking all those shell companies right back to Delaware, and right back to you. It's all going under a microscope. Every move you made in your so-called 'investigation' of Jack's murder is going to be picked apart and analyzed by people who are a lot smarter than you. You're finished!"

The detective's reaction was puzzling. The woman visibly relaxed. With eerie calm, she said, "Now I know you're bluffing."

Lucy felt rage rising in her gut.

"No one's going to believe this fairy tale. You're the one who's finished. Aggravated burglary, aggravated assault, obstruction of justice . . . you're looking at ten years, probably more."

"You disgusting bitch! I know you killed my husband!"

Lucy saw the woman's expression change.

And she knew.

She saw Scarlatti's mouth twist into a contemptuous sneer.

And she knew.

She knew, finally and horribly, that she was right.

The woman spit the words at her: *"You'll never fucking prove that!"*

Scarlatti didn't see it coming.

In a red mist of rage, Lucy pistol whipped her. She struck with so much force that she knocked Scarlatti clean off the chair. In a squeal of tortured metal, the woman's handcuffed arm almost yanked the oven door off its hinges. She landed on the floor, unconscious and bleeding, her left arm stretched to the limit, locked in place by the straining steel bracelet.

Lucy stood over her, breathing deeply. Finally, she crouched and checked Scarlatti's pulse. She peeled back an eyelid. Scarlatti groaned. Lucy checked her pockets, found a handcuff key, and released the woman's bruised wrist.

She rose. She spotted a landline phone at the end of a counter. She dialed 911 and reported an unconscious woman at 114 Collard Street. She hung up when the dispatcher asked her name.

She retraced her steps to the front door. Expertly, she field-stripped the Glock as she walked—magazine, chambered round, slide, barrel, recoil assembly, receiver. One by one, the pistol's components dropped to the tiled hallway floor.

Striding back to her car, she pulled off her belt. When she got behind the wheel, she dropped the belt on the passenger seat. She pulled away.

A rising wind buffeted her car as she drove south. At the bottom of Collard Street, she swung left onto Hopkins, a one-way avenue running east. Ahead, a dark blue Escalade sat idling at the curb on the left. As she rolled to a stop abreast of the big SUV, she lowered her window.

The Escalade's rear passenger window slid down.

"Did you get it?" Lucy asked.

Dominic Lanza held up a small digital recorder. "Every word."

"I need a copy."

"We ran a piggyback. Take this one." He handed the recorder across to her.

Lucy passed over the belt she'd been wearing. "Why do you even have gear like this?"

"How do you think we test the loyalty of our associates?" He glanced up at the sky. "Go home to your son. They say this weather's gonna get a lot worse by tomorrow."

Lucy nodded. She pressed the control to raise her window.

"Lucy . . ."

She halted her window's rise.

Lanza gave her a penetrating look. "How does it feel now, *compare?*"

Lucy cut eastward to I-78 and then fled south.

What she had just done was a shock that unsettled the whole frame of her mind.

It upended the whole frame of her being.

Her mind was a chaos of dread and pride and guilt and triumph.

She stamped down on the anarchy of her thoughts, desperate to calm the turmoil and just concentrate on her driving, pushing the speed limit, and racing back to her son.

Racing back to Kevin . . . and Jack . . . and Kevin.

"You'll never fucking prove that!"

Was one ambiguous sentence on the tape enough to finish off Jack's killer? Or was Scarlatti right? Was Lucy going to prison instead, disbelieved and despised, the half-crazed widow of a crooked cop who attacked the cop who's been investigating her?

Would this be her final night with Kevin until he was nearly grown?

She grabbed her phone and called Olivetti. He answered on the second ring.

"Lucy?"

"They're going to arrest me again."

"Lucy. NO!"

"I had to bring this thing to a head, Robert. I have a lot to tell you."

"Does this involve Carla Scarlatti?"

"Yes. But don't worry. This is going to bring in the FBI, so you can stand back when the time comes. But I want you to hear something first."

"Hear what?"

"A recording."

"Of what?"

"Of Scarlatti. That's all I want to say right now. Tomorrow? Your office?"

"Lucy, aren't you listening to the news?"

"Off and on. I've been a bit busy."

"There's a gigantic storm out there. A hurricane. They're saying it might come ashore near Atlantic City."

"Yeah. I heard. They weren't sure if it would turn."

"It has. The governor has ordered mandatory evacuations down at the Shore. And all the schools are closed tomorrow—did you know that?"

"No."

"Well, you better start paying attention!"

"I will. I'll call you tomorrow."

"Wait a minute."

"What?"

"What if Carla arrests you tonight?"

"Not likely. I put her in the hospital."

27

Forecasting Sandy had been tricky. Because of its sinuous track, the margin of predictive error beyond seventy-two hours was larger than normal. Due to superior software, the European Weather Center's medium-range forecasts, for four to six days out, turned out to be the most reliable. The European Center's ensemble was the first to predict a northwest turn when American guidance was still showing the storm remaining offshore.

While meteorologists argued, the storm made the turn predicted days ago by the Europeans, and headed for the United States.

Despite these tracking controversies, the National Hurricane Center's storm surge forecasts were right on target. On October 27, they were predicting inundations of four to eight feet for the coastlines of New Jersey, New York, and Connecticut. By late on the twenty-eighth, they were predicting six to eleven feet.

On October 29, as the center of the storm slammed ashore at Brigantine, New Jersey, it pushed nine feet of water into New York Harbor . . .

. . . and directly into Bergen Point Reach, 250 feet from Lucy's front door.

"What's happening down there?"

"The wind's not too bad. Maybe gusting to fifty, but the house is okay. There are a few tree branches in the front yard and out on the road."

"You sound pretty calm."

"Seen a lot worse in Florida."

"Maybe, but there's still the storm surge. The cops are saying Hook Road and the old Military Terminal are flooding, and there's water on the streets under the Bayonne Bridge. That's pretty close to you."

"It's still dry here. I'll keep an eye on it. Any news on Scarlatti?"

"I checked with Emergency Services. An ambulance took her to the E.R. at CarePoint. They say she was discharged the same night. That's all I know. If she's planning to arrest you, it'll have to wait. It's DEFCON 4 around here. The fire department guys are going around helping people evacuate. The PD chiefs pulled all their cops off regular duties, and the plainclothes squads were ordered to turn out in uniform. They're even calling up retired officers to help with the emergency. So, Carla's either out on the street or home licking her wounds." He paused for a second. "What did you do to her anyway?"

"I'll tell you when I see you."

"That won't be today. Probably not tomorrow either if this turns out to be as bad as they're saying. You know there's a six o'clock curfew, right?"

"Yes."

"That's less than two hours away! If you're thinking about going to a shelter, decide now, so I know where to find you if the phones go out. And remember, driving through this mess is going to be tough."

"I paid a neighbor to nail plywood over my big bay window. I've got shutters on the other ones. I'm staying."

"Okay. Be safe. I'll call you later if I can."

"Thanks, Robert."

Lucy pocketed her cell phone and climbed the stairs to the one small hallway window she'd left unshuttered. Flashes of lightning sped across the sky, thunder peeled and echoed, and all nature seemed to be in thrall of the rising tumult. Visibility was shrinking, but through the sweeping gusts of rain she could just make out the shoreline of Bergen Reach. The waters beyond were pitching and churning, but they remained constrained by the riprap barrier that divided the ship channel from the patchy lawns of Collins Park.

She felt Kevin take her hand. He stood silently at her side as they watched the violent winds torture the trees across from their house. Since they'd risen that morning, Kevin had been even quieter than usual. He had stuck close to her, no matter what her activity—sitting quietly at the kitchen table while she prepared their breakfast, waiting on her bed while she showered, nestling close by her side while they watched storm bulletins on TV. Just before noon, they'd walked through the neighborhood together, leaning into the wind gusts, talking with a few neighbors about their plans, and watching while some piled precautionary sandbags in front of ground-level basement windows.

By 5:20, the winds were ramping higher, vibrating the walls of the house and pounding on her doors and windows. Her landline phone rang, jangling her nerves. She picked up to hear a recorded message from the mayor:

"Your home lies south of Third Street and is vulnerable to flooding. I urge you to relocate your family and your vehicles to higher ground."

The mayor rattled off the addresses of the emergency shelters.

"Our hardworking responders are not going to endanger their lives to help you get out later, so please evacuate now!"

Nice of you to call before six, Lucy thought darkly. But when she returned to the upstairs window and saw walls of water flooding into the waterfront park's ball diamond, and flying blotches of sea foam racing toward the roadway below, she realized the curfew might be the least of her worries. Yes, this might be a Cat-1 storm, routine for a born Floridian, but it was starting to look like more than the Garden State was ready to handle. Cursing her stupidity, she strode to her bedroom, grabbed a travel bag from her closet, and started packing clothes.

Kevin appeared in her doorway.

"Mommy?"

"Honey, just go into your room and bring me some clean clothes, okay? Underpants, socks, everything to wear for a couple of days. And bring your toothbrush."

"Where are we going?"

"To school."

"You said it was closed."

"It's open for people who don't want to stay in their houses during the storm. We can sleep there tonight. Some of your friends might be there, so at least you'll have someone to play with."

Kevin stood for a second, processing what his mother had said. Then he wheeled and ran to his room.

They had just finished packing when they heard the pounding. It wasn't the wind this time.

There was someone at the front door.

Lucy had already closed the last set of shutters on the last window, so she couldn't look out. But then she remembered what Robert had told her . . . that the fire department was going around, helping people evacuate.

"That's probably the fire department," she said to Kevin. "They're checking to make sure everybody's okay." The boy's eyes lit up and he raced ahead of Lucy down the stairs. He was reaching for the door handle when she caught up with him.

Lucy had a sudden flash—a vision of would-be looters going door to door. She stopped him.

"Just a minute. Let me look."

She put her eye to the peephole.

Ernie Tait stood on her porch, leaning into the wind, disheveled and uncomfortable. He was dressed in full police uniform.

They're even calling up retired cops . . .

Lucy opened the door, smiling with surprise.

"Ernie? They called you out?"

"Yeah. No retirement for the wicked!" A gust of wind nearly pulled him off balance. "Can I come in?"

She let him in quickly and he helped her shove the door shut.

Kevin backed away, staring up at Tait with widening eyes.

"Came to check on you. Knew you were alone with the youngster." He looked down at Kevin. "Hello, young fella. I'm Ernie."

"I know," Kevin said.

"Really? Smart kid."

Lucy led him into the living room. He spotted the travel bag on the floor at the bottom of the stairs. "Heading to a shelter?"

"We were just leaving. What's the driving like? Is the way clear to Oresko School?"

"Pretty much. A few trees down. A few detours. More expected." He looked up at the ceiling, listening. "Your house seems to be handling it okay. Why leave?"

In the wake of the mayor's message, the comment struck Lucy as odd.

"Didn't they brief you?"

"What do you mean?"

"The park across the road is starting to flood, and we had a robo-call from the mayor, saying we need to get out now. He said if we flood, no one is coming to save us. Kind of a heartless message, actually, but probably smart."

"Hmmh. Didn't hear about that."

Lucy felt Kevin's hand slip into hers. The boy was standing next to her, but slightly behind, watching and listening.

Lucy was puzzled. "You're an emergency responder and you don't know about the evacuation call?"

"Came straight here."

"Why?"

"Heard you're still trying to clear Jack's name."

Lucy felt a jolt behind her eyes. She felt Kevin's little fingers close like a claw around hers. She felt him tugging her, urging her to back away.

"What's that got to do with—?"

"LUCE!" Kevin yelled. "RUN!"

28

Tait grabbed for Lucy, but missed. She sprinted for the back bedroom, with Kevin streaking ahead. The boy was moving faster than she'd ever seen him move before. They piled through the doorway just in time for Lucy to slam and lock the door behind them. Tait's heavy footsteps arrived outside a second later.

BOOM!

Solid core woodwork cracked under Tait's violent kick.

While Kevin tried to unlock the sliding door, Lucy cast about for something to use as a weapon.

Something! Anything!

BOOM!

The door exploded inward, carrying part of the door frame with it.

Lucy rushed to Kevin, whose small fingers were still struggling with the latch. Before she could help, strong hands seized her and threw her across the room. She smashed into the closet door, knocking it off its tracks. She slid to the floor, her head swimming.

Her son, more Jack than Kevin, leapt to defend her—an impossible task, even with the skills and knowledge of his long-dead father. Tait grabbed the boy, thumped him onto the chair at the desk, and held his small, squirming form in place with a meaty hand.

Lucy pulled herself into a sitting position next to the ruined closet door.

Tait had his gun out. He pointed it at her.

"Got a little project for you. How are you with knots?"

Lucy felt her consciousness transform. She felt the same cold clarity that had saved her from her bumbling abductors in Stephen Gregg Park. The same bloodless determination that had propelled her through Carla Scarlatti's front door.

This time it wasn't just about her. This time she had Kevin to protect.

She already had a plan, but it required extreme care.

Outside, the wind shrieked like an enraged banshee. The house seemed to shudder on its foundations.

Lucy looked up at her assailant.

"So, Tait. You and Carla, huh?"

Kevin stopped struggling against Tait's grip. Lucy realized he was trying to listen.

"I know who killed Jack," Lucy continued. "Which one of you killed Parrish? You, I'm guessing."

Tait ignored her. He pulled a length of thick cord out of the pocket of his tunic.

Lucy felt her heart contract.

Think!

Forcing herself to sound calm, she said, "Whatever you're planning, you're too late. The prosecutor's office already has all the evidence."

Tait looked unconcerned. "Evidence is useless without witnesses. You wouldn't have paid that little visit to Scarlatti if you'd found anything with her name on it. Or mine. You were fishing."

Kevin caught Lucy's eye. He had his free hand on the handle of a desk drawer, and he was inching it open.

Lucy suddenly remembered what was in that drawer.

It was something Jack had given her.

She couldn't believe the boy's coolness.

She spoke quickly, trying to keep Tait's attention locked on her. "Don't be so sure. I gave them a nice little tape recording of Scarlatti admitting she killed Jack."

"Doubt that. Woman's tough."

"You weren't there when I had her handcuffed to the stove."

"She told me. If you'd taped her confessing, she'd already be in custody."

"How do you know she isn't?"

"Because I just talked to her."

Kevin's little hand slid into the drawer.

Lucy kept the pressure on. "You're way out on a limb here, Ernie. You should be running. Maybe you can make it to Mexico before they come for you."

"I can buy a lot more time than that."

"How?"

"It's pretty simple. You were so screwed up, so obsessed about your dead husband, you finally unraveled. Lost it. Started dreaming up crazy stories about left-handed killers, and bumper stickers, and weird company names. Your son was a constant reminder of your dead husband. You'd smothered his development and screwed him up so bad the poor kid thought he *was* your dead husband."

"You sick bastard! *You* killed Clooney!"

"Only after he told us why he was seeing your kid. Some voodoo reincarnation shit. When Scarlatti conducts a second search of Clooney's office later this week, she's going to find an uncompleted referral form."

Kevin's hand came back into view.

"What referral?" Lucy asked vaguely, her mind focused on her son's careful movements.

"The one from Clooney to the Hudson South Child Protection Of-

fice, stating that in his professional opinion, Lucinda Hendricks is an un-
fit mother who is psychologically damaging her vulnerable child."

Lucy could see where this was going. "How's Scarlatti going to explain missing such a key piece of evidence on her first search?"

Tait ignored the question. He resumed his mocking narrative. "You
were so completely deranged after Clooney told you he was going to turn
you in that you killed him and dumped his body in the same place Jack's
was found. That spot had become some kind of weird shrine for you. But
you weren't finished. Next, you stalked and assaulted Scarlatti, the detective who had investigated Jack's activities after his death, and was now
investigating you for the murder of your kid's psychiatrist."

Kevin was holding an object that looked like a lipstick container.

Only it wasn't.

Lucy shifted slightly. The opening into the closet created by the
ruined closet door was now next to her hand.

Tait didn't react to her movement. He was too busy enjoying his story.
"It was too much for you. After you attacked the poor cop in her own
home, you knew you were going to jail. You knew you would lose your
kid permanently. In your demented state, you saw only one way out." He
held up the length of cord. "You strangled your kid, and hanged yourself."

"Hey, Tait!" Kevin called.

Tait turned, and five-year-old Kevin Hendricks, aka Jack Hendricks,
gave his old partner a face full of *oleoresin capsicum.*

Otherwise known as mace.

Tait roared. He swatted at Kevin. Too late. The boy was already off
the chair and scampering for his mother.

Lucy jumped into a crouch, spun, and grabbed the unsheathed dive
knife that still lay next to the boxes of dive gear after all these months.

Kevin arrived at her side. They locked eyes. He nodded.

BOOM!

A bullet whipcracked past Lucy's face and blew a hole in the back wall of the closet. The still-bellowing Tait had fired blindly, wildly, obviously hoping to terminate her existence before they could get away. Lucy flung herself across the space between them and plunged the knife into the brute's thick throat . . . once, twice, three times. As he staggered back, she thrust the blade with all the force she could muster deep into his chest.

The ex-cop coughed, spraying blood. He dropped the gun. Kevin darted past Lucy and kicked it away. Tait sank wheezing to his knees, blood pumping, and then toppled to the floor.

Together, mother and son stood over his body as it lay twitching in an expanding pool of blood.

Lucy looked at Kevin's face, expecting to see utter horror.

But in that second, behind the face of her little boy, lay the face of a man.

A man, saddened but resigned.

A man who had done his duty.

The storm was getting worse, and now they were hearing the gurgle and slosh of agitated water. Kevin, suddenly a boy again, darted to the sliding door and struggled to open it.

"No, Kevin! Wait!"

The boy rolled back the door and scuttled out onto the patio.

Lucy started to follow but then, tense with premonition, she turned back to scoop Tait's gun off the floor. She stumbled out of the house, into the tumult, seconds behind her son. The winds howled, rain lashed at her, and she tasted salt spray on her lips.

Kevin! Where . . . ?

The boy was nowhere to be seen.

"KEVIN?" she screamed.

"He's over here!"

A woman's voice, barely audible over the fury of the storm.

Lucy wheeled to her right, targeting the source of the sound.

Twenty feet away, Carla Scarlatti stood against the hedge at the end of Lucy's driveway. She was ankle-deep in water. She had one arm tight around Kevin's throat, and the muzzle of her Glock jammed against the boy's head. She screamed out: "TAIT! I'VE GOT THEM!"

"Tait's dead!" Lucy called back.

"Luce!" Kevin yelled. "She's the one!"

Lucy kept her voice calm. "How do you know, Kevin?"

"The smell!"

Lucy felt impenetrable coldness lock into place.

The sensation was familiar now, and stronger than ever.

Her mind swiftly analyzed what her eyes were seeing:

Scarlatti had her left arm around Kevin's throat. The wrist was heavily bandaged. It was the wrist Lucy had cuffed to the stove door.

She was holding her gun in her right hand.

Everything Jack had taught her on the PBA range came back. Everything he'd taught her about terminating a hostage-taker. She raised Tait's gun. She trained the foresight on a spot just above the sneering detective's upper lip.

Her hands were steady.

Scarlatti looked disbelieving. "You'll risk your own son?"

"LET HIM GO!"

"I don't think so!"

A single shot rang out . . . and Carla Scarlatti's head exploded. The woman's body flew into the hedge, and Kevin fell sprawling into the rising waters. As Lucy rushed toward him, a man appeared out of the darkness of the driveway.

The man was holding a huge revolver.

He lifted the boy to his feet.

Lucy recognized him. He was one of the men who had tried to abduct her in Stephen Gregg Park.

The one who had held her down in the back seat.

The one she had sprayed in the face.

She pointed Tait's gun at the man's head. "I'm a very good shot," she said calmly.

A familiar voice startled her from behind. "You don't need that, Lucy. Kevin is safe."

Dominic Lanza appeared at her side.

"You knew this? You knew she was coming?"

"I guessed. Sorry we got here a little late. Had to avoid a couple of roadblocks." Gently, he removed Tait's gun from Lucy's grip. The other man set Kevin on his feet on the patio. Water streamed off the boy as he hugged his mother's leg, but he remained stoic and silent, watching and listening.

"Name's Bernardo, lady," the gunman said. "Pleased to properly meet you." He added, "That's a brave boy you got there."

Lucy glanced at Dominic. "You said you'd dealt with this man."

"Bernardo did his penance. But we needed him. Like you, he's a very good shot."

"Then I guess I'm glad I didn't blind you."

Bernardo grinned. "Me too."

The moaning wind gusts were whipping their words away.

"This area is nearly cut off by flooding. Take your boy and head north. The cops are using boats and jet skis to evacuate people. They'll take care of you."

"I've got a bag packed. It's by the stairs."

"I'll get it." Bernardo ducked inside.

Lucy gestured at the doorway. "Tait's in there."

"What's his condition?"

"Dead."

"You?"

"Kevin helped."

Dominic tilted his head. "Can you deal with it?"

"You mean, guilt?"

"Yes."

"I took your advice and dealt with it in advance."

Admiration tugged at the corner of Dominic's mouth. He looked down at Kevin. He laid a gentle hand on the boy's head. "And . . . Kevin?"

"He was Jack, saving his wife. If he remembers at all, his conscience will be clear."

Dominic nodded. "We'll clean this up," he said. "The storm will do the rest."

"Clean up?"

"The cops are going house to house. How much explaining do you want to do about dead bodies on your property?"

"I don't."

"Then leave this to us."

Bernardo materialized with Lucy's travel bag. "There's a stiff in there, boss. A cop."

"You can thank our lady here."

Bernardo gaped at Lucy. "You're one tough lady."

"I'm a mother."

The water level was still rising. Lucy figured her basement was already flooded. She slung the travel bag on her shoulder and grasped Kevin by the hand. She faced Dominic. "The money my father used to buy the bar . . . that came from the family, didn't it?"

Dominic's nod was almost imperceptible. "Go now."

"How will you get out? You said the police are using boats."

"That's not everywhere. We've got a Hummer. We'll make it."

Lucy glanced at Scarlatti's body, hung up like a rag doll in the hedge. "What about their car?"

At that second, they were interrupted by the sound of wading feet, and Carlo appeared out of the darkness of Lucy's garden. He nodded politely to her and said, "Evening," as if cleaning up murder scenes for schoolteachers and their little boys in the teeth of a hurricane was just another day in the working life of a mobster. He addressed Dominic: "We found an unmarked cop car parked down the street. Jimmy hotwired it and he'll dump it somewhere up off Four-forty. Just in time, boss. Water out front's getting too high to drive through. I moved the Hummer to the back lane. We need to move fast."

Dominic squeezed Lucy's arm. "Leave this to us. You need to go. Carlo, go with her so she's on the right track. When you see the cops, come back."

Carlo lifted Kevin into his arms, and he and Lucy set out into the raging night.

Dominic called out after her. "When the storm's over, come and see me."

She turned. "I still don't get it! You were safe! Why all this? Why all this for me?"

"Not just for you, dear Lucy. For your father."

PART
III

CASTIGO

29

On the fifth day after the storm, Olivetti showed up at Nicholas Oresko School. He'd heard reports that because 60 percent of Bayonne still didn't have power, and nighttime temperatures were dipping into the teens, several hundred people were still using the school as a makeshift shelter.

The reports had been right.

He threaded his way along malodorous hallways, past throngs of morose adults and wailing children, and eventually found Lucy's classroom. Its entire floor space had been converted into a dormitory, complete with rows of army-style cots and improvised privacy screens. Despite cheerful wall decorations and whiteboard notices to students that pre-dated the storm, the pervasive atmosphere in the room was one of gloomy exhaustion.

He found Lucy sitting on a cot, folding clothes and tucking them into a travel bag. Her response to his eager hug was not quite as heartfelt as he clearly had hoped.

"I'm sorry I couldn't get over here sooner! Too many blocked roads and too many Sandy issues! We're down to half-staff at the office, and I'm up to my neck in looter files."

Lucy sincerely wanted to soften her response. She would have liked nothing better than to throw her arms around Robert's neck and just surrender to the feeling of relief. But there was no way around what she now had to face.

There was no way around the lying.

"It's okay, Robert. Kevin and I were fine."

First lie

"I tried to call you, but it kept going straight to voice mail! I don't get it—the phones were only out for a day."

"I lost my cell when Kevin and I were wading through the flood."

Second lie

"Wading? You left it that late? What about your car? What happened?"

"The car got swamped." Lucy quickly edited the truth. "The wind wasn't a problem, and I was keeping an eye on the park. But when the surge came over the seawall, the water rose so fast it caught me off guard. I realized we had to get out of there, so we escaped out the back and headed north. We made it up past Second, but then we got cut off by another part of the flooding. Luckily, two officers in a boat found us."

"Have you been back to your house?"

"No. We're going there now. The police are using a DARE van to drive people home."

"I heard the power's still out down there."

"My contractor says I can use his generator."

"Contractor? It hasn't even been a week! How could you get a contractor so fast?"

"The insurance company arranged it."

Third lie

Olivetti stared at her in disbelief. "You haven't even seen the damage and you filed a claim?"

"The adjuster's a friend," Lucy replied smoothly. "He picked up my keys yesterday, and he and the contractor went down there together."

Fourth lie

"How did you get hold of him?"

"One of the other teachers let me use her phone."

Fifth lie

"You might have called me."

"I've been a bit busy around here. They elected me dorm mother."

"I'll take you home. There's something we need to discuss."

"There'll be roadblocks."

"This is Hudson County. They'll let me through. Where's Kevin?"

"Playing in the gym."

The ride down Avenue E was reasonably clear—some downed trees, crushed fences, and a few shattered business signs blocking sidewalks. The most disturbing sight was a blocks-long lineup of people carrying five-gallon gas cans, waiting their turns at the pumps of a crowded gas station.

When they reached the intersection at Broadway and turned south, the scene began to look more and more like a war zone.

"Mommy, look at that!" Kevin was sitting in the back, with his face pressed to the window. Outside, two men were using chain saws to dismember an uprooted oak that lay across a flattened car.

When they reached First Street and turned west, they ran straight into a BPD roadblock.

"Road's in bad shape up ahead," the officer said. "And we've had some looting. We're only letting residents in."

Robert showed his ID and explained he was taking Lucy and her son to their house.

"I'll need to see some ID, ma'am. Something with your address on it."

Lucy gave him her driver's license.

The cop stared at it. "Hendricks? So that's your place?"

"What do you mean?"

"Don't know how you worked it, ma'am, but your house is the only one down here that's got a full crew working on it."

Lucy didn't reply.

The cop handed back her license and waved them through.

It was only another half-mile to the house, but the trip took them nearly ten minutes. The entire stretch was an obstacle course of marine flotsam, splintered wood decking, twisted roof guttering, and torn-up sections of pavement cordoned off by police tape.

Lucy's front yard was a huge mess—yawning gaps in her hedges, tangles of rope and marine buoys hanging in the lower branches of her red oak, and scores of sun-bleached plastic containers strewn across the lawn. There were two vans parked in the driveway and a pickup straddling the sidewalk in front.

"Where's your car?" Olivetti asked.

"They took it away. It's being dried out and repaired at a shop in Newark."

Olivetti just shook his head. He parked near the pickup and they all got out. The harsh sound of a heavy-duty generator assaulted their ears.

Olivetti strode to the pickup and studied the sign on its passenger door.

PERGUSA CONSTRUCTION LTD
"Building Your Tomorrow"

"Do you know who owns this company?"

Lucy feigned surprise. "No."

Sixth lie

"I do. The word is, they're connected."

"Oh, Robert! Not you, too!"

"What do you mean?"

Lucy needed to head this off with a little show of temper. "That was the standard accusation all through the investigation of Jack's murder! This is New Jersey, Robert! Everybody's connected! I don't care who owns this company! All I know is they're fixing my house!" She slung her travel bag over her shoulder. "Thanks for the ride." She clasped her wide-eyed son by the hand and started up the driveway.

Olivetti hurried after her. "I'm sorry, Lucy, but it's more than that! I've seen an intelligence report that said Dominic Lanza owns Pergusa Construction."

Lucy pretended to ponder his words. "So, you're saying that some people might think Scarlatti is right . . . that Jack was involved with that family, and now I am."

"Yes. It could make life difficult for you—all over again."

Lucy pursed her lips. "Well, you know what? My life's been difficult for years, and I'm pretty much sick of it. I have a house that needs repairs and a son to raise, so, I'm sorry Robert, but I don't give a shit anymore about what people think!"

"Mommy, you said a bad word!"

"Sorry, honey."

"Like it or not," Olivetti replied, "that takes us to the thing I wanted to talk to you about."

At that moment, a short man wearing coveralls and athletic shoes appeared from behind the house. He strolled toward them.

"It'll have to wait. Hi, Joe!"

"Mrs. Hendricks! Perfect timing!"

"You said the upstairs was okay, so I decided to move back."

"That's no problem, so long as you don't mind the noise." He wiped a grubby palm on his pant leg and held out his hand to Olivetti. "Joseph Tomasi."

"Robert Olivetti." They shook. "Tomasi? That name sounds familiar."

"You're probably thinking of Giuseppe Tomasi. Famous dago author. No relation, far as I know." He turned to Lucy. "The basement's pretty bad. We're stripping out the wall board and the tiling. Once everything is dry and we're sure there's no mold, we'll get the wiring checked and then replace everything. The washer and dryer are toast, but luckily you didn't have much personal stuff down there. We piled what we found on the patio. There isn't much worth saving, but I thought you'd want to go through it."

"Thanks. What about the main floor?" The spreading pool of Tait's blood was burned into her memory.

"Not too bad. Luckily your place sits a bit higher than some of the neighbors' houses. Looks like the main floor only got an inch or two of water. We'll need to replace the baseboards and maybe some of the flooring. We pulled out the living room carpeting and also"—he casually caught Lucy's eye—"that area rug in the back bedroom, and hauled them to the dump. We've just finished moving all the furniture into the living room, along with everything from your closets. We'll work on that room last."

"That's fast work, Joe! I'm really grateful for what you've done."

"Well, you were first in line. From the look of the job orders that are coming in now, we'll be working flat out until next spring." He grinned. "C'mon, I'll give you the grand tour."

It was several hours before Olivetti was finally able to get Lucy alone. Just the fact that he'd hung around all day, when there seemed to be no reason for him to do so, confirmed to her that he had something serious to discuss. She kidded herself that he just wanted to declare himself—just wanted to get back where they had been as . . . well, a sort-of couple. But her heightened senses told her it wasn't just that. That might be part of it, but there was something else.

Something to be dreaded.

She put him off as long as she could. All the lying was exhausting. She was trying to build up her strength, because she knew she'd soon be forced to lie some more.

Kevin, on the other hand, had proved himself. Not once did he mention recent events. Not once did he drop the slightest hint that he'd been witness to more violence in a single hour than most people saw in a lifetime.

As soon as cell service had been restored after the storm, Lucy had called Ricki to assure her that she and Kevin were safe. As it happened, Ricki and Jeff were visiting her father. When Ricki passed the phone to Joseph, the first words out of his mouth were:

"Lucinda! Are you taking care of that boy?"

"No, Dad."

"What?"

"I think he's taking care of me."

She didn't offer to explain.

Kevin was an enigma, and Lucy was profoundly thankful for that.

When the boy wasn't trailing the workmen around the basement, where they pretended to allow him to help out, or sharing treats they produced from their gigantic lunchboxes, Lucy kept him busy with games in his room. While she picked through the sodden contents of the boxes, suitcases, and trunks that she'd stored in the basement—eventually electing to assign the whole works to the landfill—Olivetti busied himself cleaning up the front yard. At the end of the day, after Tomasi and his men had left for the night, Olivetti went on a foraging expedition, located an enterprising Chinese takeout joint that had already reopened, and returned to the house with a hot supper.

Before Tomasi left, he'd connected the generator to the fuse box and set it to provide lights on the top floor. Lucy and Olivetti carried the kitchen dinette set upstairs and ate the evening meal in Lucy's bedroom. Kevin, exhausted from his long day, barely touched his food. After he nodded off in his chair, Lucy carried him to his room and tucked him into bed.

When she returned to her bedroom, Olivetti was gone.

While she puzzled over his absence, she heard him on the stairs. He reappeared, carrying a bottle of wine, a corkscrew, and a pair of Lucy's crystal glasses.

"I had a bottle in my car," he said.

"How convenient."

He popped the cork and poured. He passed Lucy her glass. She knew the moment had arrived. She settled back and waited.

Olivetti wasted no time.

"I need you to explain something."

"I suppose you mean my call the other night."

"You talked about the FBI. You said you were going to be arrested again. You wanted me to listen to a recording. And then you said you'd put Carla Scarlatti in the hospital."

"I went to her house. I accused her of killing Jack. She told me I'd never prove it. She didn't know I was recording her."

"Just a minute! *You accused Carla of killing Jack?*"

"Yes. And here's the thing: She didn't deny it. She just said, quote: 'You'll never fucking prove that!'"

"Lucy, you're going to have to do better than that if the Jersey City cops come to talk to you."

Lucy felt her throat constrict. "Why? Did she file a complaint against me?"

"No. If she planned to, she didn't have time."

"What do you mean?"

Olivetti took a swallow of wine. He set down his glass. "Because she's dead. Murdered."

"What!" Lucy didn't have to fake her reaction, because she was shocked that Olivetti already knew that Carla was dead.

Dominic! You said you'd clean things up!

She tried to sound deeply concerned. "God, Robert! What happened?"

"She showed up for emergency duty on the night of the storm. A few hours later she dropped out of contact. The next morning, the manager of Best Buy in Newport Plaza arrived at the store and found the front door smashed in. Carla's body was lying just inside. She'd been shot in the head. It looked like she'd tried to stop some looters."

So . . . you did clean things up.

She let Olivetti's expectant silence tick over for a few seconds before responding.

"What are you saying? Someone thinks *I* killed her?"

"Of course not!"

"Then, if she didn't file a report against me, why would Jersey City want to talk to me?"

"Her captain knows she was looking at you in that prof's murder. It's logical to expect that a detective will pay you a visit, if only to eliminate you as a suspect."

"Eliminate me." Lucy pretended to be thoughtful. "Can they pinpoint when she was she killed?"

"The M.E. says sometime between eight and midnight on the night of the storm. He also says the body had been moved. Carla was shot somewhere else, and then dumped in the store."

"Maybe in the parking lot outside?"

"Maybe. But the forensic team didn't find any sign of that."

"It rained all night!"

"Accepted."

"What about security cameras?" Her question was pro forma. She already knew the answer.

"Power was out. No juice, no cameras."

"So . . . me, a suspect. How would that work?"

"I didn't say you'd be a suspect. I just said you might get a visit. Even if Carla didn't open a file, she might have mentioned your little . . . encounter . . . to someone."

"Well, let me clear up your doubts, since you seem to have a few. I was here in this house with Kevin, and my car was sitting in four feet of water; in other words, it was inoperable. And there are two Bayonne cops who can confirm that they rescued us just a few blocks from here—a Sergeant named Lewis and a patrol officer named Laidlaw."

"What time was that?"

"Sometime between seven and eight, I think. The police will have a record of it."

"I'll check on the Jersey City investigation. I'll make sure they know that."

"Thanks. But just so you and I are clear, the fact that Scarlatti didn't arrange to have me arrested the minute she got out of the hospital tells me I was right about her. So, sorry, but if some lowlife looter put a bullet in her, that's justice."

"That sounds pretty cold, Lucy."

"Killing Jack was cold."

Olivetti swirled his wine, staring into the glass. "How do you know it was her? I mean, how could you possibly be sure of that?"

"You had to be there. I disarmed her, then I—"

"You disarmed her?" Olivetti looked incredulous. "Start at the beginning. Walk me through it."

Olivetti went a bit pale when Lucy reminded him that he was the one who'd told her where Scarlatti lived. During her outraged call to him after she'd found out about his affair with the cop, he'd mentioned that she lived in The Heights. She explained how she'd learned what shift she was working, and then waited for her to come home. When she recounted how she'd relieved Carla of her weapon and shoved the woman on her face, she detected a new level of respect on Olivetti's expression.

"I handcuffed her to her stove. I told her I knew she'd killed Jack. She didn't even bother to deny it—she just said I'd never prove it. I lost it and clocked her so hard with the gun that for a minute I thought I *had* killed her."

"That's all you've got? Just her saying you couldn't prove it?"

"It wasn't what she said, it was the way she said it. I could see it in her eyes."

"That's subjective. It's not the kind of evidence a jury would buy."

"What jury? You just said she's dead."

"I want to hear that recording."

"It's gone. It was on my phone."

Lying, lying . . .

"You must have had something on her!" Olivetti responded, exasperated. "You wouldn't have taken such a radical step if you didn't! I mean, why would Carla Scarlatti, a Jersey City cop, kill your husband, a Bayonne cop? It makes no sense!"

"I suppose I'll never know for sure, but I'm guessing she was involved in that car theft ring Jack was investigating."

"That's not a guess at all, is it, Lucy? You found something! Something that made you focus on her."

Lucy chewed her lip. She decided Robert deserved one more thing. One more thing that could never be accepted as admissible evidence.

Something that would end the discussion.

"It was Kevin."

"Kevin? You mean one of his—?"

"Yes. He remembered something. He went into one of those . . . trances. His voice changed. He sounded like Jack. He told me his killer was a woman. And that she was left-handed."

"Let me get this straight. You went after Carla Scarlatti because your son told you his father was killed by a left-handed woman."

"Because of that . . . and one other thing."

"What other thing?"

"You remember the physical evidence at the scene, and Jack's injuries? They showed that he was crushed against the wall of the garage by a vehicle."

"That's right."

"If you check, you'll find that Carla Scarlatti drives a 2005 Ford Explorer." Lucy embellished. "Even though Kevin has never seen her Explorer, he described a sticker on the bumper of the vehicle that killed him. It must have been the last thing Jack saw before he died." She paused for effect. "The same sticker is still on the bumper of Carla Scarlatti's Explorer."

Olivetti must have been holding his breath, because he suddenly expelled air. He sat there, staring at her. "So . . . no *real* evidence."

"Maybe no real evidence, but it was enough for me. Why else would that woman spend years trying to discredit Jack and harassing me? Because she was the one Jack was investigating! And because she's the one who killed him!"

Olivetti looked visibly disturbed. He was an intelligent man, and Lucy guessed that he sensed he wasn't hearing the whole story. That Lucy knew much more than she was revealing. Unless she was mistaken, Robert Olivetti had suddenly realized that his emotions were about to run head-to-head into his conscience.

Good for you, Robert. I can't afford to go there anymore.

There was one other thing she'd decided not to mention. A few hours after their arrival at the house, she'd noticed that her laptop was missing. She'd forgotten to pack it on the night Sandy hit. She doubted that any of Tomasi's men had stolen it. She wondered if Dominic had taken it. He knew she'd kept a copy of Jack's flash drive on her computer.

Not that it mattered anymore.

She sighed, and put voice to that final thought. "None of this matters anymore. I'm putting an end to it."

"Putting an end to what?"

"Everything. After this house is fixed up, it's going on the market. Kevin and I are moving back to Florida. I should never have come back here. If I'm going to have to face hurricanes, I might as well be close to my family."

"You're starting a new life."

"It's long overdue."

"Lucy . . ."

"Yes?"

"I'd like to be part of it."

Silence. Something inside Lucy softened.

Then melted.

"You're serious?"

"Yes, I am."

"Are you prepared to start small?"

"I am." His gaze drifted past her. "Is that bed small enough?"

Lucy thought about that. "Maybe. But I need a shower."

"So do I."

"There's no hot water."

"Cold shower, huh? You really do want me to start small."

Lucy smiled. "I guess I'll just have to work harder."

She was still smiling when they rolled into bed.

30

Robert Olivetti's apartment building on Beacon Way had all the cool amenities—gym, pool, Green Mountain coffee bar . . . even a billiard room. He utilized none of them. He went to work, came home, and kept carefully to himself in his two-bedroom loft. He seldom entertained guests, and even Lucy had never visited.

Twenty-four hours after the meal in Lucy's bedroom and the overnight romp in her bed, Olivetti prepared his solitary supper and sat down to eat.

To eat, and to think.

He'd left early, before Kevin woke up, telling Lucy he had to get cleaned up and attend Carla Scarlatti's funeral. Despite the ongoing disorder in the wake of Hurricane Sandy, the authorities had managed to put together a suitably solemn ceremony, complete with honor guard, emotional speeches, "Taps" at the conclusion of the Mass, and a posthumous medal of honor for the slain detective. As the attendees filed out of St. Aloysius Church, Olivetti had deliberately buried himself in the thick of the crowd, and then made himself scarce. There were more than a few members of Carla Scarlatti's family who would not have appreciated his presence at graveside.

The eerily female countertenor voice of Max Emanuel Cenčić filled his apartment. The Croatian artist was singing Policare's aria from *Tigrane*. The opera had been one of Carla's favorites. Olivetti had decided that listening to it in private was the single personal gesture he would allow himself in his ex-lover's memory.

Listening to the opera also helped him to think.

A lot of things just didn't add up. Carla's assigned police vehicle had been found behind a discount carpet warehouse, just off Route 440 in Greenville, five miles from the Best Buy where her body was found. The car's interior was clean—too clean, the forensic guy had commented, since not even Carla's prints had been found. The unit had been hotwired, so the current theory was that the perp, or perps, had shot Carla near Best Buy and then used her car to transport their stolen goods.

Kill a cop for a few dozen laptops and a flat-screen TV? It didn't make sense. And why hotwire her cruiser? Why not just take the keys off her body?

And then . . . there was this latest bit of news.

He'd decided to tell Lucy about it, just to gauge her reaction.

He knew Lucy had her secrets.

She didn't suspect that he'd already figured some of them out.

His gaze drifted across the dining area, to the chair where he'd hung his coat . . .

And to Lucy's laptop computer lying on the seat.

He picked up the file folder that lay on the table near his elbow. He'd always had a sixth sense about these things, and it had served him well. This time, there had simply been too many coincidences.

Dominic Lanza
Joseph Cappelli

Lucinda Cappelli

Lucy Hendricks

It was all in the file.

He needed to get back to his office.

There was work to be done.

31

"So when's the move?"

"Over Christmas. We're going back to my sister's place until my house sells."

Olivetti and Lucy were among a handful of customers sitting in the friendly gloom of one of the few restaurants in the Ironbound district of Newark that had reopened.

"What about a job?"

"I'm certified in Florida, but it might take a while to find a permanent position. I have no interest in substitute teaching all over Miami, so I'll wait till something comes up. My principal is pretty upset that I'm leaving, but he said he'd give me a good reference. In the meantime, I'll help Erica run the Bronte. It'll be nice to take a break. I love my students, but some of their parents are pretty exhausting."

"The Bronte?"

"My dad's bar in Coconut Grove. I thought I'd told you about it."

"Maybe you did. Guess it didn't register. Strange name."

"It started out as just a bar, but now it's a pretty popular restaurant as well. He named it after the town where his mother was born."

"Oh . . . that Bronte. Near Mount Etna."

"Very good. Not many people know that."

"My dad was Sicilian."

"You said he died when you were four."

"He did. But when I got older, I took an interest in the place."

Their meal arrived.

After the waiter left, Olivetti asked, "Will your family object if I come for a visit?"

"You mean, to Florida?"

He nodded.

"Do you mean that?"

"Yes!" He reached across and covered her hand with his. "I want to keep seeing you. If you'll let me."

Lucy took a breath, then smiled. "I think I'd like that."

They dined in companionable silence. After a few minutes, Olivetti rested his fork, sipped his wine, and casually asked, "Do you remember Ernie Tait?"

Only because Lucy was in the very act of swallowing a mouthful of food was she able to cover her shock.

Don't tell me . . . !

"Of course. Why?"

"Have you seen him since he retired from the police?"

Dominic! Where did you dump him?

"No." Lucy decided a bit of extra fabrication might help. "He called me once, after I moved back here. Said he'd seen that creepy article about me in the *Star Ledger*. He just wanted to tell me he'd never believed any of that stuff about Jack, and that I could call him if I ever needed help. We were going to meet for lunch sometime, but it never happened." She tried to look suitably puzzled. "Why are you asking?"

"He's disappeared."

"What do you mean, disappeared?"

"Just that. He showed up at BPD headquarters the afternoon before

Sandy hit. He said he knew they'd be shorthanded and offered to help out. The chief was happy to have him. He was deputized and sent out in uniform. They offered him a ride-along with one of the younger guys, but he said he'd be happy to just walk the old streets, checking doors, watching for looters. So they gave him a radio and off he went." His eyes locked on Lucy's. "The thing is, he hasn't been seen since."

Thank you, Dominic . . .

"A police officer, in uniform, just vanishes? The storm was over a week ago. Why hasn't it been on the news?"

"His wife was staying with her brother three states away. With the power out and the phones down, she figured she'd hear from him when he got a chance to call. Things were pretty chaotic after the storm, so I guess it took a few days before people started asking questions."

Lucy couldn't think of a response, so she said nothing.

Olivetti continued. "Carla Scarlatti and Ernie Tait. One killed, one missing . . . both on the same night. Makes you wonder, doesn't it?"

Lucy put down her fork. "Thanks, Robert!"

"For what?"

"For ruining a perfectly good meal."

32

The Bronte occupied the southwest corner of Main Highway and Commodore Plaza in Coconut Grove. Thanks to Giulia Cappelli's early vision and guidance, and Joseph's steady work, what began in the seventies as a déclassé hangout had been transformed by the nineties into a popular venue for locals and tourists alike. The place featured a magnificent hewn oak bar and two food service areas—an informal sidewalk café and a chic indoor dining room, complete with vintage French farmhouse furniture, rustic brickwork, and shelves lined with rare books and mysterious old ledgers held together with brown paper and twine. Due to Giulia's premature death in the late nineties, the burden of designing and implementing upgrades had fallen on Ricki's shoulders, but that endeavor had proved mostly futile. Depressed by the loss of his beloved wife, and later by his own ill health, Joseph had shown little interest in renovations aimed at staying "trendy," so Ricki's ideas had mostly fallen on deaf ears. Despite this, the Bronte remained popular, and when Lucy took up her part-time duties in early 2012, the family business was thriving.

Before she'd left Bayonne, in a moment of weakness and confusion, Lucy had made an attempt to contact Professor Jim Tucker, the director of the University of Virginia's Division of Perceptual Studies. Based on her earlier Internet research, and her conversation with Neil Clooney, she knew that Tucker was the world's leading scientific researcher into cases of children who recalled past lives.

When she called, she was told that Dr. Tucker was currently overseas, but after a brief conversation with the office manager, she was put through to Marcia Kershaw, a research psychiatrist who had recently joined the Division's staff. Based on Lucy's carefully edited version of Kevin's history of behavior—one that omitted any mention of its bloody aftermath—Dr. Kershaw was intrigued enough to suggest in-depth interviews with Lucy and Kevin.

"I would like to come as soon as possible, and bring a colleague. All expenses will be borne by the university. There will be no financial cost to you."

For obvious reasons, Lucy couldn't risk Kevin revealing too much, so she discouraged the suggestion with the excuse that she was too busy repairing her house after Hurricane Sandy, and getting ready for an impending move to Florida.

"Maybe in the spring," she suggested, with utter insincerity.

"They forget, you know," Dr. Kershaw said.

"What do you mean?"

"You said Kevin recently had his fifth birthday."

"Yes. In August."

"As these children become more firmly settled in their present lives, they almost invariably forget the past one. That usually happens by the age of five or six. Inevitably, they don't even remember speaking about an earlier life. To ensure the credibility of our research, it is important that we interview the child before that transition occurs. This way, in our later search for confirmation of facts that the child has imparted about his previous personality, our inquiries are based as closely as possible on the child's stated memories, rather than on his parents' recollections of what the child said."

"That sounds like a pitch you've given before."

The woman chuckled. "Yes, a few times." Her tone turned serious. "It's rare to come across a first-generation case like Kevin's, where the affected child carries the memories of his own deceased father, and spontaneously displays symptoms of injuries that contributed to his father's death."

"You're referring to the limp?"

"Yes! Mrs. Hendricks, we'd be very grateful if you'd permit us to investigate this case."

Lucy had already realized that her call had been a mistake and that she needed to end it. She allowed a few seconds to tick by, hoping to give the impression that she was genuinely considering Dr. Kershaw's request, and then she said, "All I can promise is that I'll contact you again after our move."

Two months later, she had not honored her promise, nor did she have any intention of doing so. While the experience with Kevin had shattered her own long-held perceptions of human existence, his memories had also been critical in solving Jack's murder. But that resolution had almost resulted in her and Kevin suffering an equally violent fate. With the blood of Neil Clooney, Ernie Tait, and Carla Scarlatti splattered across Kevin's paranormal wake, there was no possible way she would permit her son to become the focus of a scientific investigation.

And then there was the matter of Robert Olivetti . . .

Robert had already flown down twice from New Jersey. His first trip had been an abbreviated one, Friday to Monday. He'd booked into the Mayfair Hotel on Grand Avenue, a few blocks from the Bronte, tagged along good-naturedly with Lucy on Saturday when she took Kevin and Pauline on a long-promised airboat ride in the Everglades, and taken everyone out for dinner in Coral Gables on Sunday night. His quiet good looks and direct manner had disarmed the ever vigilant and suspicious Ricki, his courtroom anecdotes had immediately engaged Jeff's interest, and—most important—he'd been given the seal of approval by ever-precocious Pauline.

His second visit had lasted a week. Lucy had taken a few days off, entrusted Kevin to the care of Ricki and her live-in housekeeper, and she and Robert had driven upstate to Amelia Island. There they'd spent their days horseback riding on the beach, and their nights making love in a rustic cottage next to the ocean. Robert had originally suggested a trip down to Key West, but Lucy had demurred. She told him, a bit cryptically, that she'd been there too often. He was quick enough to divine the true reason for her reluctance, and didn't mention the idea again.

The only member of Lucy's immediate family that Robert Olivetti hadn't met was Lucy's father. That introduction was a step she wasn't ready to take. Although Lucy's dad had never been a demonstrative man, she knew he'd loved Jack like the son he'd never had. At some level, he'd related more closely to her husband, the man-of-action cop, than to Jeff, the cerebral attorney. To confront her father now, especially in his current state of health, with Jack's potential replacement seemed too much like a final step.

But in the deep of night, lying awake in her bed in Ricki and Jeff's guesthouse, Lucy knew there was another reason she hadn't introduced Robert to her father: She just wasn't sure about her feelings toward the man. With Jack, the connection had been almost instantaneous—a sudden burst of sunlight in her life that never diminished. As clichéd as it sounded, Lucy and Jack had completed each other. One of Lucy's girlfriends had once observed, jokingly, but with a tincture of wistful envy: "Just think . . . together you and Jack make a whole person."

Lucy's life with Jack had ended as abruptly as it had begun, and now she was being drawn into a relationship that seemed destined to develop in a decidedly different way. The attraction was different, because the experience was different. Robert presented her with a sort of artisanal variety of masculinity compared to Jack's full-blooded version. At times, it felt as if she and Robert were two people in an arranged marriage, reaching tentatively, almost experimentally, toward each other. Seeking common ground beyond atavistic lust or arctic loneliness. Seeking understanding, appreciation . . . and laughter.

Sometimes it felt like a growing love. They talked on the phone three or four times a week, and Lucy's heart beat a little faster when she saw Robert's name on the screen. Despite her doubts, she was looking forward to his next visit.

But she couldn't shake the memory of a quote from Proust that she'd read years before. Because of her durable relationship with Jack, she'd told herself at the time that the dictum had no application to her life. Despite that, she'd never forgotten the line: *"It is always thus, impelled by a state of mind which is destined not to last, that we make our irrevocable decisions."*

Her experience with Robert was very different from her experience with Jack. What if her state of mind was "destined not to last"?

There was also, of course, the small matter of *necessary lies.*

Fortuitously, but, as it turned out, grievously for Lucy, her son had already shown signs of forgetting his past life memories. In fact, it was almost as if Kevin—or Jack, as Lucy insisted on telling herself—had signaled the coming end.

Two weeks after their move south, Kevin had fleetingly manifested Jack's persona. As she dried him after a bath, he had told her, quite matter-of-factly, that he was sorry.

"Sorry for what, dear?"

"I'm sorry that we won't have time to go back to the Mir . . . Mira . . . mar."

Lucy flashed on her final vacation with Jack, at the Avenida Miramar in Key West. Tentatively, she asked, "Why won't we have time?"

His little fingers clutched her forearm. " 'Cause I think I'm going away soon. I'm sorry, Luce. I love you." The boy's eyes widened. "Oh, Mommy, I love you! I love you so much!"

He threw himself into her arms, weeping.

Luckily this incident had happened while they were alone, because she hadn't mentioned a word about Kevin's "condition" to Ricki and Jeff.

But now she had something else to grieve over in her solitary moments.

The final departure of Jack.

Even though her son's memories of her deceased husband had gone quiet, she was acutely aware of the fact that the dual investigations into Carla Scarlatti's murder and Ernie Tait's disappearance were ongoing. If some inconvenient piece of evidence happened to turn up, Robert might show up at her door with something more than romance on his mind.

In these circumstances, how could she ever imagine a committed, trusting relationship?

Then her phone rang, and it was him.

"Hey, beautiful!"

Hearing his voice, Lucy's qualms momentarily fled. "Hi. What's up?"

"I've just been invited to address a law enforcement conference in Coral Springs. It's at the Marriott from the eighth to the eleventh."

"How did you manage that?"

"It took a bit of maneuvering. Let's just say I have low friends in high places. Any chance we can get together while I'm there? I could tack on a few extra days."

"Like you need to ask? I'll talk to Ricki about my shifts. I'll have to tread carefully. I'm already living at her and Jeff's rent free."

"Any news on the job front?"

"Broward School District wants to interview me. I'm waiting for the e-mail with date and time."

"Good sign. Listen, I'm heading for court now, but I wanted to let you know about the conference right away since it's only a week away. I miss you, Lucy."

"I miss you, too."

"It's time I met your dad, don't you think?"

Hell!

"Maybe. But it'll have to be up to him. You know, what with his health . . ."

33

At three o'clock in the afternoon on March, Lucy was drudging through household chores when her cell rang. It was Ricki, calling from the bar.

"There's a man here looking for Dad."

"Okay . . ."

"He says he knew him back in the day."

"Which day?"

"Sicily."

"You haven't told him where Dad is!"

"I'm not an idiot."

"Why are you calling me?"

"He's got a big guy with him, and a woman. He said they're not leaving until he sees Dad."

"Then call the cops."

"From the look of them, I don't think we'd want to . . . attract that kind of attention."

"You mean . . . ?"

"Yeah. I thought, with your connections, you might—"

"—scare them off."

"Yeah."

"I'll be right down."

When Lucy walked into the Bronte, Ricki was serving two men at the bar. Her eyes cut to the left, to the dining room. "In the back," she murmured.

Lucy took a deep breath and stepped through the archway. Most of the late lunch trade preferred sidewalk tables, so the dining room was almost empty. Only one table was occupied. A trio sat in the gloom in the far back corner, conversing quietly. There was an older man with silvering hair, his back to her; beside him, a woman; and, on the opposite side of the table, facing her, a big man with a receding hairline and an expressionless face.

Lucy barely suppressed a laugh. She walked toward them.

Carlo rose to his feet, followed by Dominic, who turned to face her with a mischievous grin. "Dear Lucinda. I had hoped our visit would smoke you out of hiding."

The woman turned in her seat and smiled uncertainly as Lucy, despite herself, gave Dominic a big hug.

"I haven't been hiding."

"You've been hiding from me. You didn't come to see me before you left."

"The truth?"

"Usually the best choice. Not always."

"The truth is that I had a feeling you were planning to tell me something about my father that I didn't want to hear. And that is still the case, Dominic. I don't want to know my father's secrets."

"There is one secret that I think would delight you." He turned to the woman, who now rose to her feet. Lucy found herself facing an attractive, impeccably dressed woman in her forties. "Allow me to introduce you to Anna Jefferson, formerly Anna Lanza."

Lucy held out her hand. A beautifully manicured hand accepted hers.

"Lucy Hendricks—" she glanced at Dominic and added "—formerly Lucy Cappelli."

Anna's eyebrows migrated upward. She turned to Dominic. "Father, you always said—!"

"Later, my girl. Later."

As Lucy puzzled over this exchange, Ricki appeared. She took in the sociable scene before her.

"Lucy?"

Lucy realized this was going to take some explaining. Months ago, she'd revealed to Ricki in a telephone call that Dominic had contacted her. Later, she'd been forced to come up with a story. Once again it had come down to *necessary lies*. She'd told Ricki and Jeff that she'd only met the man twice. The first time, he had visited her and offered his personal word that Jack had never been involved with the Lanza Family. The second time had been on the night of the storm, when Dominic and Carlo had shown up at her house and helped her and Kevin to safety.

"I think we've had a little joke played on us here, Ricki."

"What joke?"

"This is Dominic Lanza . . ."

Ricki's eyes widened.

". . . and his daughter, Anna. And"—she leaned theatrically against the big man—"this is Carlo, who carried Kevin through the flood on the night of the storm."

Her sister appeared momentarily mollified. But this was Ricki, and she wasn't born yesterday.

"Our family is very grateful for that, Mr. Lanza—for keeping Lucy and my nephew safe. But that raises questions."

"Why we helped Lucy and Kevin, why we're here now, and why we want to see Joseph."

"Yes!"

"Lucy has said that your father is ill."

"He is."

"Is this a terminal illness?"

Ricki swallowed.

Lucy answered for her. "Stage four emphysema. His doctor calls it a grim, stalking death."

"That's why we are here. Anna has only met your father once. It was a long time ago, and she deserves to meet him one more time. It is important to Anna, even though she doesn't know the full story, and I believe it will be important to your father."

"I don't understand." It was Lucy who spoke, but she was clearly speaking for Ricki as well.

"You will. Both of you should be there for this reunion." He looked at Lucy, then at Ricki. "Will you take us to him?"

The sisters exchanged a look.

"Michael can take over the bar," Ricki said. "I'll call Dad."

There was a big SUV parked in the lot behind the Bronte. Carlo drove. When they arrived at Joseph Cappelli's apartment, Carlo waited for everyone to get out and then he drove away.

"Better not to draw attention to your father's residence," Dominic explained to Lucy.

"I thought the car was a rental."

"It is. And this is the digital age."

They went inside.

When Lucy saw her father yank his oxygen line from his face; when she saw him jump from his chair with a burst of energy she hadn't seen him display in months; and when she watched him and Dominic kiss each other's cheeks, all her fears came back. All her fears that her father had once been a Lanza soldier, a loyal and valued servant of a Mafia don, and that now she was going to hear the worst.

Her confusion increased when her dad turned to Anna.

"This is Anna?" His eyes filled. "This is really you?"

Anna burst into tears. "Yes, it's me, it's me! Dear Joseph!" She hugged Lucy's father tightly. "Thank you for my life!"

The embrace lasted a few seconds too long. Dominic broke the spell. "Joseph . . ."

Joseph looked up from Anna's shoulder. Before him stood his two daughters, their expressions a clash of shock and fascination.

"The time has come for Erica and Lucinda to know the truth."

Lucy had a frightening thought . . .

Are you our real father?

. . . followed by another, equally chilling:

Is Dominic our father?

Joseph Cappelli collapsed back into his chair. His hands trembled as he tried to refit his cannula. Ricki finally intervened to help. When it was done, he said, "Please. Everyone sit. Coffee?"

The three women shook their heads. Dominic said nothing.

Joseph tilted his head back, taking in an extra few breaths of oxygen. Then he looked at his daughters and said, "First of all, our name is not Cappelli. It's Tartaglia."

34

It took Joseph Tartaglia much less time to tell his story than it did for Lucy and Ricki to absorb the impact of it all.

He told them about his life in Sicily; about his life as a *picuneri* in the sulfur mines; about the merciless mine owners, about the *soccorso morto*, and about the boys, the exploited *carusi* and their ruined lives. He told them about the day his little friend Peppino died in the mine. He told them about his utter dejection and his helpless rage—still an indelible memory after forty years—as he trudged along Via Roma's narrow corridor toward his dismal home.

He'd been passing the forecourt of *Chiesa Madre* when it happened. The incident that had changed his life.

The incident that had changed all their lives.

"They were *Mafiosi*. They dressed like priests, but I knew right away what they were. And they had Anna." His eyes locked on hers. "You were a beautiful child, screaming with terror. One of them punched your mother. I heard her nose break."

"I remember," Anna said. "I remember that man hitting Mama."

"Your mother . . ." Joseph looked suddenly confused. He turned to Dominic. "Chiara? Where is she?"

"Gone, Joseph. It was a long illness."

"So, a mercy?"

"Yes, a mercy. In the hospital, she made me promise. She made me promise to find you, and to thank you. I do that now. I do that now for Chiara."

"And I do that now for me," Anna added.

"Find me? But, Dominic, you always knew where to find me! Your messenger . . ."

"Cowan."

"And those other men. All the visits. That extra money, for the renovations."

"Yes. But I stayed away. I wanted to keep you safe. You, and your family."

Alarm bells went off in Lucy's head. She butted in. "So, what's different now?"

"A lot, Lucinda. I will explain later."

Lucy had spent enough time with Dominic to recognize the warning. She segued quickly so Ricki wouldn't ask questions. "Okay, but will one of you *please* explain what happened that day?"

"There were three men," Dominic said. "They were sent by the Mazzaras to abduct Anna. She was only five. I had just stepped into the church to take a look. Anna and her mother were outside. Your father saw what was happening. He killed two of the men with his miner's pick and rescued Anna."

"You helped," Joseph interjected, looking suddenly uncomfortable.

"I came out of the church a few seconds too late," Dominic explained. "The man who attacked my wife was about to shoot your father. I took care of him."

"The driver," Joseph said. "Are you saying he died?"

"Brain hemorrhage. Your pick handle."

"I didn't know."

"You never asked."

Ricki interjected. "Let me get this straight! You *killed* people?"

"They were trying to kidnap a little child, Erica. I had to stop them!"

Lucy looked at Dominic. "You said somebody sent those men."

"Antonio Mazzara. He was the head of a Sicilian group that was allied with certain . . . business rivals of my uncle in New Jersey. They were planning to use Anna as a hostage in order to extort control over some of our operations."

"Don't try to dress it up, Mr. Lanza!" Ricki blurted. "This was part of a war between two crime families, wasn't it?"

"If you wish."

"Why were you in Sicily in the first place?"

"Visiting family. And getting some suits made. Valguarnera is renowned for its tailors—last year one of them was hired to make clothes for the Pope. I would not have taken Chiara and Anna had my visit been for . . . business purposes."

"So, I'm guessing that because of our father's intervention, he became a target of the Mazzara family."

"Correct."

"Is the Mazzara family still in business?"

"Yes, but much diminished. The Italian *carabinieri* and their judicial police have been unusually effective in the last few years. Antonio and his three top capos are doing life in Opera Prison in Milan."

"With assistance from you, perhaps?"

"You're very perceptive."

"Tell us the rest, Dad," Lucy said. "You're a miner with a pregnant wife, and now your name's on a Mafia hit list. What happened next?"

"Dominic embraced me and asked my name. He said he'd clean up the mess." Lucy shot a look at Dominic, who responded with the shadow of a smile. "He knew I would be a marked man, so he told me to run home, get my wife, grab whatever we could carry, and meet him at an address on Via Toscana. When we got there, a doctor was treating Chiara. Two of Dominic's men drove us to a *casolare* near Gangi, in the Madonie Mountains. We stayed there for nearly a month."

"We used our contacts in Palermo to arrange new identities," Dominic said. "That's how you became Cappelli. My Uncle Tommaso used a friend in the U.S. government to secure immigration clearances for Joseph and Giulia to enter the States. We gave Joseph money to start a new life. Both of you may have had your suspicions, but I want you to know that your father never worked for us. He and your mother made their own decision to settle in Florida. You know the rest."

"We don't know the rest!" Lucy replied heatedly. "We don't know what happened to our grandmother! You and Mom always said she died before the immigration papers came through. A heart attack, you said! But last year you told me Nonna gave her life to keep us safe! *All of us!* What did you mean by that, Dad? What did she do?"

"Your mother and I . . . we wanted to bring her with us. Dominic offered to get her the right papers, a new identity, all the clearances. But she refused to leave. She refused to leave the country—" his voice faltered "—a country that had abused her and ground her down from the day she was born. She would only agree to move away from Valguarnera . . . back to Bronte. But after she moved, she started getting reports from our relatives about strange men asking about her. She knew the *Mafiosi's* methods—she knew that if they found her, they would torture her to find out where I was. So she changed her mind and decided to join us. I had a phone number for Dominic. He started working on the paperwork. But the Mazzaras found Nonna first." Tears welled in his eyes. "It was weeks before we found out what happened." Words caught in Joseph's throat. He waved a hand at Dominic.

"Your grandmother had moved into a cottage on the outskirts of Bronte. Our people in Palermo were taking care of the rent. But the Mazzaras eventually found out where she was staying."

"How?" Lucy asked.

"Mazzara had a man in Palermo's *cosca*. He was flushed out later." He resumed his narrative. "Every night before she went to bed, your grandmother spread snail shells on the floor inside her front and back doors. It's an old Sicilian trick, and it worked. She heard them coming. She had a *lupara*—a shotgun. She killed two of them, and then ran out the back door. But there were more men waiting. When they grabbed her . . ." He hesitated. "Your Nonna was a brave woman."

"Tell us!" Ricki demanded.

"She had a grenade. Where she got it, no one knows—thousands of them were stolen from the Allied Forces after the 1943 invasion. When they grabbed her, she pulled the pin. The blast killed her, and two more of the men."

"She would never have given us up," Joseph said, proudly and through his tears. "That bastard Mazzara sent five men after her, and only one of them walked away."

"Not for long," Dominic said. "We found him."

After a second of uncomfortable silence, Ricki asked, "What about over here?"

"Over here?"

"You said the Mazzara family is weakened in Italy. What about in the States? Are they over here?"

"They have a presence, but it's almost invisible. They work through one of the New York families."

"Invisible . . ." Lucy said. "Isn't that what you want to be?"

Dominic shot her a warning look. Addressing Ricki, he continued: "If you're asking if there's any danger to your father today, after forty years, I would say the risk is very low."

They ordered Chinese and stayed for dinner.

While they were waiting for Carlo to deliver the takeout order, Dominic and Joseph sat together on the patio, talking in low tones. When they returned inside, Lucy noticed Joseph's demeanor was even more somber than usual, and Dominic's expression was cold and thoughtful. When the food arrived, Anna took her leave. She hugged each of them, kissed Joseph on both cheeks, and left with Carlo.

"Why didn't she stay?" Lucy asked quietly, after she'd gone.

"He's taking her to the plane. Anna lives in Houston. She's married to an architect and they have two teenaged boys. She needed to get home."

"So, she's not part of your world."

"I didn't want her to be."

"You said, 'the plane,' not 'the airport.'"

"One of my companies leases a jet."

"Nice."

He shrugged. "Being rich costs money. Which brings me to another subject . . ." He addressed her father, who was sitting at the other end of the table, poking at a container of ginger beef. "Joseph, do you have any interest in seeing home one last time?"

"Home?"

"Sicily. Valguarnera . . . and Floristella. The mine property has been converted into a historic park."

"The whole valley?"

"Everything. The *calcuroni*, the *decentiria*—everything preserved as it was. Except, now, there are trees, Joseph. A forest."

"There were no trees when I worked there. Nothing. Just heat and sweat and death."

"The baron's palazzo is still standing, up on the hill."

"That family . . ." Joseph's voice was bitter, his memories grim and far away.

"I have a Gulfstream. It's on its way to Houston right now, but it will be back on the apron at Kendall by morning. If we leave tomorrow night, we'll be in Catania early on Monday." As he continued, Lucy felt him give her leg a warning squeeze under the table. "Lucinda should come as well. To take care of you, and make sure you take your medications."

"Maybe . . . maybe it is time I visited my mother's grave."

Joseph had answered too quickly, and Ricki was no fool. Her eyes cut back and forth between the two men. "Okay," she demanded, "what's this really about?"

Silence.

Lucy was no fool either. She recalled the two men's expressions when they came in from their private conference on the patio. She realized that their last exchange had been rehearsed.

"Sister . . ."

"What?"

"I'm not sure myself, but I don't think you want to know."

Ricki searched faces. "Fuck . . . the past *is* coming back, isn't it?" she asked. No one answered. After a few seconds, she grumbled, "Guess I'm taking care of Kevin."

Later, as they were leaving, Dominic took Lucy aside. "Mr. Olivetti . . ."

"What about him?"

"You're more than friends again, aren't you?"

Lucy sighed. Apparently nothing escaped this man.

"Don't call him tonight."

"Why?"

"I'll explain tomorrow . . . Carlo will find you."

35

The entrance to The Barnacle Historic State Park lay directly across the street from the Bronte. Just after ten on Sunday morning, Lucy threaded her way along the park's familiar pathways. She knew these trails; she had played here as a child. As she eased past stands of moss-draped live oak, poisonwood, and slash pine, she was aware that Carlo was somewhere behind, watching for followers. That such a possibility existed was itself a bit unsettling, but she duly paid for a day pass and strolled on, playing tourist. She paused occasionally, pretending to read botanical information signs, glancing at the trail behind her.

She was actually enjoying the intrigue. *You're getting too comfortable with this stuff*, she thought.

She meandered past the meticulously preserved residence of nineteenth-century yacht designer Ralph Munroe, whose oddball nickname for his home, "The Barnacle," had supplied the park with its name. From here on, the bush and hammock terrain yielded to a vast manicured lawn that ramped down to the shoreline of Biscayne Bay, five hundred feet away. In the distance, a half-dozen day-sailers swung on their moorings in the shallows.

Dominic Lanza was waiting on a weathered bench that appeared to have been dropped at random near a dense stand of bamboo. As she approached, he said, "Good morning," and patted the seat next to him. Lucy sat.

"Why am I here?"

"Patience. First, we wait for Carlo."

They sat in silence. After a few minutes, Carlo appeared. As he sauntered past them, he gave Dominic a quick nod. He took up a position on another bench, forty feet away.

"You're here," Dominic said, gazing at the bobbing sailboats, "because we have unfinished business."

"Tait and Scarlatti?"

"Yes."

"Scarlatti could have been handled better."

"Mistakes tend to happen when we're working against the clock."

"You mean the storm?"

"The curfew. And the fact that one of our men was driving Scarlatti's police car. He couldn't afford to get stopped, so he dumped the cruiser early. All things considered, they did well."

"What about Tait?"

"He was easier. He won't be found." He turned to her. "Do you understand why we dealt with them differently?"

"I'm listening."

"If both were found dead on the same night, someone might have made a connection."

Lucy completed the thought. "Or . . . if both of them disappeared on the same night, same result."

"You have fine instincts, my dear."

"*Fine* might not be exactly the right word. I'm sitting with New Jersey's most feared *capo famiglia* discussing our recent killings."

Dominic grunted. "Good point."

"Can we get back to why I'm here?"

"Because someone may have already connected those two."

Lucy's stomach tightened. "You mean Robert?"

Dominic didn't answer. He didn't have to.

"You told me not to call him. But we're leaving for Sicily tonight, and he's arriving here on Thursday night for a conference. He expects to see me, so I need to tell him something."

"A conference. Is that what he said?"

"Yes. Why?"

"Before we get to that, do you remember Tigrane Holdings?"

"The shell company in Delaware."

"We know who's behind it."

"How did you get that information when the FBI couldn't?"

"We found Parnell, the manager of that wrecking yard. Squeezed him. Not gently, I admit," he added, with a pat on her leg, "but no lasting damage. He gave us the final link, from Tigrane in Delaware to a company in Belize." He handed her a folded sheet of paper. "Names, shareholdings."

Lucy unfolded the paper. She read out loud. "Noel Parnell, Carla Scarlatti, Ernest Tait . . . fifteen, fifteen, fifteen. Raffaello Mazzara . . . fifty-five percent?" She straightened. "*Mazzara?*"

"He's one of Antonio's nephews. He dropped out of sight years ago."

"Does this have something to do with our trip to Sicily?"

"Yes."

"I don't understand."

"You will."

"You always say that! Tell me how taking my father back to Sicily will—?"

He cut her off. "First, I have something else to show you." He unhooked his cell phone from his belt and handed it to her. "Watch the video."

There was a single video saved in the phone's library.

Lucy thumbed *play*.

The opening footage shocked her. After a few seconds, she hit *pause* and studied the frozen frame. She was looking at a man in a police officer's uniform. From the angle, she couldn't read his shoulder patch. He was tied to a heavy chair, and appeared to be unconscious. His mouth was duct-taped, but what appeared to be a long drinking straw led from under the tape to a breast pocket in his tunic. The pocket bulged with a rectangular shape.

"I asked the boys to record that. For you."

"For me?"

"To show you that no one was hurt. That we don't kill without good reason."

"He looks in bad shape."

"Pentothal. The shot wears off in fifteen, twenty minutes."

"What's with the straw?"

"Pentothal can leave you with a hell of a thirst. They put a juice box in his pocket."

"Who is he?"

"Night security at the Hudson County Prosecutor's Office."

Lucy gaped at him. "The one on Duncan Avenue?"

"Yes."

"That's where Robert's office is!"

"That's why they were there."

"A lot of cops work in that building!"

"Not at four in the morning."

Lucy re-started the video. She watched with rising concern as the camera navigated familiar hallways.

"What about the alarm system? Security cameras?"

"All taken care of. We learned our techniques from the best."

"Who?"

"The FBI. They have tech guys; so do we. Twenty-first century, remember?"

As if to prove Dominic's point, a member of his entry crew came into view on screen. The man was wearing a swat hood and surgical gloves. He swiftly bypassed the lock and entered Robert's office.

"When was this?" Lucy asked.

"Four nights ago."

"Why?"

"Keep watching."

The lockman walked directly to Robert's desk, knelt down, and opened the door in the right-hand pedestal, revealing the hotel-style room safe hidden behind it. Using a flashlight, he examined the safe closely. Then he tapped in a code on the keypad. The safe door opened.

"How did he know the combination?"

"He didn't. Every one of those safes has a default master code when it's shipped. It's a feature designed for emergencies. It can be re-set after delivery, but most hotel managers can't be bothered. They hang on to the original master code as a backup in case guests forget the one they set and can't retrieve their valuables. We took a chance that your friend never bothered to change the default."

"Is every manufacturer's code the same?"

"No. But my man knows them all."

As Lucy watched, Dominic's man removed something from the safe. It was the exhibit envelope that held the USB drive that Jack had hidden in their house. The field of view expanded as the camera zoomed in for a close-up.

The seal on the envelope had been broken.

The man reached back into the safe. One by one, he removed its contents and laid them out in sequence on Olivetti's desk: a notebook, a typed document that appeared to be a chronology, a booklet of photographs, copies of birth certificates, an airline flight itinerary . . .

Abruptly, the video ended.

"Go to the still library. He photographed everything."

A few minutes of reading and scanning was enough. Lucy immediately understood the full extent of her peril. Ashen-faced and numb with shock, she sagged against Dominic Lanza. He slid a protective arm around her shoulders.

He waited.

He waited for what his careful observations of Lucinda Arianna Tartaglia assured him would come next.

Lucy let out a long, rattling breath. "He'll know he was the target of the break-in."

"Doubtful. They didn't leave a paper clip out of place."

"So what? They drugged a cop!"

"There are more obvious targets in that building than a prosecutor's office. There's a homicide unit, a gang unit, and a narcotics squad. Our people used a pry bar to break into a room on the second floor. It's where they keep court exhibits. They loaded a knapsack with drugs and guns. The cops are chasing their tails, trying to figure out if it was random, or if someone went in there to help out a particular defendant."

Lucy didn't speak, didn't move.

"Lucy, I'm truly sorry I got you into this."

"You didn't. I went in with my eyes open."

"Maybe, but now I'm going to make sure I get you out."

She twisted to face him, leaned forward, and kissed him on the cheek. She fixed him with her eyes, hard and cold as malachite, and said: "Let's get something straight right now. We'll be doing that together."

Dominic's patience had been rewarded, as he'd known it would be. "Good," he said. "We'll need you."

"You told my sister the risk to our father was low."

"Why worry her?"

"You don't mind worrying me," she observed.

"You're different, Lucy."

A second passed.

"I am, aren't I?"

"Yes."

"You have a plan."

"Yes."

"And I'm already included in it."

"Yes."

"Does my father know?"

"Not every detail. In his condition, I didn't—"

"—want to stress him."

He nodded.

"So how is this going to work?"

"I'll explain everything on the plane."

"No, explain it to me now," Lucy ordered. "And don't hold anything back."

And so he did.

For the last few minutes, Carlo had been keeping an eye on his boss. He knew what was being discussed, and he was watching for the young woman's reaction. For that reason, he didn't appear to notice a tourist standing under a massive, vine-choked oak a few hundred feet away. The man was holding a camera, and it was pointed in their direction.

The man's name was Raffaello Mazzara.

36

"But why such short notice?"

"The opportunity just came up! He's an old friend of Dad's who made it big in some kind of tech business. Something to do with renewable energy. He'd already scheduled this charter, and he'd heard my father was pretty sick so, out of the blue, he showed up and offered to take him along. Dad figured it's his one last chance to see home, so he agreed. I'm used to helping out with his oxygen and meds, so I'm elected to go as his nurse. I'm scrambling right now to get us both packed."

Lucy kept her tone upbeat and the lies rolled on, but she didn't flinch. From here on it would all be lies.

"When are you back?"

"Not sure. Four or five days . . . maybe a week."

"So you might get back when I'm still in Florida?"

"Hope so, but I can't promise. I'll call as soon as I know."

"Okay. I guess you've got to do this, but I'm really disappointed. I miss you, Lucy."

Sure you do, you scheming bastard . . .

"I miss you, too."

"I'm in love with you. You know that, don't you?"

Lucy felt her gorge rise. She forced herself to stay silent, to let a few seconds go by, and to make sure there was no telltale tremor in her voice. "Love you, too," she replied brightly. "I'll talk to you soon." She ended the call.

Lucy had been pacing back and forth on the patio of her dad's apartment, with Ricki watching the unfolding conversation from a chair. Their father was inside, taking a nap.

"Bit of storytelling going on there," Ricki observed. "Renewable energy?"

"I can't trust him anymore."

"Oh, yeah? 'Love you, too'? 'Call you soon'?"

"He can't know what I'm doing."

"You mean, what you're *really* doing."

"That's right."

"You've been acting like this guy was capital-T, capital-O, The One. Like you'd finally moved on. Meeting the family . . . Amelia Island . . . what was all that?"

"Sis . . ."

"What?"

"There are things you need to know. About Bayonne."

"Yesterday you said I don't want to know. What changed?"

"I met with Dominic this morning."

"And?"

"And, if Dad and I don't come back from Sicily, things might get a bit uncomfortable for you and Jeff."

"What do you mean, '*don't come back*'?"

"We're going there to fix something. If it doesn't work, you might receive a visit. An unwelcome visit. You need to be ready."

Ricki studied her sister's face. "Am I going to need a drink?"

"Maybe more than one."

They opened a bottle of Chianti, and Lucy began.

She told her everything.

When she finished, Ricki sat very still, staring, her fists clenched, her face a kinetic mix of fear, amazement, and mystified respect.

Then Lucy witnessed something she hadn't seen since the day their mother died.

Her sister wept.

Erica Barnett, née Cappelli, née Tartaglia, wept uncontrollably for one long minute. Then she stood up, wiped her eyes, hugged her sister so hard she nearly crushed the breath out of her, and went inside to sit by their father's bed.

Two hours later, Carlo delivered Dominic, Lucy, and Joseph to Kendall Executive Airport.

37

Just before noon on Monday, the Gulfstream G550 made a long banking turn past the lava-blasted slopes of Mount Etna and landed at Catania-Fontanarossa Airport.

Dominic had given Lucy's father the aft stateroom and he'd slept like a baby. The flight had taken eleven hours, and he'd slumbered on through eight of them. Oddly, he had slept more soundly on the jet than he normally did at home.

But Lucy was exhausted. She'd lain on her divan in the main cabin, restlessly thinking and reviewing and preparing. She'd only dozed in snatches, and now she was worried that jet lag was going to undermine her faculties just when she needed them most.

After they disembarked, Dominic took the lead, piloting Joseph's wheelchair, and fast-tracking them through the formalities in fluent Italian. Within twenty minutes of touchdown, they were exiting into the cavernous main terminal. The noisy, teeming foreignness of it all was the first thing that struck Lucy—the babel of languages and the unfamiliar smells assaulted her unprepared senses. Outside, they were met by a beefy character named Lucca. His oily hair, pockmarked face, and vulpine eyes made him look like a walking mugshot. Ignoring Lucy and her father, he spoke only to Dominic as he led them to a waiting seven-passenger BMW X5. Despite Lucy's draining fatigue, she couldn't resist pointing out to Dominic that their guide looked a bit more stereotypical than she'd expected.

"Not exactly the twenty-first-century look you've been advocating," she murmured.

He shrugged. "It's the old country, Lucy. They live under the weight of generations."

"Is this guy a relation?"

"Third cousin. Maybe fourth. Don't remember which."

But Dominic's reply barely registered in Lucy's weary brain because she had just seen an apparition.

At first, he'd been a tall man angling through a swamp of tourists milling around a row of tour buses. A tall man with a familiar build. A familiar gait.

Then she'd glimpsed his face.

Jack's face.

Jack's eyes, watching her.

Jack, smiling his love.

And then the face was gone.

It wasn't Jack. It couldn't be him, and it wasn't. Lucy knew it. Maybe it was a man who resembled him. A man who had noticed an attractive woman, and smiled.

That was it. She was just hallucinating from lack of sleep.

Unaccountably, the experience calmed her. Because of that fantasy of Jack, that fleeting illusion of the beautiful man whose life had so thoroughly suffused her own, she was able to relax on the long drive to their destination.

Not just relax. Sleep.

She conked out before they hit the *autostrada*. She didn't stir until the car came to a stop, ninety minutes later, in front of a huge ironwork gate just off *Strada Statale* 640, ten minutes past Caltanissetta on the road to Agrigento. She awoke just in time to see the gate swing silently inward, revealing two unsmiling men sauntering toward them, each carrying a *lupara*. That sight brought her upright and fully alert, generating a laugh from both Dominic and her father. She suppressed an ill-tempered impulse to chide them both about yet another throwback scene, this time from *The Godfather*.

The two armed men bent to scrutinize their faces, and then nodded for Lucca to drive through. A long unpaved driveway wound through ordered groves of olive, past a dark mass of irregular outbuildings, and finally arrived at a second, smaller gate, this one set in a high, vine-covered stone wall. As they approached, the gate swung open and they eased into a paved courtyard. On three sides rose the walls of an attractive manor house; on the fourth, a long, low building with a tiled roof sealed the quadrangle.

An erect old man with white hair stood waiting. He was holding a cane with a silver handle. At his side was a slender, good-looking young man in his thirties.

"That's Silvio?" Joseph asked, referring to the older of the two.

"Yes."

"I wouldn't have recognized him."

"The years are not always kind, Joseph," Dominic replied.

"I guess I'm proof of that."

Forty years earlier, at the safe house near Gangi, Silvio Lanza had been entrusted with the lives of Joseph and Giulia Tartaglia. According to Joseph, he'd been quick and resourceful, and an attentive host to the endangered couple. Today, assisted by his son, he presided over eighteen hundred hectares of orchards and vineyards. Before they left Miami, Dominic had explained that Silvio would again act as host, only this time in more comfortable surroundings.

Silvio and Dominic embraced and kissed cheeks. Then, while Lucca retrieved Joseph's wheelchair from the back, Joseph approached his former protector on uncertain legs. They embraced and kissed cheeks with much emotion.

"And dear Giulia?" Silvio asked in Italian. "I am told that she passed."

"Yes. It's been many years now."

"She was a fine, fine woman, Giuseppe. I am truly sorry."

"Thank you."

Silvio turned to Lucy, and switched to English. "And this beautiful young woman is your daughter?"

"This is Lucinda. Our youngest."

"You are most welcome in our home, Lucinda." He leaned closer. "But I must warn you to beware of Nicolò," he added, in a theatrical whisper. "He seems to have taken great interest in your arrival."

Pointedly, Silvio now took his own sweet time, introducing his son to each of the men in the party. When at last he came to Lucy, Nicolò interrupted. He took Lucy's hand, squeezed it gently, and said in unaccented English, "Please. Just call me Nicci."

"I'm Lucy," she replied, smiling.

"It is a pleasure to meet you."

"And you, Nicci."

With that, everyone went inside.

The vast manor house was a miracle of simplicity and charm. Nicci commandeered Lucy and, with obvious pleasure, he took her on a fifteen-minute tour through corridors paved in marble, finely appointed sitting rooms, a chapel lit by lofty windows of colored glass, a vast kitchen and pantry, a cavernous wine cellar, and a dining room filled with antiques—the latter rendered more fascinating by a row of wall niches displaying brightly colored ceramics.

"Let me guess," she said. "They're from Caltagirone."

"You know their work?"

"My mother left me a piece. It had belonged to her mother."

"These aren't that old. They were made to order. One of the arti-

sans in Caltagirone had a problem. My father . . . made it go away. The
man showed his appreciation."

Lucy thought she detected a note of disapproval in Nicci's voice.

Finally, he showed her to her bedroom. It was tucked away on the
southwest corner of the second floor. Sunshine lay in bright patches on
the carpet, and her travel bag sat waiting on the bed.

"This definitely looks like a girl's room," Lucy ventured, taking in
the satin coverlet, the pillows edged with lace, and a hand-painted doll
propped on the dresser.

"It was my sister's. Her name is Gemma."

"Where is she now?"

"Salerno. It's near Naples." He paused. "I'd better tell you. Don't mention her in front of my father. She married against his wishes."

"Sounds like there's a story there."

"This is an ancient, secretive land, Lucy. There are many stories."

"That sounds almost poetic."

"I read a lot." He knitted his brow. "Is it correct, what I have been
told? That you are a schoolteacher?"

"Yes."

"And yet you are here, with Dominic Lanza."

"Yes."

"Why?"

"Because he offered to bring my father back for one last visit. As you
can see, he is ill. I'm here to take care of him."

"And that's all?"

"Yes."

Nicci was plainly skeptical. He switched subjects. "How would you
like a tour of the estate? I can take you around, show you how we make
wine, olive oil . . ."

"I would like that. But what I need now is a few hours' sleep."

"Of course. Supper's at eight. Shall I have the housekeeper wake
you?"

"Yes, please. If I haven't shown my face by seven, ask her to knock on my door."

Supper might not have been such a trial if Lucy didn't have so much on her mind. Only Silvio, Nicci, Dominic, Joseph, and Lucy attended the meal. The others on the estate, whatever their roles, apparently took their evening meal elsewhere. Lucy forced herself to participate cheerfully in the toasts, and tried to appear engaged, but it was a losing battle. It didn't help that, in true Sicilian fashion, the food kept coming. Silvio left the room occasionally to consult with the kitchen staff, and he returned each time with a satisfied look on his face.

As the meal progressed, Lucy noted an odd contrast between the old man's interactions with the serving staff and those of his son. Silvio was polite and considerate to a fault, and his employees' responding affection was clearly sincere. Nicci, on the contrary, tended to be short with them, leading to tight faces in response.

By the end of *primo*, the third course, Lucy was done. By her ancestors' standards, this was the first substantial course—hence its name—but that was no consolation. She was dog-tired and had already lost all interest in food by the time the *antipasti* had been cleared away. She struggled through *primo* and then—to the obvious disappointment of Oscar, Silvio's smiling, impish chef, who kept finding excuses to enter the dining room so he could gauge their reaction to his creations—she excused herself, pleading exhaustion, and dragged herself back to her bedroom.

There was another reason she'd been happy to leave early. As she slipped under the covers, her mind replayed a tense exchange between Silvio and his son.

"Dominic and I have much in common," Silvio had intoned gruffly, after a toast. Perhaps lubricated by vino, he had added, "We may be the men in the dark, but we own the men in the light."

"Those days are coming to an end," Nicci responded.

"We've had this conversation, Nicolò. Many times. We shall not repeat it in front of our guests."

Nicci ignored the admonition. "You are trapped by history, Father. I am not."

"I send my son to university," Silvio said to Dominic. "You see how I am repaid."

"I, too, have a college degree, Nicci," Dominic interposed. "And I have put that education to work."

"This estate"—Nicci waved a hand at their surroundings—"these lands . . . they should be enough. Why aren't they enough? Why the perpetual plotting, the unending conspiracies?"

"With these lands came responsibility. Responsibility to the many families we employ and support. After I am gone, Nicolò, unless you are careful, you will lose these lands. You will lose them to other men. Men in the dark. Men who care little for the people under our protection. There will always be such men. In Sicily, you are an owner, or you are owned!"

As Lucy left the table, she went away with the distinct impression that Nicci had engineered the argument to impress her.

If so, he had misjudged Lucinda Tartaglia.

38

For Joseph Tartaglia, the visit to the cemetery was an emotional one.

Less so for his daughter. Lucy had never known her grandmother, who had died before Lucy was born. She knew her only as an enigmatic character in family lore and, more recently, as the indomitable protagonist in Dominic's horrific account of her violent end. Her attachment to Nonna was dutiful, but it lacked the connective tissue of deep emotion.

Despite that, she was moved by the experience at the graveside.

Before their arrival in Sicily, and at Dominic's request, Silvio's aides had made some inquiries. With great difficulty, and with no small reliance on the element of intimidation associated with Silvio's name, they had finally discovered where the unfortunate Pietronella Tartaglia had been laid to her final rest—in a cemetery behind an abandoned sixteenth-century convent near Pietraperzia.

Accompanied by Dominic, Lucy wheeled her father through a narrow gate in a discolored stone wall, and into a vast maze of ornate, above-ground crypts. They navigated along row upon row of elaborate marble mausoleums, all, by the look of them, erected and maintained at great expense. Engraved grandly into the lintel of each structure were family names right out of a history of the *Cosa Nostra* . . .

Famiglia M. Filippello . . .
Famiglia A. Bonanno . . .
Fam. Rocco Calderone . . .
Famiglia P. Leggio . . .

They passed one crypt where otherwise padlocked steel doors stood wide open. Inside, in a space that could easily have accommodated a respectable private chapel, a squad of uniformed workmen toiled away, polishing and cleaning.

"I've heard it said that Sicilians devote more time and money to the dead than they do to the living," Dominic observed.

"By the time this is over, we might be doing the same," Lucy replied.

Lucy's humble grandmother, they knew, was not to be found among the prestige funereal addresses in this section of the cemetery. Aided by a hand-drawn map, they finally arrived at the miserable plot near a rear wall where Joseph's mother lay buried. After a long moment of respectful silence, and after Lucy had gently dabbed a tear from her father's cheek, she and Dominic left him there with his thoughts and his memories. As they departed, Lucy could hear his voice, low and halting. He was speaking *Sicilianu*—the centuries-old dialect of Sicily that northern Italians couldn't understand, and Lucy had never mastered.

Joseph was talking to his mother.

They returned to their borrowed Mercedes.

"We've heard from Palermo," Dominic told her, as they waited. "They're on their way."

"So . . . it's on."

"Thursday, at four."

Today was Tuesday.

"And, today?"

"Get some rest."

"I will. But first I'm going to accept Nicci's offer and take a tour of the estate."

"He could be a problem."

"Why do you think I'm going?"

"Very good."

Twenty minutes later, Lucy's cell rang once. She walked back through the cemetery to meet her father.

"How are your nerves?" Joseph asked, as she wheeled him along.

"That's the first time you've asked me that, Papa."

"Papa? You never call me that. Not since you were—"

"We're in Sicily now."

"You know I didn't want you involved in this."

"Well, I am. It's a little late to argue the point, isn't it?"

"I'm old, Lucy. It doesn't matter what happens to me."

"It does to me. It does to Ricki."

They arrived at the car.

"How are you so calm?" Joseph asked Lucy as she helped him out of his chair.

"All those years ago, at the *Chiesa Madre* in Valguarnera . . . did you hesitate?"

"No."

"Neither did I . . . with Tait. So I guess it's in our blood, Father."

"What about Tait?"

Lucy glanced at Dominic, who was stowing Joseph's chair in the trunk. "You didn't tell him?"

"Left that out," Dominic replied.

Her father repeated the question. "What about Tait?"

"Later, Papa."

"Lucinda, tell me! *What about Tait?*"

She faced him. "I killed him! With Jack's dive knife. And I'd do it again, believe me!"

Her father sat in the back of the car, behind Dominic, on the drive back to Silvio's.

Lucy could feel him watching her.

Joseph Tartaglia was sitting very, very still, looking at his youngest daughter through newly opened eyes.

39

Lucy spent the rest of the day with Nicci Lanza, touring his father's vast landholdings in a golf cart. He arrived at her room wearing a polo shirt, skin-tight jeans, turquoise running shoes, and a designer scarf wound around his neck in the rather vain style favored by other young men she had noticed on the streets of nearby Caltanissetta. There was a faintly metro-male air about him, which was only enhanced by his liberal use of some heavily fragrant hair product.

The vernal equinox was still two weeks away, but already a harsh sun was flaying the hillsides. Flocks of noisy starlings wheeled and dipped above them as they bounced along the estate's network of tracks and lanes.

"Everything we do is certified organic by the European Counsel of Agricultural Ministers. The regulations are very strict—stricter than in America. Getting that certification was my doing," he told her. "My father resisted me every step of the way because he couldn't cut through the red tape like he usually does. We had to go by the book."

The planted lands were a mottled carpet in every direction, readily surveyed from a succession of hilltops where Nicci stopped their cart and launched into what sounded like practiced monologues.

"Those green fields are all in wheat," he told her, waving an arm at a vast stretch of bottom land where foot-tall grasses ducked and rippled with each stray current of the hot, dry air. "We plant it in early December, and it's usually ready to harvest by June. One of the big organic food companies in Germany buys our entire crop every year."

They drove to the next hilltop.

"None of our other crops have really gotten started yet. Our workers are spending their time pruning back the olive trees and the vineyards, and spreading fertilizer. It's a good time to fertilize because we usually get a few good rains in March."

Lucy had seen no sign of rain since her arrival. In fact, what had struck her was the impossibly clear air of central Sicily, and the spectacle of a deep blue sky that was utterly free of clouds from horizon to horizon. But she vaguely recalled her father once saying that terrible storms—sometimes death-dealing storms—seemed to come out of nowhere in the ancient land of his birth.

She had the night of Hurricane Sandy to remind her that sometimes the death-dealing came from agencies other than the weather.

As the day wore on, Lucy found herself impressed with Nicci's intelligence and determination, but she found his conversation an unsettling combination of fine-tooth comb and steamroller. On the subjects of organic farming, wine making, and soil chemistry his knowledge and interest level were granular. On the subject of his father's businesses, his pronouncements were blunt, sweeping, and unforgiving. He seemed oblivious to the fact that he would one day be the beneficiary of it all. In the wake of extensive land reforms in post-war Italy, Silvio Lanza's estate—over four thousand acres of rolling countryside—was comparatively unique. On the flight over, Dominic had explained that his cousin had assembled the estate from smaller landholdings. At times Silvio had paid a fair price to willing families whose puny allotments could not support them. At times he'd used more traditional *Cosa Nostra* methods to achieve his ends. That his blatant reversal of the regional government's land reform process had been allowed to proceed unhindered was not really surprising.

After all, this was Sicily.

Ironically, and entirely at odds with Nicci's incessant assertions of righteousness, this grown son of a Sicilian *capo* displayed a depressingly aloof lack of concern for the dozens of farm workers in his father's employ. At their various stops along the tour, he tended to address these people abruptly, and at times imperiously.

Lucy did not fault him for rejecting his father's lifestyle.

But she did fault him for an arrogance bred of the privileges that that very lifestyle had brought him. And she faulted him for blinding himself to danger—not only the risk his egotism would bring to himself, but the risk to all the workers and their families who would depend upon him for protection after his father was gone.

The Mafia was many despicable things, but above all else it was family.

Family at all costs, yes.

Family soaked in blood, yes.

But family.

Lucy's reaction to Nicolò Lanza was unalloyed. By the end of the day, she pitied him.

Ignorant of the impression he had made, he asked her to dinner.

"You mean, not here at the house?"

"No. Just us. There's a place near San Cataldo. A traditional farmhouse. They accept only a few diners each night. You eat outside, under the trees. I thought you would like it."

"Thank you, Nicci, but I shouldn't leave my father."

"I'm still not understanding. This visit . . . you . . . your father . . . Dominic Lanza. He is a much-feared man in your country, is he not? A *padrino?*"

"I suppose, if you believe the Internet. I don't care. He's been a good friend to my father, and to me."

"To you? *Tu sei insegnante!* A teacher!"

"Yes."

"How?"

"That's all you need to know."

"Tell me why you're really here!"

Lucy swung her legs out of the golf cart. She stood up and faced him. "You'll have to ask your father."

Nicci's tight smile told her that he already had.

Dominic was waiting when she returned. He touched his lip, warning her not to speak. He led her through the main house to an isolated portico that looked out over the western hills, where sunset had become a fiery pageant of glowing clouds.

Her father was sitting there, bathed in ruddy beams of dying sunlight.

"Now . . ." Dominic said.

"You need to keep him out of it," Lucy stated bluntly.

Dominic nodded. "That was our assessment. Fortunately, his own father agrees. Silvio has arranged an errand. He's sending him to Castelvetrano tonight."

"He'll be suspicious."

"Maybe, but he's all talk. He won't disobey his father."

Joseph seemed to be barely listening. He reached for Lucy's hand. "I remember these sunsets," he said, emotion in his voice.

The entire western sky had turned a deep crimson.

"When the sky looked like that, Nonna would say to me, 'We might not live at the ends of the earth, but you can see it from here.'"

40

He had been keeping careful watch.

He had an impression of preparations.

Quiet, careful preparations.

Another vehicle had shown up in the compound. A nondescript three-year-old Fiat.

Silvio Lanza had always scorned "nondescript." It wasn't in the old man's nature to tolerate second rate. The cane he carried said it all. Gleaming ebony and shining solid silver. A cane, carried but never used, had always signified one thing in Sicilian society, and one thing only:

Power.

Then, just after noon on Thursday, the Fiat emerged from behind the iron gate and picked its way down the broken pavement of the access road, past the sprawling vineyards, and joined SS640, heading northeast, toward Caltanissetta.

There were three of them in the vehicle: the two old men and the young woman who had arrived with them.

The daughter of the man in the wheelchair.

He followed them, staying three or four cars back, sometimes five or six. Tailing a vehicle was an easy task on Sicilian highways. There were always nervy, impatient drivers, tailgating, passing on double-solid lines and on corners, if only to gain a car length, oblivious to the ultimate futility of their actions on roadways clogged with giant, crawling trucks.

So he let them overtake, and from time to time he passed them himself in order to stay in position. He knew his driving would blend in; that anyone alert and watching mirrors would see nothing out of the ordinary— just cars and vans, passing and jockeying and dodging in and out.

Before the Fiat reached Caltanissetta, it took the Enna-Gela exit. At the bottom of the long hill, it took the second exit, looping around and under to join SS626 north. The next exit, eight kilometers ahead, would lead to the back way into Enna. He doubted they would take the longer route via the *autostrada*.

He followed.

But then they started doing something strange. They drove right on the speed limit.

Like tourists.

If he paced them, he would stand out.

On the next curve, he eased off on the accelerator, slowed, and let a string of vehicles pass him. Then he sped up. He could just make out the Fiat now, in the far distance. The exit for Enna was coming up. He watched for their turn signal.

There it was.

He relaxed. He wasn't concerned that the Fiat was lost from view by the time he took the exit himself. There was a good chance he would catch up within five kilometers. As he knew, a long section of road repairs just this side of the Borgo Cascino turnoff had reduced the highway to a single lane. A red light could hold them up for as long as five minutes.

His gamble paid off.

He joined a line of vehicles, six cars back from the Fiat. After about thirty seconds, the light changed to green and the line began to move. He was able to keep the Fiat in view all the way to the outskirts of Enna—the modern outskirts, below the old city on the mountain.

Then, at the junction with S561—the turnoff to Pergusa, and Valguarnera beyond—the Fiat swung across the oncoming lane, pulled into an Esso station, rolled past the pumps, and stopped.

It was facing back the way it had come.

Caught by surprise, and left with no choice, he drove on.

By the time he had found a spot to turn around, out of sight of the filling station, reversed course, and returned, the Fiat was gone. As he turned into the station and stopped, he saw a pair of white vans pulling away from the area where he had last seen the Fiat.

Then he saw it.

The Fiat.

It was passing the station, heading in its original direction, up the hill toward Pergusa.

But what he didn't see confused him even more.

The woman, who had been sitting in the back behind the driver, was no longer there. All he could see were the graying heads of the two men.

He rolled his car forward, craning, looking around, checking his mirrors.

The insolent woman who had refused his invitation to dinner was nowhere to be seen.

He made a decision.

Tires squealing, he swung his car around the pumps, sending a fist-shaking attendant scampering for safety, and exited through the *solo entrata* ramp, nearly causing a collision.

Motor whining, he raced up the hill.

He was halfway to Pergusa before he regained contact with the Fiat.

When they made their final turn, he drove by, parked at the roadside and waited for ten minutes. Then he turned around and took the same unpaved road the Fiat had taken.

He parked at a picnic site and started walking.

41

Il Parco Minerario di Floristella-Grottacalda was the largest industrial archaeology park in Europe. It had been created as a museum of the Sicilian sulfur mining experience. As Joseph Tartaglia well knew, that history was a horrific one—a story that never sat well against the pastoral romanticism of homeland memories perpetuated by the island's immigrant communities in America. Few had believed Joseph when he'd mentioned the brutal experiences of his early years, and he had long ago ceased talking about them.

And, until five days ago, he had never described them to his daughters.

It was here at Floristella that he had labored in the hot and poisonous galleries of the scores of mines that dotted the sinuous network of hills and valleys. It was here that he had witnessed the beatings of children, the scorching of young legs with hot lanterns to rouse them from collapse. It was here that he had witnessed the agonies, and the shrieks, and the deaths.

Decades before Joseph was born, strict laws had been passed against the *soccorso morto*, against the employment of children under fourteen, against the underground work of the damned. But those laws had been ignored. The mine operations had simply been moved farther back into the hills, far from the prying eyes of government inspectors.

In those years, Baron Pennisi—the absentee owner who preferred to spend his time lounging in his palace at Acireale, on the coast— had relied on a Mafia family to oversee and protect his mines. It was the hard men of that family who had perpetuated the true hell of Floristella.

The Mazzaras.

The road into the park from the main highway was a kilometer-long dusty track. Joseph and Dominic arrived at the park headquarters, an ancient building that had formerly housed the estate's grape press, and stopped behind it. The parking lot was empty. Dominic emerged from the car into warm air and silence. There was not a soul to be seen—not even a park attendant. He ambled over to the headquarters building and tried the door.

Locked.

He caught Joseph's eye through the open passenger side window. Joseph nodded.

Dominic returned to the car. The Fiat rolled out of the parking area and started down a sloping drive, past a carved wooden sign that read:

PALAZZO PENNISI
SOLO PER IL PERSONALE ADDETTO

Joseph had earlier explained to Dominic and Lucy that Palazzo Pennisi was the fortified manor house that had once served as home and office to the mine's overseers. His descriptions had been helpful, but forty years out of date, so to ensure familiarity with the layout, Dominic, accompanied by Lucy, had driven to the site on the previous afternoon.

The unpaved service road the Fiat was now following was little more than a track. It made a long, descending loop through the forest, finally debouching into a graveled clearing in front of the building.

Though now a vast, boarded-up shell of whiskey-colored block and stone, it was not difficult to visualize how Palazzo Pennisi must have appeared in its neoclassical heyday.

Dominic parked near a steel barrier that blocked a tributary road—one that appeared to descend deeper into the Rio Floristella valley. He was about to press the rear hatch release when he felt Joseph's restraining hand on his arm.

"Leave the chair," he said. "I can walk."

They stepped from the car. Dominic helped with a small backpack that contained Joseph's oxygen supply, threading the cannula line under his friend's jacket collar.

As they moved toward the manor house, Joseph stopped. He pointed at the opening of a trail that ascended, die-straight, up through the surrounding forest. "They used to call that the 'wine road.' It connected the grape press to the palazzo. There was a tiled sluice running down beside that path that went straight into the cellars."

They resumed their walk.

"Over three hundred windows—and gun ports covering every angle of approach," Joseph offered tonelessly, waving an arm at the building. "It was designed as a fortress, in case men like me decided they'd had enough."

They were nearing the entrance. It consisted of a chain-link gate, set in an imaginary chain-link fence—a fence that consisted solely of evenly spaced metal posts, without a single scrap of fencing material connecting them. Beyond the ineffectual gate, through a stone archway, could be seen a main door. It stood partly ajar.

There was no sign of a custodian.

They entered. The huge foyer was cold and empty. The light from the open doorway barely penetrated to the far corners of the space. It was empty of furniture or decoration except for one feature. Arranged along one wall at the base of a flight of stairs leading to the upper floor was a grouping of framed pictures. On closer inspection, they turned out to be photographs—some out of focus, some clear, all in black and white.

Photographs of naked boys, filthy, bathed in sweat, toiling at the working face of an underground gallery.

One picture caught Dominic's eye. He leaned closer. In the background, at the edge of the picture, he recognized a familiar frown.

Joseph's.

"The boy on the right is Peppino. That picture was taken two weeks before he died."

"I'm surprised they were taking photographs. If laws were being broken, and the pictures were discovered, they could be used as evidence."

"The mine director had a little side business. He rented some of the boys to certain men. Men with perverted tastes. He kept a catalogue. If the government is planning to convert this building into a museum, they'd better do their research."

"We should keep going," Dominic said. "Can you handle the stairs?"

"Yes."

They climbed to the second floor, where they took a moment, while Joseph recovered his breath, to admire the polished pitch pine ceiling beams. Then they moved on, through light and shadow, to a doorway that led to a wide balcony. The valley of the Rio Floristella lay spread out below. Interspersed with recent growths of pine, eucalyptus, and rare Nebrodi fir lay the rotting remnants of three centuries of reckless mining. What the trees and wildflowers were now reclaiming had once been a barren scene of blasted, sulfur-scorched earth.

"That's Pozzo Number Three—one of the vertical shafts," Joseph said, pointing to a fifty-foot-high gantry of rusting metal. "Those workings were too easy for the inspectors to check, so the boys were kept in the oldest area, the *Zona Galazzi*. It's up on those hills." He pointed across the valley. "We *picuneri* made our own shafts up there, the *decentiria*, and they made the boys sleep underground, out of sight."

The bright afternoon sun, sharp as a stiletto, cast a skeletal shadow of Joseph's gaunt form on the wall behind them. It was emblematic,

Dominic reflected sadly, of the man himself, now a shadow of the robust miner who had rescued his daughter.

He stood in silence, allowing his old friend a few moments of bitter reminiscence.

But they both knew there was another reason for their presence on this patio.

They were deliberately making themselves visible.

Finally, Dominic checked his watch and said, "It's time."

They reentered the main building, retraced their steps to the ground floor, moved to the rear of the building, and descended a narrow, curving stairway to the labyrinthine network of cellars below.

42

The cellars at Palazzo Pennisi consisted of a series of separate galleries that covered the entire footprint of the building. The largest rooms were located at each of the four corners of the vast rectangle, where immense oaken wine vats had once stood.

Dominic led Joseph to the gallery at the northwest corner. The concrete floor was mainly dry, but mottled stains spoke of recent intrusions of water. In one corner, a low archway led to a stone-lined shaft that, in turn, led upward to the surface. It terminated at a metal grating outside the palazzo's main walls, thus providing a dusky facsimile of daylight below.

Three straight-backed chairs had been placed in the middle of the room. A lamp sat on a small side table. It appeared to be a battery-operated replica of an old-style oil lamp. It gave off dim but adequate light. Even so, and despite the muted glow from the vent shaft, most of the space they occupied remained in murky darkness.

Joseph removed his pack and hung it on the back of a chair. He and Dominic sat down, side by side, facing in the direction from which they had come.

They waited in silence.

Minutes passed.

Dominic kept checking his watch.

Ten minutes . . . fifteen minutes . . .

After eighteen minutes, they heard footsteps.

"They're coming," Dominic said.

The footsteps were on the stairs. Four, maybe five pairs of feet, one of which seemed scuffling and irregular.

"Don't like the sound of that," Joseph muttered.

After a few seconds, three men wearing dark clothing entered through the archway. Two of them were holding a fourth person, a struggling male figure. They frog-marched him across the room and shoved him headlong to the floor. He lay there, his breaths shallow, his face a smashed and bleeding ruin.

Nicolò Lanza.

Each of the three men drew a weapon—two autos and a revolver, as Dominic carefully noted. Immediately they moved aside as another man joined them.

Raffaello Mazzara.

"We found him outside," Mazzara said with a twisted smile. "He claimed he didn't know anything. We tested that. Guess he was telling the truth. Surprising . . . considering you two are staying with his father."

If Mazzara had expected a reaction, he was disappointed. Dominic's expression revealed not a hint of concern. He gestured toward the third chair, which had been positioned facing the ones he and Joseph were occupying.

"Please. Take a seat."

Mazzara ignored the invitation. Instead, he fixed his gaze on Joseph, who was sitting perfectly still, his assisted breathing marked by the faint click of the oxygen apparatus.

"So, we meet at last, Joseph Tartaglia. I have waited a long time for this day."

"How old were you?" Joseph asked. His voice was barely audible.

"Four. I was four years old when you murdered my father!"

"Preventing an armed man from abducting a five-year-old child is not murder, Mr. Mazzara," Dominic interjected. "We don't know what your mother or your uncle told you about that day . . . but Joseph is here of his own free will to explain exactly what happened."

"Is that what you expected, Lanza? A friendly talk? Is that why you sent that message to my uncle?"

"*Carcere di Opera*. It's a fitting name for an Italian penitentiary. But we both know how it works. Even from a high-security prison—even from solitary confinement—Antonio Mazzara controls your family. And he has sent you here to listen."

Mazzara looked incredulous. "You expected my uncle to agree to an old-fashioned sit-down? You expected me to come here, listen to this old bastard's excuses for killing my father—Antonio's only brother!—shake hands, and go away? *You expected that?*"

"No. I didn't expect that. Joseph did, at first. Unlike us, he has led a blameless life and, perhaps, a guileless one. So, as I say, at first he agreed to come, hoping that you in turn would agree, in our Sicilian way, to put a stone on it. *Sperando di mettere una pietra su di esso.*"

"At first?"

"He changed his mind when I told him everything. When he realized his family would never be safe from you."

"And yet, here he sits."

"Yes. He has come to watch you die."

Mazzara stared in stone-faced disbelief. "Watch *me* die!" He splayed his fingers, indicating the armed men at his side. "Four of us, and two of you! Two old men, weak and"—he stabbed a finger at Joseph—"barely breathing!"

A soft voice spoke from the gloom behind Joseph's chair.

"Two old men . . . and me."

Lucy stepped into the pool of light.

"You were late, Mr. Mazzara. We were concerned." She glanced down at Nicci Lanza's prone form. "Now I understand."

Mazzara and his men had jumped at the sound of her voice. Now his thugs had their weapons up and pointed at her, glancing at their boss, looking uncertain. As for Mazzara himself, Lucy had the supreme satisfaction of observing a look of confounded incomprehension on his face.

On the face of the man she knew as Robert Olivetti.

"LUCY?"

"None other."

Recovering quickly—*too quickly*, Lucy warned herself warily—he asked, "How long?"

"How long have I known you were a liar and a murderer?" she responded icily. "Since Sunday, when you were sneaking around Coconut Grove, taking pictures of me and Dominic."

"You've been following me?"

"Newark, Miami, Rome, Palermo," Dominic interposed. "It's not difficult to follow a man who never looks behind."

"I'll work on that." He addressed Lucy. "What happened on Sunday?"

"I saw your birth certificate. Imagine my surprise when I discovered that Olivetti was your mother's name."

"Birth certificate? How could—?"

"Easy. You keep it in that safe in your desk, along with a few other interesting treasures. Like the flash drive I gave you, with all its contents erased! It wasn't hard to work out who took my laptop."

"The break-in. So that's what that was about."

"You ran the car theft operation that Jack was investigating. The bracelet the M.E. found in Jack's throat was from one of your old cases. I'm guessing you stole it from the exhibit locker and gave it to Scarlatti. So it's also a pretty good guess that you ordered Ernie Tait to kill Cal Parrish. *And that you ordered Tait and Scarlatti to kill Jack!* It was *your* name that Jack got from Mulvaney, wasn't it?"

"None of this will do you any good, Lucy."

"Prosecutor, huh? I've got to hand it to you, Robert—it was a great cover. How many cases did you make go away?"

Olivetti said nothing.

"How many cases did you use to undermine the other families?"

Olivetti said nothing.

"You and Scarlatti—was all that staged for my benefit? Good prosecutor, bad cop—was that it?" She spit the next words at him. "Were you still sleeping with her when you were sleeping with me?"

A look of deep regret clouded Olivetti's face. "I'm sorry, Lucy. You shouldn't have come."

"After you and I had those first drinks at The Starting Point, you tracked down the retired Immigration agent who had helped smuggle my parents into the country. You blackmailed him to get my father's real name. That puzzled me, until Dominic told me your father didn't drown in some lake up north—that he was killed in Sicily. In Valguarnera!" She laid a hand on her father's shoulder. "Killed by a miner who risked his life to stop a kidnapping."

"We Sicilians have long memories, Lucy."

"Yes. And I guess that means you and I are here for the same reason."

"And what would that be?" Olivetti sounded calm, but as he spoke his hand slipped behind him. It reappeared holding a gun.

"*Castigo*," she replied.

"Retribution."

"That's it, Robert. That's it exactly." She took one step and placed herself directly in front of her father. "But only one of us will face that today."

"I've got to admit, Lucy, you're pretty impressive, standing there, all cool, doing the talking for these two old men. But what did you actually think was going to happen here? That you were going to mediate? That your soft presence would change the outcome? That the presence of park custodians would prevent any violence? There are no *Forestales* here to help you! We paid them to take the day off."

"So did we," Dominic rumbled. "Before you did."

"You haven't been listening," Lucy said.

Olivetti's brow darkened. "So, enlighten me . . . why set up a meeting down in this dungeon where you have no way out?"

"Because you're too young to understand that it is you who has no way out," Dominic replied. "And from the look of your uncle's men, so are they."

"What the fuck do you mean? We have people outside! The building's sealed! You're not getting out unless I let you out. And"—he shifted his gaze to Lucy—"I'm sorry, but I can't think of a single reason why I should."

"As I was saying," Dominic stated, "you're too young, and clearly too arrogant to learn from your elders. We counted on that, so thank you."

Olivetti leveled his weapon at Dominic. "Maybe you'd like to explain that statement!"

"Happy to. If you'd paid any attention to your family's history, you'd know that your grandfather ran the Floristella mine for the Pennisi family. When the *picuneri* got sick of his brutal methods and tried to unionize, he started worrying about strikes and riots. He persuaded the owners to fortify the palazzo. That's why you see all those gun slits in the outside walls. But, just to be safe, he also created a number of secret exits. Fifteen of them, in fact."

As Dominic uttered those final words, the vast room was filled with the unmistakable sound of coordinated footsteps, and a dozen armed men stepped into view. Simultaneously, Carlo materialized next to Dominic's chair. The big man was holding a MAC-11 .380 machine pistol, and it was aimed directly at Olivetti's chest.

"You see, Mr. Mazzara," Dominic continued, "the thing about exits is that they can also be used as entrances."

A deafening barrage erupted, echoing through the chamber. Stitched with automatic fire, Olivetti and two of his men dropped where they stood. The third man sprinted for the stairwell. A shotgun boomed and he went down, his chest in flames.

It was all over in less than five seconds.

Lucy strode over to Olivetti.

He was still alive.

She bent and picked up his gun.

He blinked up at her in agony and disbelief. Coughing blood, he gasped, "You set me up?"

"You sound surprised. You came here to kill my father." She kneeled. "And you murdered my husband." She jammed the muzzle of Robert Olivetti's gun into his blood-choked mouth. *"Did you really think I would never find out?"* she hissed. *"Did you really think you could walk away alive?"*

Lucinda Tartaglia pulled the trigger.

When she rose and turned away, the first thing she saw was a capsized chair and her father down on his knees, cradling Dominic's head. She rushed over.

"He was hit?"

"Probably a ricochet. He'll be fine."

"How can you know that?" she snapped, tugging at Dominic's jacket, searching for blood.

"Because we're wearing protection," Joseph replied quietly. He unbuttoned Dominic's shirt, revealing the matt texture of a Kevlar vest.

"You both wore vests? *What about me?*"

Dominic's eyes fluttered open. He grunted a reply. "Too restrictive. Thought you might need to move fast." Forcing a smile through lips marbled with pain, he added, "And your boyfriend might have noticed the unwelcome change to your fetching figure."

"Nice to hear you have so much confidence in me," Lucy replied, touchily.

"That's just it, Lucinda. I do."

Carlo materialized above them. "Boss!"

"I'm okay. Help me up."

Carlo lifted his boss off the floor and lowered him onto a chair. As he opened Dominic's shirt, Lucca and several hard-looking men emerged from the shadows. "We're cleaning things up outside," he said, speaking Italian. He glanced around. "There'll be lots of room for these pigs at the bottom of the *Pozzo*."

"You can start by putting that fire out," Lucy ordered, pointing at the body of the man who had been shot near the stairwell. His skin and clothing continued to smolder, infusing the cellar with an acrid odor. "If that smell goes all through the building, someone's going to start asking questions."

"*Si, Signora*," Lucca replied, eyeing her with dark amazement. At a wave of his hand, two of the men jumped to comply.

"And why the hell is he still burning?"

"Lucca waxes the barrels of his *lupara*," Carlo informed her, as he pried a deformed bullet out of Dominic's vest. "He says it sends a stronger message."

"We're not sending this message. We're dropping it down a mineshaft." She turned to Dominic, who was watching her with an expression of grave amusement. "We should leave now."

"Aren't you forgetting someone?" He nodded toward a cowering form. Nicci Lanza had somehow managed to scramble away from the action. He was sitting with his back propped against a pillar, watching and listening.

Lucy walked over. "Can you get up?"

He accepted her offered hand. When he was on his feet, she grabbed him by the shirt front and marched him over to the archway, where she used the spill of gray daylight from above to assess the damage to his face. The skin was split in several places, and one of his eyes was swollen shut.

"We'll get you to a doctor. But I wouldn't want to be around when your father finds out."

He stood before her, silent, trembling, and humiliated.

"You surprise me," she said quietly. "You grew up with this."

"And never wanted it," he whispered. "You didn't, but look at you now."

For a few fleeting seconds after Nicolò Lanza uttered those words, it seemed to Lucy as if she had a sudden recollection of a previous existence.

Then it was gone.

She turned to face the silent, watching men.

"Get to work! There's a little boy in Florida who needs his mother."

ACKNOWLEDGMENTS

Readers who know something about the unfolding history of notorious Mafia families may not be entirely surprised at the thought processes that led me to dream up this story. I'm not talking about the "Medicare Mob," as one media outlet described the recent string of "Old-fellas" arrests by FBI investigators. I'm talking about changing times, and the possibility that a few farseeing scions of the old families may have turned to CIA-style tradecraft, and MBA-inspired business models, to elude law enforcement interest. Although I have no direct, firsthand knowledge of such devices, I began to wonder how much the authorities were missing while they were busy applauding themselves for taking down a handful of sclerotic wise guys from yesteryear.

Storm Rising is partly the result of those ruminations.

Despite my own background in criminal prosecution and defense in *non*-U.S. jurisdictions, my roving imagination would not have been much use to me without significant help from a number of knowledgeable people, most notably my good friends in—yes—U.S. law enforcement. And so, a big thanks once again to Sgt. David Conte of the Bayonne, New Jersey, Police Department—my perennial guide and advisor. David not only assisted me "on the ground" in New Jersey in too many ways to catalogue here, but he also introduced me to Lt. Stephen Antisz (B.P.D., retired) and, through a mutual friend, to Sgt. Maria Dargan, who works at the Hudson County Prosecutor's Office. Stephen's firsthand experience of the terrors of Hurricane Sandy was of great help in developing the narrative, and Maria's detailed and informative guided tour of the County Prosecutor's Office was equally valuable. Thank you both for your time and your patience.

There is another law enforcement officer whom I wish to single out for specific honor. She or he must remain anonymous, so I will refer to her/him as J.S. I may only say that this courageous officer has spent most of the past twenty years working serial undercover operations for U.S. federal, state, and local forces, and has been responsible for successive high-value arrests and prosecutions across the entire breadth of the nation. That J.S. agreed to meet with me on more than one occasion, agreed to share with me enough inside information for a dozen novels, and continues to respond to my (occasionally dumb) questions, is a gift I can never repay. Wherever you are, my friend, my heart is with you.

I also wish to single out the following friends and colleagues for their invaluable assistance and support:

In Bayonne, New Jersey: A big thanks to Susan Metelski, bartender at The Starting Point Bar & Grill, for making every visit to your establishment an adventure in itself.

At the University of Virginia: Jim B. Tucker, M.D., Bonner-Lowry Associate Professor of Psychiatry and Neurobehavioral Sciences. Dr. Tucker is a certified child psychiatrist, and is director of the UVA Division of Perceptual Studies, where he is continuing the work of Dr. Ian Stevenson with children who report memories of previous lives. Jim's two utterly compelling books on that subject, *Life Before Life—A Scientific Investigation of Children's Memories of Previous Lives*, and *Return to Life—Extraordinary Cases of Children Who Remember Past Lives*, were directly responsible for inspiring the character of Kevin Hendricks in this novel. Readers who found Kevin's character intriguing could do no better than to read Dr. Tucker's astonishing collection of case histories.

In the Cayman Islands: David Baines, the Commissioner of the Royal Cayman Islands Police Force. In years past, David was a member of Special Branch, an elite law enforcement agency in the United Kingdom, and his anecdotes, insights, and advice have been invaluable.

And now we come to Sicily! Let me just say that on that fabled isle, my wife, Melody, and I met, and came to adore, some of the most warm-hearted people anyone could hope to encounter on Planet Earth. Our joint heartfelt thanks must first go out to Silvia Sillitti and Silvia's husband, Dr. Bruno Fantauzza, and also to Silvia's brother Giuseppe, and her nephew Antonio. Over three lengthy visits to their farms near Caltanissetta, this wonderful family provided us with home and hearth, boundless affection, and vast amounts of local knowledge. We are eternally grateful.

I also wish to pay tribute to geologist and teacher Enrico Curcuruto. This most singular Sicilian gentleman opened my eyes to the fascinating geology of Sicily, and thereby inspired a critical aspect of *Storm Rising*. Dr. Curcuruto is professor of geology at Mining Technical School "S. Mottura," and director of the Mineralogical Museum of Caltanissetta (more properly: "*Museo Mineralogico Paleontologico e Della Zolfara, Caltanissetta*"). Thank you, Enrico, for your time, your hospitality, and the amazing depths of knowledge that you so freely shared.

I would also like to express my gratitude to Genny Trovato, our guide—not once, but twice!—through the complex industrial archaeology of *Il Parco Minerario di Floristella-Grottacalda*. And thank you too, Genny, for arranging a private tour of Palazzo Pennisi. You are truly a gem!

Finally, and as always, my deepest love and gratitude go to my dear wife Melody, who year after year, and without complaint, accompanies me on various madcap research trips, and who never fails to patiently point out the often glaring flaws in the tales I propose to weave. So it's hats off to you, my love—and to our keen-eyed editor and friend at St. Martin's Press, Daniela Rapp—for keeping my stories just barely inside that blurry line between fiction and unreality.

Okay . . . almost.